Some risks were not worth taking and my lord Strensham was one of them.

'If I catch you out in one more misdeed, your mistress will hear of it,' he warned, and his mistrust hurt.

'Maybe she'll wonder why you care,' Thea was stung into replying pertly, questioning why that threat tormented her so much she had to blink back tears.

They could never be more than master and housemaid after all. The Winfordes had seen to that.

Author Note

In households like the ones in my story the housemaids would be at work by five or six o'clock in the morning, and they scrubbed, cleaned and carried until their 'betters' went to bed. Without vacuum cleaners, and with bathrooms and indoor plumbing almost unknown, the endurance of the young women who undertook such labour now seems phenomenal. Even so, my heroine would have considered herself lucky to find such work without references.

Housemaids were the unsung heroines of the elegant Regency house, and without them the airy rooms and delicate furnishings we still admire would soon have become squalid and dull. My heroine is lucky enough to meet her hero despite her humble position, but she learns a great deal about friendship, hard work and humanity when she becomes a housemaid heiress. I hope you enjoy her eventful journey from spoilt miss through runaway maid to beloved wife.

HOUSEMAID HEIRESS

Elizabeth Beacon

MILLS & BOON®

Pure reading pleasure

First published in Great Britain 2007
Large Print edition 2008
Harlequin Mills & Boon Limited,
Eton House, 18-24 Paradise Road, Richmond, Surrey TW9 1SR

© Elizabeth Beacon 2007

ISBN: 978 0 263 20145 1

Set in Times Roman 15½ on 16½ pt.
42-0408-85380

Printed and bound in Great Britain
by Antony Rowe Ltd, Chippenham, Wiltshire

HOUSEMAID
HEIRESS

Elizabeth Beacon started daydreaming about handsome and brooding heroes while she was still at school and should have been paying attention. After being distracted by them during a short career in the civil service, and whilst teaching, temping and managing a garden centre, she has finally given up and written about some of those heroes and their feisty heroines, and hopes her readers will enjoy meeting them as much as she did.

Elizabeth lives in the West Country, with an eccentric rescue dog who could easily be half Springer Spaniel and half hearthrug. When not immersed in every historical romance she can lay her hands on, or looking for the perfect setting for her next book, she can be found enjoying other people's gardens, or walking through the beautiful countryside around her home, musing about a new hero.

A recent novel by this author:

AN INNOCENT COURTESAN

Chapter One

'You will have to marry Granby now,' Lady Winforde observed with undisguised satisfaction.

'I'd sooner wed the boot boy!'

'Your low tastes are irrelevant.' Lady Winforde contemplated the bedraggled figure in front of her with distaste, and Thea forced herself to meet those cold, colourless eyes as if it cost her no effort at all. 'It's not as if you have any claim to breeding, and my son will be taking a step down by marrying the granddaughter of a foundling.'

'Your son is a gambler and a drunkard. No female with any regard for her comfort or sanity would willingly marry him, whatever her birth.'

'Ah, but such a lady would not be shut in a gentleman's bedchamber all night in the first place. How on earth you expect me to believe a door could stick at night and open freely in the morning I shall never know, but you have no choice but to accept my son's offer. The poor boy thinks himself very hard done by I fear, having been trapped in such a distasteful fashion by a designing female with no pretensions to rank.'

'No doubt unfettered access to my grandfather's fortune will help him endure.'

'How well you understand the matter. Now it's high time you retired to your room to contemplate your undeserved good fortune.'

'If you recall, Lady Winforde, my room is being refurbished. How unfortunate that such a catastrophic flood should force me to take up residence in the attics at such a time,' Thea said drily.

'Yes, the roof on that side is sadly neglected.'

'How convenient.'

'Oh, no, my dear, highly inconvenient when it puts you so far from my care and guidance, as last night's escapade amply demonstrates. Never mind, once you are married to Granby you can join him in the master suite quite respectably.'

'I'd rather share it with the lunatics at Bethlehem Hospital.'

'Would you, niece? I'm sure that could be arranged, if you persist in showing such stubborn disregard for the conventions.'

'I am not your niece.' Thea had steadfastly refused to call the woman aunt from the day she and her repulsive son arrived under Grandfather's much-maligned roof. 'And my trustees would never believe such shameful lies.'

'I think you might be surprised. Refusing such an honourable offer of matrimony, after being discovered in my son's bedroom in such a state of disarray, will hardly convince them of your sanity. Especially when such impeccable witnesses discovered you in that dreadfully compromising situation.'

'And just how were the vicar and his wife so conveniently to hand?'

'What more natural in a worried aunt than to scour the countryside for her missing niece? It was hardly to be wondered at that a man of the cloth should rush to my side to offer support and succour at such a time.'

'And his wife's curiosity was the icing on the cake I suppose?'

'What strange turns of phrase you possess, a legacy of your peculiar upbringing one can only suppose.'

'There was nothing wrong with my upbringing,' Thea was goaded into protesting and one of Lady Winforde's plucked eyebrows rose incredulously as she let a smile fleetingly touch her thin lips.

Drat, she had let the scheming witch win another bout, and once upon a time she had thought herself so very clever.

'Perhaps not for the granddaughter of a cit, but you are ill prepared to follow in *my* footsteps,' her ladyship informed Thea haughtily. 'Still, we must make the best of the inevitable. You will return to your room and compose yourself for your wedding to my son. A bride must prepare for such a solemn occasion.'

Thea was marched back to captivity by one of the thuggish servants the Winfordes had brought in when Grandfather was hardly cold in his grave. Somehow she must lull them into thinking her defeated; in the hope they would relax and give her a chance to escape.

Not that she feared another visit from Granby; even last night he did no more than half-heartedly molest her, until her virulent, and fluently expressed, disgust sent him back to his beloved brandy bottle. What an idiot she had been not to take the unscrupulous rogues seriously from the outset, when she might have stood a better chance of confounding them.

Thea plumped down on the narrow bed that was the only furniture in her dreary attic, apart from a broken joint stool. Tempting though it was to fall into a despairing stupor after such a night, she refused to give in. Somehow she would find a way out of this trap, even if it killed her. At least that would frustrate the conniving rogues after her fortune!

'Confound it, Nick, I should have left you in Southampton,' Major Marcus Ashfield, the new Lord Strensham, announced as he regarded his gaunt companion through narrowed eyes.

Even in the fading light of a March afternoon, he could see the stark pallor of his cousin's thin face, and bitterly reproached himself for listening to the idiot's demands to get him away from the sawbones.

'Damn it, man, I should have let them take your arm off after all.'

'Not losing my arm,' his cousin mumbled, 'nothing wrong with it.'

'Only a festering slash from a French sabre to add to the bullet wound in your shoulder, and when did you study medicine?'

'Know more about it than that bumbling fool,' Captain the Honourable Nicholas Prestbury muttered darkly.

Marcus heard the slurring in his voice and noted his pig-headed relative's feeble attempts to pretend he wasn't about to fall out of his saddle. Evidently they could go no further today, but in the midst of this wilderness, where on earth could they safely stop?

'Luckily even I know enough to tell you can go no further.'

'Ride all night if I have to—never gave in when we marched over the Pyrenees.'

'Maybe not, but you lacked two wounds and a fever to slow you down then.'

'Won't slow me down now.'

'Stow it, you ass, of course they will.'

'Sweep!'

'Hyde Park Soldier!'

'Always were an idiot,' Nick muttered and finally lost the battle with his reeling senses.

Marcus was only just in time to steady his cousin's slumped body and calm his spooked horse.

'Thank heaven you have some manners, Hercules, old fellow,' he murmured as his own horse stilled, obedient to the pressure of his rider's legs, which was all Marcus could currently spare to control him.

The spirited bay snorted his disapproval of all that was going on around him, but fortunately made no attempt to gallop off when Marcus slid out of his saddle, while at the same time somehow keeping Nick in his until he could secure him.

'We're in the devil of a fix, old man,' he informed himself as much as his long-time mount.

He finally managed to calm both horses to the extent where Nick's precious black stallion was as quiet as he could ever be accused of being. Hercules nuzzled his owner's shoulder as if to remind him there were more important things to think about than wayward cavalry officers and their restless mounts, such as oats and water, probably in that order.

Yet the woods were thick on either side of the track and it was at least a couple of miles since they had passed a run-down wayside tavern Marcus suspected must be the haunt of thieves, mainly because no one else would bother to go there. Maybe he should have insisted they stay for the night nevertheless, but he doubted his ability to guard his cousin and their horses so they could leave it again come morning. All he could do now was tie Nick to his saddle—as they sometimes had the lesser wounded on the march—and hope to find some sort of make-shift shelter for the coming night.

It was darker here than it would be in the open, and from the look of the overcast sky there would be no kindly moon to mark their path later. Marcus was contemplating making camp on the edge of the road when at last he caught a slight whiff of wood-smoke on the chill air. Used to moving in hostile ter-ritory, he was still too cautious to rush toward its source. This might not be Spain or France where hostile armies sometimes camped within yards of one another, but he wasn't fool enough to think everyone in England a bluff John Bull, waiting to welcome the Marquis of Druro's officers with un-alloyed delight.

Cursing their vulnerability, he kept the horses as quiet as he could and listened intently. Nothing but the normal sounds of nature, which did little to help or hinder his attempts to plumb the darkness. Deciding all he could do was proceed with caution, he led the horses forward as quietly as possible. Of course it could be charcoal burners, but he was unsure they would be any better off with them than the rum company he might have found at the wayside inn. At last the scent led him down a ride and deeper into the forest, and he had no choice now but to follow it, for Nick was beginning to groan in his uneasy stupor and Marcus was desperate.

'Idiot,' he murmured, wishing now he had never

listened to his cousin's pleas not to be left behind in France for the surgeons to practise on when Marcus was forced to sell out and come home himself.

He was so busy wondering if there was a way to safeguard Nick's limb from the knife that he almost missed the hut. Even in the twilight he could see how humble it was, but beggars couldn't be choosers, so he rapped on the warped door. After a couple of very long minutes he grew impatient with waiting and called out.

'We are benighted travellers and mean you no harm.' His voice sounded unnaturally loud in the still clearing, but he was certain someone was inside pretending not to be and felt so thoroughly exasperated he didn't much care if he frightened them. 'Confound it, we need help!'

The householder seemed to consider his less than humble demands for shelter. 'We ain't got nothin', go away!' an anxious voice finally quavered, as if its owner was on the edge of panic.

'Just open the door, child,' he ordered more softly and waited with what little patience he could now summon.

Still the door stayed stubbornly closed and he finally had enough of standing outside like some frustrated lover pleading for admittance to his lady's bower. Another groan from the direction of the now-tethered horses made him barge the warped barrier out of his way and force himself on the squatters, who must be the only ones desperate enough to want such a tumbledown shack in the first place.

'I did say we needed succour,' he said sharply as he stood on the threshold and surveyed the mean space within.

'An' I told yer we 'ad nowt,' a surly voice mumbled in the darkness.

Instinct warned him to expect an attack of some sort, and he hastily raised his arm to take the blow from a bolt of wood instead of letting it hammer down on his head. Marcus shot out his hand to pin a slim wrist with merciless fingers until the improvised club fell to the floor and he forced his attacker's arm up his back.

'Ouch! You brute!' the supposed child squeaked and he nearly let the girl go as he finally realised he had a slender and decidedly feminine body clamped against his own and not that of a scrubby youth after all.

'Fortunately for you, ma'am, you are quite out in that assumption. Now shall we begin again?'

'That fib would be a sight more convincing if you was to let me go.'

'I may not be the villain you were anticipating, but neither am I a complete flat, my girl. So, do you promise to behave?'

'Mumchance when you'm twice as big as me, your lordship.'

'Never mind obfuscation, wench, promise not to attack again and I'll let you go.'

'I promise,' she spat and the fury in her voice re-assured him she meant to honour her word, as she was so furious about giving it.

Cautiously they stood like disengaged duellists, trying to assess their new positions in virtual darkness.

'This is ridiculous, you must have the means to produce a light of some sort to have lit a fire in the first place.'

'And wasn't that a big mistake?' the girl mumbled irritably as she fumbled about in the darkness to find the dark lantern that should have made him even more suspicious of her.

While it would have been a gross exaggeration to say the hut was flooded with light, the glow of a single tallow candle revealed the grim details.

'There's nothing here,' Marcus exclaimed in dis-appointment, visions of getting Nick settled comfortably out of the cold and damp of an English spring vanishing like his breath on the chill air.

'Told yer,' the girl told him gleefully, arms folded across her skinny body as she nodded her triumph.

'Which means you have naught either,' he pointed out with excusable exasperation.

'True,' she acknowledged cheerfully enough and nodded in the direction from which he had come. 'Road's that way.'

'I have no intention of dragging a wounded man any further along it tonight, so either you tolerate us for the night or leave yourself.'

'I was here first,' she said sulkily, the wind apparently taken out of her sails by the thought of a night in the open.

'And ordinarily I should gallantly leave you to your solitude. However I have more important things to worry about tonight than a sullen runaway maid without a feather to fly with.'

On the point of impulsively informing the hateful creature that she actually had two pounds and ninepence ha'penny to her name, Thea just managed to keep her tongue between her teeth. Since that was all she had left of the few guineas she had managed to hide from the Winfordes, she had better keep quiet about her available fortune. She bit down on the urge to spark back and eyed the intruder balefully through the gloom.

She should never have given in to temptation to light that fire in the first place. Although she had let it out once her scratch meal was eaten, the damage was done. Still, she could have brought far worse down on herself than an officer in search of a billet for the night. Come to think of it, she could yet if she wasn't more careful.

'Am I correct in assuming that the "we" you spoke of was a lie to see off the fainthearted?' he asked and she shivered.

Nobody would come to her aid if this man proved rather less of a gentleman than he appeared.

'Maybe,' she replied cautiously.

'Either way you are the only person who can help me, so hold that lantern a little higher to guide me to the horses, will you?' Seeing that she did not move, he made a noise of acute impatience and informed her sharply, 'You'll have a man's life on your conscience before morning if you don't help.'

'And who says I've such a luxury?'

He sighed and took a shilling from his pocket and held it so it caught the poor light. 'This does,' he informed her so wearily that Thea almost dropped her guard and did as he bid her out of fellow feeling.

After three weeks of running and hiding and walking until she could walk no more, she had a lot of sympathy with the weary. Reminding herself she must not drop her guard, she eyed the shiny coin as if it represented nigh-irresistible temptation. It should of course, for heaven alone knew when she would have a chance to earn another one, so she nodded as if coming to a purely mercenary decision and signalled him to follow.

Complete darkness had fallen while they had stood arguing, but as her eyes adjusted to the night she saw a shadow move at the edge of the woods. Nervous of what she could not clearly see, she fought the urge to run back inside the hut and hide in a dusty corner.

'My horse is wondering where on earth I got off to,' the soldier's voice reassured her gruffly.

His presence reassured her more than words and she relaxed a little as she let him lead the way. While she would find it unbearable to be ordered and bullied like a raw recruit in his regiment for long, for now it was oddly appealing.

'Ah, but he's a beauty, ain't he?' she murmured and reached out a gentle hand to the great horse so patiently awaiting his master.

'Reluctant though I am to interrupt such a touching scene, more light would help me judge my cousin's condition better.'

'There's no need to be sarcastic,' she murmured as she held the lantern aloft and saw the vibrancy of gold braid and dash that was a Hussar's uniform, but which now only emphasised the thinness and pallor of the gentleman wearing it.

'There's a lean-to round the back of the hut where the charcoal burners kept their beasts,' she volunteered and would have taken the bay's reins, if the first soldier had not put out a hand to stop her.

'Light the way while I lead them.'

Knowing he thought she would ride off with his horse, she flounced along the overgrown track to the hovel, where the few ancient bundles of hay might serve to bed the animals for the night, even if they could hardly eat it. The officer hitched the black's reins to the sturdiest post he could see and untied the ropes that held his friend in the saddle. Thea forgot her anger at being so mis-

trusted and hung the lamp on a nail driven in for
the purpose.

'I can manage his feet if you hold his arms,' she
offered, only to step back in awe when he hefted the
unconscious man out of the saddle, setting him
gently on the nearest pile of hay.

She shook her head in astonishment at such
mighty strength united with gentleness. It flew in
the face of all her experience and she didn't want
to soften toward his sex, unless some miracle led
her to sanctuary. Even then she would probably
do well to avoid this abrupt gentleman. Silently
she moved to soothe the restless black until he
calmed down enough to let her rub him down with
a wisp of hay.

'You have a way with horses,' the man said, and
if he was expecting her to fall at his feet in delight
at his compliment, he would be disappointed.

'I like them,' she told him, wishing she could hate
him.

'He must be able to tell. I've often seen the bad-
tempered brute lash out when he has a mind to be
awkward.'

'Shame I can't be a groom then, ain't it?' she
replied lightly and went back to reassuring the
restless stallion.

'Yes, it's a lot safer for a boy to wander about unprotected than a girl.'

'I don't need nobody's protection,' she lied as he

lifted the packs the horses had carried and took out nosebags and a good supply of oats.

'Soon as we get your friend bedded down we'll water them,' she observed. 'He looks about to wake.'

'The sooner we get him inside the better. Are you good with people?'

'Can't abide 'em.'

He chuckled and she tried not to smile, even if he couldn't see her.

'I thought not. Bring my pack along like a good girl, will you?'

She scowled and tried not to show the slightest awe when he hauled his lanky comrade into his arms and bore him as if he weighed little more than a child.

Chapter Two

'Light the fire again,' the tall rifleman ordered, when they were inside the hut with the door safely shut behind them.

'It'll give us away.'

'I have a rifle, four pistols, a sword and a cavalry officer's sabre at my disposal, so I think we can deal with any intruders, don't you?'

'I dare say Boney's too busy to call tonight, so likely we can.'

'A wench with a sense of humour, how refreshing,' he said drily and Thea subsided into mutinous sulks once more.

As she reached for the precious kindling she had gathered in case she could not get through the night without the comfort of a fire, she wondered just what the pampered girl of a few months ago would have made of this ridiculous situation. In all likelihood silly Miss Hardy would have thought a dark stranger in rifleman's green deliciously overwhelming, and fallen headlong in love with him at first sight.

'Silly clunch,' she murmured at the very thought.

'Who is?'

'Who is what?'

'I may be a clunch, but I'm not a deaf one.'

'I meant someone else,' she said, surprised to find she didn't want to hurt his feelings after all. 'A young lady at the last house I was in. She insisted her fire must be lit three hours before she got up every morning, so there was no risk of her delicate little feet getting cold. The maids had to rise early in the winter just to do as she bid us.'

Ashamed of the memory of that unnecessary demand, Thea was glad the subdued light would hide her blush. What an inconsiderate, objectionable female she had been, before the Winfordes took a hand in her education.

'Cold-hearted bitch,' he growled, and, if it had not been her true self he was traducing, she might have been warmed by his partisanship.

'I dare say she's learnt her lesson now. They say she's to be wed for the sake of her fortune.'

To her surprise she saw a blush fire *his* tanned cheeks as the fire caught properly and began to warm the room at last.

'We need hot water. There's probably a shaving mug somewhere in my pack if you can find nothing else to boil it in.'

'Then you find it. I'm not putting my hands in there. They might come out without some fingers.'

His teeth flashed white in the firelight as he grinned at her maidenly refusal to search a soldier's possessions, and for once did as he was bid.

'You really are a most unusual female,' he told her as he handed her the tin mug, almost as if he approved of her rather odd behaviour.

She filled it carefully from the handleless jug she had made sure was full to the brim earlier, so she would not need to venture outside until morning. A precaution she might just as easily have not bothered with, as it happened.

'Because I like my fingers where they are?'

'Because you don't mind saying so.'

'They always said I had a big mouth,' she acknowledged with an answering grin, and for a moment felt a peculiar heat run through her like warm lightning as he laughed and his rather sombre personality was temporarily transfigured.

Suddenly she could picture him, light-hearted and welcoming as he bid guests welcome to his home. War and responsibility had made him serious, but she imagined him transformed—galloping that great horse of his through summer meadows just for the joy of it, as he laughed with the lucky female who rode at his side, matching him pace for pace. Putting herself into that very attractive picture, she knew her heart would be in the smile she returned, that earlier jag of fire that had spread through her growing ever sweeter....

'There, and won't you look at that!' she exclaimed with every excuse for annoyance, as a spark flew out of the fire when she poked at it unwarily and scorched her disreputable skirts before she could slap it out. 'They said I was clumsy as well.'

'They?' he asked companionably, glad of any diversion from the task of discovering the state of Nick's wounds.

'The folk at the Foundling,' she improvised, fervently hoping he knew less about such charitable institutions than she did.

'No doubt very worthy people, but not given to spoiling their charges, perhaps?'

His voice was gentle as he contemplated the privations of an orphan's life, and Thea felt guilty once more as she considered her very privileged existence as one until just lately. Grandfather had given her everything she asked for, apart from stubbornly insisting she must wed a man with a title. He even specified it in his will, and of course Granby had a title. She shuddered at the very thought and moved closer to the warmth of the fire.

'They didn't hurt you, I hope?'

He had evidently seen that shiver. She felt the burden of untruth weigh heavy on her slender shoulders, but too much depended on her staying out of the Winfordes' clutches to resort to the truth now.

'No, but I had to run away from my last place.'

'Considering you find this place preferable, I can only imagine that the alternative must have been dire indeed.'

'It was,' she replied and could not hold back another shudder as she recalled the repulsive feel of Granby's damp hands roughly thrusting at the neck of her gown as she gagged from sheer horror.

'Not all men are brutes, you know.'

'No, some try honey before resorting to vinegar,' she said cynically, recalling some of the titled suitors Grandfather had lured to Hardy House.

Those poor and desperate men had soon put her off becoming Lady This or the Marchioness of That.

'You have been unfortunate. Somewhere there must be an honest young fellow just waiting to value your youth and wit.'

'Yes, most of them can't wait to stone me from any parish that might be burdened with the burying of me, after they let me starve to death within their bounds,' she said bitterly.

'With a chance of earning an honest living, you might meet someone.'

'And, if wishes were horses, beggars would ride, now what of this poor man you were supposed to be so concerned about?'

'Is the water hot yet?'

'Any hotter and it'll do him more harm than good.'

'Hold that light as steady as you can then, while I see what the idiot's done to himself this time.'

Thea gulped and reminded herself that she was a soldier's daughter, even if she could hardly remember either of her parents. Her mother had eloped with a handsome subaltern, so perhaps this ridiculous attraction to the military was in her blood. Within five years both her parents were dead and her grandfather insisted she carry his name, then made the best of a bad job.

It took all her flagging courage to do the same now, and she gasped in shock when the warm water finally soaked the poor man's dressing off, and revealed the angry slash marring the length of his upper arm. She gazed down at the puckered wound and the number of stitches holding it closed, and wondered how the unconscious man could have borne the jarring that riding must have inflicted on his wounds.

'He should be in bed!' she exclaimed.

'If I hadn't brought him with me, he was threatening to set out alone as soon as my back was turned. He always was stubborn as a mule.'

Thinking of this man's determination to get his own way by fair means or foul, Thea raised her brows sceptically in the useful gesture she had learnt from her bitter enemy. He flashed her an unrepentant grin, then distracted her from thinking about the leap of her heart that it had caused her by bending down to sniff the wound.

'According to his long-suffering doctor, if it starts to smell sweet I'm to get him to a sawbones as fast as I can tie him to his horse and force him there. Otherwise the damn fool stands as much chance of keeping his beloved arm as he might if he had had the sense to stay in bed in the first place.'

'In other words, he's getting better?'

'So I concluded, but when he fainted on me tonight I began to think he was as big an idiot as his physician.'

'And instead he's just a run-of-the-mill idiot?'

He chuckled. 'Nothing about Mad Nick is commonplace.'

'Nevertheless you are very fond of him, I think?'

'Maybe,' he said, but Thea had seen his affection for his relative in his actions tonight and perhaps he thought it was too late to pretend to mere duty. 'We both suffered for our respective mothers' sins, so I understand him better than most, I suppose.'

'I don't see how *you* could be made to suffer for your mother's deeds.' She forced bitterness into her voice by remembering her grandfather and his twin brother, abandoned on the doorstep of the foundling hospital.

'Oh, we weren't, at least not in the way you must have been. Anyway, I must get this mess cleaned and rebandaged, so, for the sake of Nick's sensibilities, perhaps you could water the horses and give him freedom to swear like one of his troopers?

Not even he can sleep through that, and you will inhibit him sadly.'

She hesitated, fighting her fear of the dark wood.

'Take this if it'll make you feel better,' he offered, handing her an evil-looking pistol, which she examined as if it might bite. 'It's loaded, so just draw this back and pull the trigger when you're close enough to disable your quarry.'

Thea gulped as she contemplated actually using a gun on her fellow man. Even if Granby was lurking out there in the darkness, she would not be able to shoot him, so she pulled back from it with horror.

'Couldn't I scream for you?'

'It might be too late by the time I find you, but since this is England and black night I dare say you'll be safe enough.'

'Yes, I dare say,' she said, with the oddest feeling of disappointment she had ever suffered in her life because he didn't think her worth protecting.

'Well, then, if you would not mind, Miss... We appear to have omitted to introduce ourselves. The gentleman on the floor is Captain Nicholas Prestbury of the 10th Hussars and I am Major Marcus Ashfield of the 95th Rifles and at your service, ma'am,' he said with a half-mocking bow.

She bobbed him a perfunctory curtsy, copied from those long-suffering maids at Hardy House. 'Hetty Smith, Major,' she lied.

'Pleased to meet you, Miss Smith.'

'I doubt that, sir.'

'How did you come to that conclusion, my dear?' he asked, acute interest suddenly lighting his dark gaze.

'I ain't your dear.'

'Odd how that accent of yours comes and goes, is it not?' he mused and Thea cursed her own carelessness, even as she wondered how she could explain her lapses.

'Now then, children, I'm not up to playing referee,' a weak voice chided from the floor where the sufferer lay.

'The devil—how long have you been awake?'

'Long enough, Marco, long enough.'

'You always had peculiar ideas of entertainment.'

'I hail from a peculiar family.'

'And are commonly considered the pinnacle of our eccentricity.'

'I don't usually waste time interrogating pretty girls in the middle of the night, so I could argue with that, were I feeling up to it.'

'No doubt you soon will be, so if you will excuse us, Miss Smith?'

'You'll come if I scream?'

'Trust me,' he said with a rueful smile that did something to her heartbeat.

Dazed, Thea went out into the night without her usual feeling of dread dogging her every step. She doubted Granby's thugs would be a match for her tall rifleman and his fearsome artillery, so at least tonight she was unlikely to be captured and forced up the aisle.

Murmuring soft endearments to reassure the nervous black charger, she carefully untied his reins. The stream ran only yards from the back of the hut and she knew Marcus would never have sent her out here if he thought there was the faintest degree of danger, but he was not to know what devils stalked her footsteps.

She caught herself thinking that, if only some of the lords Grandfather lured to Hardy House had been more like him, she might have wed before Granby's mother realised what an opportunity was going a-begging. Anyway, the Major wasn't a lord, so there was no earthly reason why he should want to marry her. If she did not wed a titled man, her fortune would be tied up so tightly only her grand-children would receive more than a pittance.

Now her reputation was so comprehensively ruined, no self-respecting gentleman would marry Miss Alethea Hardy, and she instinctively knew Major Ashfield was one of those. All she could hope for was to stay out of the Winfordes' reach until her twenty-first birthday, then live in obscurity on her hundred a year. It was so much less than her once-grand expec-tations that she almost sat down and cried.

By the time she had repeated the process of gently leading a horse to water and letting him drink with

Hercules, she was resolved to be on her way as soon as dawn lightened the way.

'I was beginning to think you a figment of my fevered imagination,' Nick joked weakly when she crept through the ill-fitting door at last.

'Funny, I hoped I was having a nightmare,' she replied, wondering crossly why his darkly romantic looks had no effect on her silly heartbeat.

'I like your waif, Marcus.'

'You liked every pretty female you ever set eyes on.'

'Well, they like me,' he replied smugly.

Thea chuckled and got a penetrating stare from his cousin that she met with proud contempt, in case he thought her susceptible.

'Will the Captain be fit to ride tomorrow?' she asked at last.

'He wasn't fit today, but that didn't stop him.'

'You'll be on your way at first light, then?'

Marcus frowned. 'I shall be, but I hope you'll stay while I fetch our cousin's carriage to take him to Rosecombe.'

'To the Park?'

'Yes, do you know it?'

'I saw it on my way,' she said casually, trying not to sound wistful.

From the road she had caught a glimpse of the beautiful neo-classical mansion through still-bare trees and thought it everything she could never have.

Elegance and harmony, she thought now, and the protection of a loving family. These two men were inside that family, and she could not keep a twist of bitterness from her lips.

'You dislike the aristocracy?'

'No, I just wish they'd give me a job in one of their grand houses, but no respectable family employs a vagrant maid.'

'Oddest vagrant I ever set eyes on,' Nick observed faintly from his makeshift mattress.

'Oh, for heaven's sake, go to sleep,' his loving relative ordered sharply.

'Don't see how I can with you gossiping.'

'I'm going out, so I suggest you recruit your strength. Lydia won't be best pleased with you as it is, without working yourself into a high fever.'

'No, the little darling will no doubt give me the scold of my life.'

'Then get some sleep, instead of fantasising over Cousin Ned's wife.'

'Got to be fresh tomorrow to greet the flower of the regiment,' Nick said irrepressibly and closed his eyes at last.

After a few minutes they heard his breathing deepen and knew he was genuinely asleep at last. Marcus put a finger to his lips and quit the room with a significant nod at his patient.

Did he think she would make a bolt for the open road in the middle of the night then? Thea tried hard not to feel insulted. It seemed that the rifleman's trust was hard won, and she wanted it for some reason. Which was ridiculous, she decided, stoking the fire from a dwindling reserve of logs before she sat against the wall next to the primitive fireplace.

The rifleman's bedroll was under his cousin along with his own. Their cloaks lay over him, with Thea's cherished blanket, but she didn't expect to sleep. It wouldn't hurt her or the Major to pass the night in a draughty shed, but their patient was a very different matter. She focused her tired eyes on the pallid oval of his sleeping face. She was supposed to be watching him, not thinking about his arrogant cousin.

Hours later, Thea felt someone shake her gently and came awake, panic stark in her startled face. Gracious! She was leaning confidingly against Marcus Ashfield's mighty torso. No, she had snuggled into his warmth like a shameless hussy in her lover's arms. Thea tried to put as much space as possible between them and her hair promptly fell out of the knot held in place by her diminishing supply of hairpins.

'If you have a particle of sense you'll hold still, if you don't want to make me into the rogue you seem determined to cast me as,' Marcus gritted as if an armful of bedraggled woman fighting sleep represented limitless temptation.

Finally realising her dishevelled state, she flushed

and shook her head to try and clear it of the nonsense his coming upon her last night seemed to have stuffed it with, and felt her heavy locks fan out in an untidy cloak that threatened to enmesh them both.

'Why?' she managed to whisper at last, nodding at his scandalously positioned arms.

'For warmth,' he said abruptly and her heart sank ridiculously.

'Of course,' she mumbled and rubbed sleepy eyes before stretching against his muscular chest, feeling a terrible temptation to rub up against him like a luxuriating cat.

'I could not have you catch your death, Miss Smith.'

'No, I would be for ever on your conscience, I suppose.'

'I think you could be anyway,' he replied with a sombre look and Thea's heart plummeted; she didn't want to be numbered among an officer's obligations, especially not his.

'I'm an independent woman,' she informed him crossly and felt him chuckle through the warm connection of their still-entwined bodies.

'You're a penniless runaway,' he corrected and the growing daylight revealed that his grey eyes were shot through with hot silver sparks she should definitely be wary of, since excitement and curiosity were coursing through her in the most immodest fashion.

'I still have my pride,' she assured him crossly.

'Does it keep you warm at night?' he asked huskily and the feel of his superbly fit body lying so close said the rest for him.

He had kept her warm all through the night, and for the first time in her life she felt the traitorous stir of passions she did not understand, and could not hope to resist if she spent much longer in his arms.

'No, but it ain't so likely to land me back at the foundling's in nine months' time.'

'I told you I honour my obligations, I believe,' he informed her rather coldly and in turn shook his head as if to clear it of incendiary thoughts. 'I must apologise if I have behaved in an ungentlemanly fashion toward you, Miss Smith. I promise I am not a vile seducer.'

No, a wayward voice informed her, he would probably prove all too pleasant a one. She tried to rein in scandalous images of being locked in his strong arms, and learning things a proper young lady would never picture. Her baser self told her that if she was to lose her virtue, how much better to do so to a virile and attractive man like Marcus Ashfield rather than Granby. She shuddered at the memory of the night she spent in the dissolute baronet's bedchamber, and tried not to protest when Marcus misinterpreted her revulsion and let her go, as if he had just unwarily touched a burning brand.

'Will you stay?' he asked abruptly.

'How long will you be gone?'

'I should reach Rosecombe by breakfast time, if I set off now. Unless yon lunatic wakes up and insists on coming too.'

The subject of lunatics reminded her what she was running from, and panic threatened, heedless of the injured man only feet away. Fighting it cost her a bruised lip as she bit down on her full lower one, but she managed it and looked up into his questioning eyes.

'Please hurry,' she pleaded in an urgent whisper she hoped would not wake the sleeping Hussar.

'Don't worry, I will, and you can keep my armoury.'

'Take it, I will stand less chance of shooting myself.'

'Nick could shoot the pip out of an ace left-handed even in his current state. If anyone sinister appears, wake him up and he will shoot for you. I would not leave you if I thought you were in danger. Oh, and if he decides to importune you with unwanted attentions as well, just squeeze his bad arm.'

She managed a weak smile, and watched him perform an abbreviated *toilette* by running his fingers through rebelliously curling dark hair and rubbing a rueful hand over his unshaven chin. Then, with a last look and a quick gesture of farewell, he left the hut with his boots in one hand and his rifle in the other.

The place seemed cold and empty as she listened to the faint noise he made resuming his boots and the jingle of Hercules's tack and the indistinct murmur of a deep masculine voice reassuring both horses as he mounted, then rode away. Never had a room felt so silent and bereft as this ramshackle shed, despite the man sleeping in the dying light of the fire and the strengthening daylight round the ill-fitting door. Thea reminded herself of the realities of her new life and sat down to wait in the cold dawn for the injured man to need her, or his rescuers to come.

Chapter Three

Marcus rode away from the tumbledown hut with contrary feelings. Of course it was normal for a man waking up to a delicious armful of slenderly curved woman to be aroused by her. Just because the wench had stirred his baser instincts, he did not have to act on them. After all, he was a gentleman— no, he was a nobleman now, and one did not always preclude the other.

His grandfather's death, only ten days after that of his direct heir, had brought the new Viscount Strensham home to try to sort out the havoc his father's wild spending had wrought. Julius Ashfield must be turning in his grave now that the son he had despised had inherited the title he had coveted so long for himself. Although, according to the family lawyer, his father had made damn sure only crushing debt accompanied the family honours— maybe he was having the last laugh after all.

There was one clear solution, and he would take

it if there was truly nothing left, but a man who was contemplating matrimony to the richest woman he could cozen into becoming his viscountess had no business seducing the first attractive female to fall into his arms. He considered Miss Hetty Smith with a reminiscent smile. No doubt the fiery little creature would read him his fortune if he offered to set her up as his wife in watercolour, and he couldn't afford her even if she surprised him and said yes.

A picture of her, flushed with sleep and delightfully ruffled, rose in his mind's eye. With his attention wandering from his quest, it was just as well that Hercules had realised comfortable stables lay close as they neared Sir Edward Darraine's country home. She had looked enchanting with that heavy mass of tumbling nut-brown curls falling about her slender shoulders and down her back, Marcus remembered with a wolfish glint in his eyes. Yet the sleepy mix of puzzlement and heat in her blue-green eyes indicated she was an innocent, in that if nothing else.

He reflected on the presence of his untouched purse in his pocket and decided he did her dishonour. She was certainly no thief, nor willing to earn her bread on her back. The grim truth was that she would starve without recourse to one of those undesirable occupations, and he found the idea of her being forced into either repulsive.

It went against his baser instincts, but he must

provide her with an escape from poverty if he was not to exploit her vulnerability to get her into his bed. Shocked by the potent drag of desire at the thought of having her under him, he knew he must reject such a venal notion out of hand. If either of them was to come out of this with any self-respect, the less he saw of her, the better for both of them.

A very resolute Major Ashfield rode into Ned Darraine's stable-yard ten minutes later and issued a set of precise orders to the staff, who found themselves running to obey before they questioned his right to hand them out as if he was with his old brigade.

'Marcus, good to see you, old man!' The master of the house greeted him as if they had parted yesterday, instead of over a year ago when Ned had inherited his own title under very different circumstances.

'Same goes for you, Ned, but where's Lyddie when I need her?'

'Getting dressed of course. Where else would she be at this unearthly hour of the morning?'

'In the old days she would have been up and about for hours. You have become a fine pair of slug-a-beds since you came home.'

Ned just smiled an extremely smug smile. 'One day you'll understand,' he assured his cousin, and the memory of where he had awoken himself drove all desire to tease from Marcus's mind.

'I need you too,' he insisted instead and Ned knew he wouldn't ask if he didn't need it.

A plan was taking shape in Marcus's mind for rescuing both his charges, so he had better get on with it before his baser self gave in to temptation.

Luckily it took less than half an hour for the Darraines' travelling carriage to be fitted out with quantities of cushions, an ominous-looking box from Lady Lydia Darraine's stillroom and the noble lady herself.

'Marcus will come with me,' she told her husband, who meekly ordered a groom to lead the second-best hunter in his stable for the Major to ride back.

'Ned hates being cooped up in a coach, but now you can tell me just what you have been up to,' her ladyship informed him. 'And don't leave anything out.'

Marcus left a considerable amount out; after all, he needed Lydia's sympathy for his waif, not her abiding mistrust.

'You ordered the poor little thing out into the dark to water your horses, after forcing your way into her refuge and terrifying her half to death? Marcus, how could you?'

'Nick was faint and there was nothing but a disreputable hedge-tavern for miles.'

'If you had had a woman with you, things would have been so much easier on the girl.'

'No, they wouldn't, Lyddie. You know very well

women can play up like the very devil if they scent a rival.'

'I didn't mean one of those blowsy creatures who used to shamelessly chase you and Nick in Spain. A lady of quality would have put the girl at ease, and made sure you were the one fumbling about in the darkness, attending to two great horses.'

'Such a lady would have been compromised the moment we set out from Southampton,' he pointed out helpfully, or so he thought.

'I was speaking hypothetically.'

'Then please don't, it confuses me.'

'Doubtless your waif is a runaway, and I will have some unprincipled employer turning up on my doorstep and demanding her return if I take her in. Anyway, how would I convince Ned she will not try to run off with the silver, or, even worse, one of his precious horses?'

'I can't argue with the first. The wench admitted she ran from her last place because of some man who wouldn't take no for an answer. She also let out that she was raised in a foundling hospital.'

'Poor thing. They raise those unfortunate children to be deeply ashamed of their beginnings. It made me cross whenever I visited one of the places with Mama to take clothes and books. I knew they would strip any ornament off the clothes and sell the books to buy improving tracts.'

'Surely not all of them are so austere?'

'You should try visiting one, but that's beside the point. We must do something about the poor girl if she truly is respectable. You can put your mind to finding some practical way to reward her for looking after Nick, presuming he and his kit are there when you get back.'

'They will be,' he said confidently and in that at least he was right.

By the time they got to the clearing, Lady Lydia had come to a decision. After insisting two strong ex-army officers were quite sufficient to heft Captain Prestbury out of his hut, she ordered the grooms to stay and protect the coach from marauding villains.

Sweeping into the dilapidated hut, she took a comprehensive look around and sniffed loudly. Thea almost flew to the defence of her makeshift home for the last two days, but she was eager to escape it and kept quiet. One look at this stunningly beautiful golden-haired creature, dressed in the very latest kick of fashion, had made her feel more like a beggar-maid than usual. Watching the Captain being carried out by Major Ashfield, and his cousin, at least she could be sure he was safe. It was high time she put as much distance as possible between herself and the acute major's family.

She hesitated too long, cravenly fearing what lay ahead and not wanting to leave behind the first sense of security she had experienced in months. Trying to melt into the shadows and slide out of the door while her ladyship was preoccupied with gathering Nick's possessions, she cannoned into a familiar broad chest.

'And just where do you think you're going?' Major Ashfield demanded sternly, putting out a hand to stop her bouncing backwards into Lady Lydia.

She swung round to stare at him with pleading eyes, hoping he would let her slip off into the woods.

'Yes, you cannot just leave, my dear!' the beauty added in the mellow contralto voice that had almost made Thea dislike her—she was so perfectly everything her various governesses always insisted she was not. 'You have cared for poor Nick, after all.'

'I did nothing more than keep the fire burning, watch his sleep and give him water whenever he wanted it,' Thea protested.

'Something he will thank you for himself when he is feeling better, but won't you speak to me in private, my dear?'

Thea hesitated, unsure that a lady could have much to say to a homeless nobody. At last the mixture of her ladyship's pleading smile and imperious manner disarmed Thea into staying when Major Ashfield went to stop Nick's black stallion kicking down his makeshift stable.

'Don't worry,' her ladyship told her airily, when Thea protested about the waiting carriage and her ladyship's entourage, 'they can look after themselves for five minutes.'

'I'm sure they can, my lady,' she agreed, trying to hide a smile at the idea of three stalwart gentlemen who had held his Majesty's commission in crack regiments being unable to organise a simple expedition without this vital female's assistance.

'Although I probably shouldn't leave them for ten, so let's get to more important matters. I am fond of both my husband's cousins, and you rendered them a service I want to thank you for.'

'When I realised they were real gentlemen, I was glad of the company, my lady. It's very lonely here after dark. I was too scared to sleep the first night.'

'You couldn't induce me to stay here half an hour in the dark for a handsome bet, let alone a whole night, but are you hard working and honest, Hetty? Marcus says you were brought up a foundling, so you must be, if their teachings have any effect at all.'

'I'm as honest as I dare to be, my lady.'

Lady Lydia shot her a penetrating look, but seemed convinced by Thea's steady gaze.

'If you truly do not mind hard work, my third housemaid has left to look after her little brothers and sisters now her poor mother has died. You can have a month's trial in the post, if you care to risk not suiting me?'

'I wish for nothing so much as a roof over my head and a place in the world, my lady.'

'Even such a very humble one? You speak well and seem used to better things.'

'I shall hardly find them lurking in woods or being moved on by the constables in every village where I dare show my face.'

'True, then you will accept my offer?'

'Gladly, Lady Lydia, and I promise you will never regret your kindness in making it to one in great need.'

'Your hard work will be thanks enough for me. Follow this road north for about six miles, then cross Rosecombe Common. The village edges on to it and the first cottage on the green belongs to my husband's old nurse. She will happily take you in when I explain what you have done for Nick. Then come to the Park tomorrow to see if you might suit. It will sit better if the other servants think you a connection of hers.'

'You are very considerate, Lady Lydia.'

'See if you still think so in a few months' time, when the Park is full of guests and you have to tramp up and down the stairs half a dozen times an hour. Now we must say goodbye, Hetty, and there must be no familiarity between us in future, if you wish to be accepted by my household.'

'Certainly not, my lady,' Thea said, managing to look shocked in the style of all the best servants she had ever come across, who considered such encroachments a cardinal sin on both sides.

'Although I might give in to curiosity when we are

alone,' her ladyship joked, as Thea resolved to be as unobtrusive as possible.

The walk in broad daylight, over ground where her pursuers could have easily caught her, had been an experience Thea never cared to dwell on afterwards, but it had passed without incident. Maybe the Winfordes had given up, or thought she could not have got so far from her home in Devon alone. Once they might have been right, but fear and loathing had spurred her to self-reliance. Grandfather would hardly have believed his indulged granddaughter could change so much, so little wonder if the Winfordes thought her so feeble.

Thea presented herself at the back door of the great house at Rosecombe the next morning, dressed in a print gown she and Nurse Turner had spent the previous evening taking in. Having subjected her to a grilling that would have done justice to Bow Street, the housekeeper conducted her to my lady's sitting room, so she could interrogate her as well.

'Any relative of Nanny Turner's is worthy of a trial,' Lady Lydia declared at last, 'but make sure she is trained all over again, Meldon. You know how particular I am about having things done my way.'

'Of course, my lady.'

'The usual wage, and find her something decent to wear,' her ladyship concluded and they curtsied and silently left the room.

'The head housemaid will send down your new clothes, and you will be expected at six o'clock sharp tomorrow, ready for work.'

'Yes, Mrs Meldon. Thank you, ma'am.'

'Thank me by doing your duty and learning our ways quickly.'

'I always do my best, ma'am.'

The dignified woman just sniffed in the proscribed style, and Thea went out of the side door with a lighter heart. She managed to walk down the path that led to the village without dancing a jig, but it was a close-run thing. Maybe she would evade the Winfordes for the five more months she needed after all. Even if she had to live on very little a year after she came of age, at least it would be her choice.

'I take it your mission was successful?' a deep voice she wished she could forget asked as she rounded the corner that would take her into the Park.

'Major, you startled me.'

'Miss Smith, I could hardly bid you farewell in front of your future colleagues or the lady of the house, now could I?'

He was going, then? A traitorous voice within told her that would take the shine off her new life quicker than anything, but she silenced it and faced him with composure.

'You should not be talking to me, sir. I could lose my place.'

'Since I have no intention of doing you such a backhand turn, will you walk with me?'

'Aye, sir,' she could not resist saying, even knowing she was courting a danger that had nothing to do with her enemies for once.

It was two miles to the village and she was glad of company. She tried to believe any would have done and failed miserably. This morning he was fresh shaven and his dark mane subdued to strict military order, and he looked even more handsome than he had done dishevelled and weary that first night.

I spent the night with this man, she mused, a wry smile quirking her lips at the very thought. If the starchy housekeeper ever found out, Thea would be out the back door faster than Mrs Meldon could say 'trollop.'

'Do you think you will suit, Miss Smith?'

'I'm sure of it, desperation is a fine teacher.'

'Oblige me by not abusing Lydia's trust. I didn't finagle this place for you so you could run off with the family silver.'

'I thought it was Lady Lydia's idea to offer me a job?'

'So did she. The only way to handle her ladyship is to let her have the ordering of everything. Ned always does, so long as it suits him. I learnt my strategy from a master, which is something else you would do well to remember. My cousin is very far from being the slow-top he often does his best to appear.'

'Why should I take advantage of either?' she protested hotly, stung by his assumption that she would abuse the trust of people who had taken in a stormy petrel.

'Who knows, Miss Smith? I certainly do not. That is a conveniently common name, by the way.'

'Only when it's not yours, Major.'

'You are either a steadfast liar or exactly what you seem, and at the moment I can't quite make up my mind which.'

'Then put me out of your mind. You did your duty and provided a sanctuary that lets me keep my honour. Any obligation is satisfied, and I do not intend to lose a place where I have no need to fight off my master.'

'Ned hasn't noted another female's existence since he met Lydia.'

His voice was warm as he spoke of the lovely Lady Lydia and his guarded eyes softened. Thea wondered with a fierce pang of jealousy if he was in love with his cousin's wife. Not that it mattered of course, he would never feel more than fleeting desire for humble Miss Smith, and heaven forbid that he should discover her real identity. Then she would see his clear grey eyes cloud with distaste and his firm mouth straighten in revulsion. She would rather face Lady Winforde than that particular scenario.

'And I would be an idiot to endanger such a place for a life crime.'

'Yet I can't help but be struck by the fact that you speak very much better than your peers, and express yourself in surprisingly sophisticated language. Who are you really, Miss Smith?'

She was a fool, she silently decided, and tried hard to pretend he had not shaken her composure. She could not seem to draw back behind a mask of humble ignorance when she was with him, which meant she cared what he thought. Nonsense of course, they could not mean anything to one another.

'I am nobody,' she replied bleakly.

'At some stage you must have been somebody, to acquire such a vocabulary.'

'I might have thought I was, but I was mistaken,' she admitted, suddenly tempted to pour out the whole unsavoury story after all. 'My first mistress was a good woman, who wanted her servants to read and write, however humble their origins,' she improvised hastily instead. 'She taught me to read fluently when her eyesight began to fail.'

As lies went, it sounded convincing, she thought miserably, and tried to believe it under the acute scrutiny of Major Ashfield's steady grey eyes.

'And when she died you went back to domestic service?'

'Yes.'

'Then why are your hands those of a lady who has recently suffered a reverse?'

He took those offending hands in his and she

jumped as a lightning beat of responsive heat shot through her at his touch. Hoping he would take it for a flinch of revulsion, she stared numbly at her hands cupped in his.

'I take care of myself,' she offered hopefully.

'Without noticeable success.'

'In this case I seem to have done better.'

'So you do, but I suspect you were a ladies' maid in this former life, and this role will be a comedown,' he finally concluded.

Thea had to bite back a sigh of relief. 'I shall learn to bear it,' she said truthfully. 'Destitution is a fine teacher.'

His grip on her slender hands gentled, some of the feelings she longed to inspire in him lighting his gaze, or so it seemed. 'I'm glad Lyddie saved you from starving or selling yourself even so.'

'I would starve,' she breathed.

'You would be surprised what a person can be driven to, when there is no alternative,' Marcus replied bitterly and dropped her hand to step away.

'I probably wouldn't, you know.'

'But you aren't driven by the need of others,' he murmured, almost as if he was reminding himself of some significant factor she knew nothing of.

'No, luckily I only have my own to consider.'

Unless she could describe herself as driven by the Winfordes' greed, and she refused to do so.

'And as you are no spoilt miss, accustomed only

to eating sugarplums and reading gothic novels, I suppose you will do well enough here.'

'I shall,' she agreed serenely enough.

If she had been such an idle damsel, she never would be again. She didn't regret her uselessness, but mourned her blackened reputation. If not for that, she would have faced her major as someone more equal. She might even have told him the truth, which would have been folly of the finest order.

'Once I thought I could order the world at my own convenience,' he continued absently, as if he was thinking out loud. 'And rapidly discovered the error of my ways when I joined the army. Now my father and grandfather have made me a pawn in their game. God knows they have been playing it all my life, and I thought Grandfather would win. He delighted in conundrums and his treasure hunts were famous all over Gloucestershire at one time. Playing games where you do not know the rules can be the very devil, Miss Smith.'

'Perhaps we are all pawns in a much larger one?'

'Maybe, but now I must go and perform the new role set out for me. Just as tomorrow you take up yours.'

'And you consider my lot the easier of the two?'

'You are too perceptive by far, but I would rather say it is the simpler. I have seen too much of hardship lately to dismiss yours as easy, and I shall adapt. Here we are at the crossroads already. Even you can hardly come to any harm between here and

Nurse Turner's cottage, so we will say goodbye. Being seen walking with me would do your reputation no good.'

Thea felt a bitter smile tug at her lips, but managed to banish it. He had dismissed her with one shrug of his mighty shoulders. Instead of learning to love him, she could just as easily hate a man who could so casually say his goodbyes to her.

Chapter Four

'Goodbye, then, Major, and thank you for my new post. I did little enough to earn it.'

'Goodbye, Hetty, and thank you. Would that I were a different man.'

'Should you not say if I were not so humble, or so poor?' she challenged, and let out a great shush of breath when she was clipped into a powerful embrace and kissed ruthlessly.

'Say rather if I were a better, more worthy man,' he told her in a dangerous undertone and despite all his warnings that they might be seen, he obviously enjoyed the experience and promptly did it again.

Now she knew why she had never responded to the half-hearted overtures of Grandfather's fortune hunters, she decided hazily, and if she had a shudder to spare it might go on Granby's revolting embrace. As it was, she was too consumed by the explosion of heat that seemed to course back and forward between their greedy mouths. Of course she could not possibly have felt such intimacy with another man, she decided dazedly. He was the one designed to unlock the passionate nature she hadn't known she had until that morning in the hut, and she was more than half inclined to wish it imprisoned again. This would come to nothing, despite the heated magic that bound her to him as if for life itself.

If she had not loved its presence so deeply, she might have bitten his sensual mouth for awakening her to such need, such endless, unmet need, when she might easily have gone through life never knowing what passion was. He nibbled a line of infinitely gentle bites along her lower lip, then smoothed them away with his tongue, running it along her soft damp skin as if he loved the taste of her.

She whimpered, and a stern part of her longed to think it was in protest against what he was doing, but what she really wanted was more; more of him; more of his kisses, just simply more. She moaned her approval as he once more deepened his kiss and this time opened his wicked, wonderful mouth on hers and probed her velvet warmth with his tongue. All the steel seeped out of her bones and she arched towards him ever more closely, binding her soft curves to hard muscles and strength without any menace but the one she wanted.

For all her lofty resolutions that she would stay untouched for a lifetime in memory of a man who would soon forget her, she suddenly knew that she was wrong. To be loved and left by Major Ashfield of the 95th Rifles would warm those stark and lonely years that were all the future seemed to offer her now. She could never have his respectable attentions, so why not simply melt into his powerful embrace and save her regrets for after he was gone?

Now he was trailing more urgent kisses down the exposed length of her throat, and when exactly had he exposed it? She felt fine tremors of heat shake her and knew they were both on the edge of being consumed. Could the fact that they were standing on a public highway where anyone might see them go hang? Could she ignore the last whisper of caution that warned against this? Could she throw away all the kindness Lady Lydia was offering her for one tumble with that lady's handsome relative?

Probably, she conceded, as his wondering hand trailed a line of fire down her backbone, but she could not do the same for him. Despite those bitter words that seemed to condemn him as a heartless philanderer, she knew her seduction would haunt him once he found out he was her only lover. The only one she would ever have, for how could other men follow ardent desire combined with such tenderness? Yet the thought that he would wake up one morning in his new life and remember what he had done, and feel it as a betrayal rather than a glory, was one she could not live with.

Forcing her dazzled eyes open, she saw how his

molten grey gaze dwelt on her disgracefully open gown, apparently fascinated by the rise and fall of her creamy breasts. She catalogued the flush of heated desire across his hard cheekbones and the wondering curve of his shapely mouth, that looked as if it remembered hers and wanted more. Then she drew back and shook her tousled head. His dark hair was disordered once more, by her wandering, wondering hands. I did that, she told herself in awe. I was his lover for just a brief, uncrowned reign of mere minutes. And now I am not.

'No,' she whispered when she could find enough breath even for that feeble objection. 'I would not have you dishonour yourself, Major.'

With an almost animal sound of denial and possession, he went to tug her back into his strong arms and cover her all-too-willing lips with kisses, so they could both forget her 'no.'

'Nor would I have you dishonour me,' she added inexorably, scant inches from the ultimate temptation of surrender, and still he seemed ready to read actions rather than words.

That earlier promise he made about honouring his obligations bit like acid into any lingering dream she was clinging to. 'And I could not let you tarnish your name, Major Ashfield.'

He stepped back from her as if she had slapped him and stood, chest heaving and looking as if he had just run a heat with the devil.

'Tarnish?' he rasped out. 'How could I tarnish a name my father dragged through every patch of filth he could mire it with?'

'By muddying your own along with his.'

'Oh, preach me no such piety, Miss Smith. Just tell me no and mean it, then have done with me.'

'I can't,' she whispered miserably and for just a few seconds felt useless, hateful tears salt her eyes.

'At least that's honest,' he told her fiercely.

'As am I,' she informed him proudly, and for the first time in weeks truly meant it. She had been in danger of taking herself at the Winfordes' valuation.

'Then you cast your bait in dangerous waters, madam. You must be more careful what you catch.'

Sending him a look of pure hatred, Thea decided she would never forgive him for what he had done today, then looked down her nose at him as if he was Sir Granby Winforde himself and stalked away without another word.

'You had best do up your gown and tidy your hair if you don't want to be run out of this village as well,' his deep voice taunted behind her.

Overcome by an irresistible impulse, she swung round and stuck her tongue out at him like a street urchin.

'Goodbye to you too, my dear,' he called cheerfully, then turned on his heel and strode away whistling, as if not a single kiss or caress of that steamy encounter had meant a thing to him.

'I am not your dear!' she yelled defiantly and stormed up the wooded bank and on to the Common, completely forgetful of her safety and the dictates of everyday good sense for once.

'I hate you, Marcus Ashfield. I hate you every bit as much as you want me to, and I wish I could forget you as easily as you will me,' she raged. 'When you find a more deluded female to warm your bed, I hope she leads you a merry dance, then walks away as if she hasn't a care in the world.'

She calmed down at last and returned to her temporary home and scrubbed and dusted every corner of Miss Turner's cottage in return for her kindness. By the time the woman came back from clucking over her precious Master Nick that evening, Thea was calm again and ready to share their simple supper. They retired early, for Thea had a brisk walk to look forward to and a hard day's work. It was a very long time before she slept. When Thea did, she was glad her hostess was rather deaf, for she had woken from a nightmare on a panicked scream.

It was strange living on the wrong side of the myriad of doors designed to hide servants in the service of their betters. The sun rose and set on her labours, but Thea got used to her duties. The news that Major Ashfield was the new Viscount Strensham galled her more. Of course it made no difference. With her name besmirched she couldn't marry him, although his title would free her fortune. Yet could she have lived with his cold logic, if he had found out who she really was and offered marriage for mercenary reasons? Yes, the instant reply came, then she contemplated such an unequal match and shuddered.

The great idiot had already hurt her more than the Winfordes had succeeded in doing by stripping her of home and worldly advantages. Marcus Ashfield had left her without the luxury of hope. Some last childish part of her had harboured the delusion that one day she might meet a man who valued her for herself alone. She did not have that vague hope now and, if she hadn't been so busy, she might have been miserable.

She found comfort in the thought that, even if she were a lady, he would dish out the same hurt. The deluded girl she had been could well have gone into a decline, so at least she was saved making that discovery too late.

Then one April morning the sounds of church bells pealing out joyously interrupted the calm of Rosecombe, and such small considerations as a bruised heart faded into unimportance. The now nearly recovered Captain Prestbury rode out with his cousin to find out what was going on, to be met with the joyful news that Bonaparte had surrendered to the Allies. The cousins galloped back to Rosecombe with joy in their hearts.

'Peace at last, my love!' Sir Edward shouted, and

threw himself off his horse to share the glad news with the woman he loved so much.

'Oh, Ned, is it truly all over?' her ladyship gasped breathlessly, as he seized her and swung her round, all the time laughing with joy.

'Unless Farmer Boughton has been at the apple brandy, which I doubt as he has been a teetotaller ever since I can remember.'

'Then we must ring the bell so we can share the news, my love.'

As they were standing in the hall under the bemused gaze of most of their household, there was no need, and there was much cheering and chattering with joy and relief. They were given a half-day to celebrate and by nightfall bonfires were blazing for miles around.

'Not celebrating, Miss Smith?' Captain Prestbury asked Thea as she melted into the shadows where he watched joy being unconfined.

'Of course, Captain, who would not?' she replied cautiously, wishing she had checked the darkness before she tried to melt into it.

'Someone who finds it hard to believe it's all over I suppose.'

'It does seem strange.'

'Strange is too mild a word. After so many years of fighting that genius of a madman, I can't believe it's over.'

'You think Bonaparte mad?'

'Not in the sense poor old Farmer George is, but anyone who seeks to rule the world is unhinged.'

'I see what you mean.'

'Do you, Miss Smith?' The light mockery was back in his voice and Thea wondered if anyone was allowed to catch more than a glimpse of the real Captain Prestbury.

'Only a fool refuses to acknowledge his enemy's strengths.'

'And you are far from being a fool.'

If only that were true. 'Neither am I very wise.'

'Yet, does a hard start explain your contradictions, I wonder?'

Now his voice was speculative and Thea felt her heart race for a very different reason than it had in Marcus Ashfield's company. Both cousins were dangerous in their own way.

'I must leave you, sir, lest we be seen.'

His grip was surprisingly firm for a man who was recovering from dreadful wounds. Most unattached females in Wiltshire were in love with this tall, dark and handsome Hussar, but she just felt a twinge of regret that they could never be friends. His cousin had dealt with any weaknesses she had for rogues ready to break her heart and leave without a backward look.

'Just a warning from one adventurer to another,' he continued, his grip impersonal and his gaze steady.

'I'm no adventuress.'

'Yet you're not what you seem either, are you, Miss Smith?'

'I am *exactly* what I seem, sir. Someone who needs a job to stave off destitution.'

'Those are the plain facts,' he agreed, but she could still see the glint of cynicism in blue eyes that were dark in the distant light of the flames. 'Yet it is my business to look beneath them, even if my intentions are pure for once.'

'You can hardly expect me to believe that, now can you, Captain?' she told him, with a significant glance at his long fingers fettering her wrist.

He chuckled and let her go, trusting his words to keep her.

'You have a way of looking adversity in the face and defying it that says you are a kindred spirit, Miss Smith. Would I had met you on the dance floor.'

'You must have a touch of fever, Captain. Housemaids hardly ever go to grand parties.'

'I observe, my dear. I don't report unless my commanders decree it, and even if you were Boney's best spy it could hardly signify now.'

'Well that's a relief.'

Thea saw him smile by the intermittent light, but he was sober and unsmiling when he finally came to the point. 'My cousin Marcus is a fool, but a very determined one,' he said gently.

She held up a hand in protest, feeling as if

someone was probing a wound as tender as the one finally healing in his arm.

'I'm not always so fast asleep as I seem, Miss Smith. With the number of stitches in my arm, I am often pressed to do more than doze.'

'You have the habit of deceit, Captain,' she told him disapprovingly.

'True, but perhaps we had best not to examine that trait too deeply, since you share it. At first I was sparing the great oaf worry by staying still, then I nearly ended up blushing like a schoolgirl.'

'Serves you right.'

'True, but I was glad you finally remembered my presence.'

'I recalled my own good sense, you had nothing to do with it.'

'I'm suitably mortified, but nevertheless you did well. Marcus decided long ago to have nothing to do with love. I doubt anything less would seem worthy of throwing your bonnet over the windmill.'

'I realised that for myself.'

'Yet it can't hurt to say he's as stony hearted as I'm thought to be.'

'No, Captain, the gossips are wrong.'

'That they're not. Marcus is quieter than me, but he's still dangerous, and your sex has a way of yearning for the unattainable.'

'That's not what I meant,' she said softly and reached a gentle hand up to touch his still-thin cheek. 'Lord Strensham is essentially cold, but I think you, Captain, are far from it.'

He looked uncomfortable, more used to brazening out misdeeds than fielding praise. 'I leave at the end of the week to continue my recovery at my grandmother's house in Bath,' he said with every sign of revulsion.

'Poor Captain Prestbury.'

'Oh, confound it, why not call me Nick?'

'Because I'm the under-housemaid.'

'My friends call me by my given name.'

'Thank you, Nick, but when we meet again, please forget you ever set eyes on me?'

'Aye, but a letter to the Dowager Lady Prestbury in Sydney Place will find me.'

'I will remember,' she said softly and with a gesture of farewell, went to find the solitude she needed. If only she had a brother like Nick Prestbury, how different her life would be.

At the end of April the Darraine family left for the capital to enjoy the Season and to join the peace celebrations. Although most of the senior staff went too, the rest stayed at Rosecombe. Which could hardly be described as a holiday, Thea thought one sunny day at the end of June, considering the housekeeper would pounce on any neglect of their duties. Yet, if she made up her work in double time, a few minutes could be stolen from the day.

* * *

'You'll get caught one day you will,' Carrie, the head housemaid, informed her cheerfully when she came upon her second lieutenant illicitly reading one of Sir Edward's beloved books.

'Caught dusting the library? That's what we maids do.'

'The rest of us don't read the books while we're dusting them, but you'd best be more careful, now.'

'Why?' Thea got on very well with the cheerful country girl and doubted her warning was a threat to reveal her secret.

'Family's coming home, and bringing guests with them.'

'I thought they were off to Brighton.'

'So did I, but we was both wrong. His lordship and the Captain will join them later, or so Mrs Meldon says, and she wants their rooms got ready before we start on all the others, just in case one of them takes it into his head to arrive before we're ready.'

Thea's heart thumped at the mere mention of the new Viscount Strensham, but she told herself not to be a fool. He had made his feelings, or lack of them, clear last time they met. He was just another stranger who would fill her days with work as Lady Lydia had promised.

'I'd best hurry up in here, then,' she said calmly and put her book back.

'I'll help, then we'll find Jane and make a start.

Let's hope the missus don't expect us to do it all ourselves, or we'll be dead on our feet.'

Plenty of help was forthcoming, but Thea was
soon wondering if they might not all drop from exhaustion, just running about satisfying the guests'
constant demands. Lady Lydia and Sir Edward
Darraine cultivated a very odd set of friends. A
bullying and humourless heiress whose father made
his money in the cloth trade in the north; a lively
widow with a merry eye; and a very young lady so
shy she hardly spoke. They didn't seem to have
much in common and would surely have been better
entertained by the protracted victory celebrations
the newspapers were full of.

Miss Rashton's demands and constant complaints
about country servants and their uncouth ways was
wearing everyone's nerves to tatters. Thea kept out
of her way, and tried to consider the wretched
female her punishment for once also being a demanding and inconsiderate miss. Then the maids
were ordered to help in the hall one day and the
reason for the lady's presence became clear as glass.

She saw a tall and immaculately dressed gentleman climbing down from a hired carriage, just as an
artlessly disordered Miss Rashton came drifting
down the stairs as if by pure chance. For a moment
Thea's ears buzzed as if she might actually be in
danger of fainting, but she refused to give him the

satisfaction. Not by one look or gesture would she reveal she even remembered him, she told herself, and folded her hands behind her back where nobody could see them shaking.

'Oh, the dear viscount is here,' the chief heiress breathed in the softest tones anyone at the Park had heard since she arrived. 'Now we shall be merry again,' she added, with an eager sparkle in her hard eyes, and the unscrupulous rogue greeted her with a wicked smile and a bow that would have done credit to a Bond Street Beau.

'Miss Rashton, and Mrs Fall,' Lord Strensham said, bowing just as gracefully and smiling just as wolfishly at the widow, who emerged from the music room where she had probably been hiding from the tone-deaf Miss Rashton. 'London was a veritable desert without you, ladies, so I escaped Prinny's celebrations as soon as I could.'

'Indeed, it must be nigh unbearable by now, what with all the noise and heat and that vulgar crowd turning out to see the Sovereigns off,' Miss Rashton said rather wistfully.

'Yes, you would not have liked it at all,' he returned, and Thea wondered if she was the only one who detected mockery in his grey eyes.

He was here to marry one of these creatures. At the moment she fervently hoped that he saddled himself with Miss Rashton for the rest of their days. Such a cynical alliance would suit him perfectly.

She stood, head bowed and waiting for orders, trying to pretend the man standing so close and so remote meant nothing to her. Her battle-worn major had become the sort of fastidious aristocrat who might turn a menial into a rabid Jacobin. This cynical rake really didn't appeal to her at all. Or at least not very much.

His broad shoulders were encased in a coat of dark blue superfine that fitted him without a wrinkle, his cravat was perfection and his linen as spotless as if he had just stepped out of his dressing room. She was in an excellent position to know that his mirror-polished Hessians were unblemished by so much as a speck of dust, and his pantaloons were designed to emphasise rather than disguise the muscular strength of his powerful legs. If he had become as idle as he looked, very soon he would run to fat, she concluded vengefully, and just remembered in time that she was not superior enough a servant to give vent to a sniff of disapproval.

'Before I join the delights of the drawing room, you really must let me get rid of my dirt, ladies,' he drawled and Thea longed for the pail of dirty water she had recently washed down the drain, after scrubbing the pristine marble under his fastidious feet.

No, he could bring all the heiresses in Britain into his cousin's house and shamelessly flirt with them in front of her, then cynically make his choice for all she cared. She set her face in an indifferent mask as the butler ordered her to help with his lordship's luggage. Her gaze fixed on the middle distance as was only proper and she spared the tall figure at the centre of all this fuss not another glance; he wasn't worth it, after all.

Chapter Five

Wishing he could be as serenely indifferent to the little wretch as she appeared to be to him, Marcus ran upstairs and tried to reorder his world again. It had cost him weeks of turmoil to forget the hurt in a pair of unique turquoise eyes, and harden himself to this task. He would not let the mere sight of her throw him off course now. Three months spent turning this way and that like an animal in a trap, and he was held as fast as he had been when he began. Still, now he knew he had no alternative but to marry the money he needed to drag his estates out of River Tick.

Despite the immaculate attire that made Thea itch to muss and muddy his splendour, he stripped off and shaved himself once more, before donning pristine breeches and a spotless linen shirt. He was absently tying his neckcloth when he reminded himself of Nick's cynical advice.

'Look like a ragtag without sixpence, Marco, and you will be taken for the desperate man that you are.

Dress like a top o' the trees and you will be fighting off the rich little darlings in droves.'

A smile fleetingly softened his austere mouth. Few believed Nick had a kindly bone in his body, but gain his loyalty and he was steadfast as granite.

Nick had come to town to consult the doctors about his arm, and ordered his own tailor to outfit his cousin. 'And if he don't pay you out of his ill-gotten gains, send the bill to me and I'll dun him instead.'

He had gone on to countermand the modest wardrobe Marcus had ordered, and thus he stood here, dressing in fine feathers to charm the gold out of the heiresses' dower chests. He probably deserved Miss Rashton he decided, and at least her iron determination to wed a title would work to his advantage. He could make her a viscountess and she could save his bankrupt estates. They might have been made for one another.

He shrugged himself into the elegant waistcoat and beautifully tailored coat Nick insisted no self-respecting fortune hunter should be seen without, and wondered what his lordly ancestors would have made of their latest descendant. Not much, he determined grimly. The Ashfields had been a shrewd race, until his father gambled, drank and caroused his way through every penny he could lay his hands on, and a good many that should have been safely out of his reach.

Hastily running a brush through his thick dark

hair, Marcus knew he looked as elegant as a gentleman could without the services of a skilled valet, and decided it was high time he wrote to his lawyer again. Surely something must have escaped his father's headlong pursuit of pleasure? After all, his grandfather had outlived his only son by ten days, so it wasn't as if the Honourable Julius Ashfield had ever inherited the title and estates. He had been borrowing against expectations, so how had he managed to beggar his heirs?

Preoccupied with this dilemma, Marcus forgot his promise to join the ladies in the drawing room and marched downstairs with a determination his former brigade would have recognised, even if the light-hearted Major Ashfield they knew off-duty had vanished along with his dark green uniform. He was halfway down the room in search of a decent pen and hot pressed paper when he finally took in the picture before him.

The humblest female in the entire household was taking her ease in Ned's favourite chair. Marcus blinked and wondered if too many sleepless nights and occasionally drinking too deep to escape harsh reality, had caught up with him. No, his eyesight was sharp and his senses stubbornly unclouded, so the troublesome wench really was sitting reading some solemn tome with such intense concentration she hadn't noticed him come in.

'And what the *devil* are you up to now?' he

barked, and watched her start violently with an unworthy sense of satisfaction.

A faint feeling of shame made his expression all the more forbidding as he stood in judgement over the female he had fought so hard to forget. How could the annoying little witch be so wrapped up in her studies, when he had been so ridiculously conscious of her every move the instant he stepped over the threshold?

Thea glowered back at him, Lord Strensham was a fortune hunter of the worst sort—a man who could easily earn his own wealth if he could be bothered to do a day's work now and again. To prove that he meant nothing to her, she had slipped away from the furore his coming had caused and taken this ridiculous risk. Ten minutes of forgetfulness were needed to erase the image of dashing, self-sufficient Major Ashfield from her mind, and set foppish, useless Lord Strensham in his place.

'Improving my mind,' she snapped as he continued to wait for her explanation like examining counsel. 'An example you might follow, if only you could spare the time.'

'And you obviously spend yours avoiding the job you're paid to do. I should never have told Lyddie you needed work, for you quite obviously don't value her kindness in taking you without a reference.'

Maybe he was right. If he had let her slip into the

woods that day, she would never have suffered the hurt and humiliation of being rejected by this handsome idiot. Of course she might also have starved to death or been caught by the Winfordes by now, but sometimes even that seemed better than yearning for a man who did not want her. It was his fault of course—if he had stayed away just a little bit longer she would have forgotten him. Anyway, he was changed, if the trappings of a fashionable fortune hunter and the indolent, impudent manner he affected were anything to go by.

'Her ladyship knows we're run ragged by that virago of yours.'

He looked conscious, and so he should. If he was really planning to wed the confounded female for the sake of her bulging coffers, he was selling himself short. After all, if a fortune was all he wanted, he could have married her. By reminding herself that she would have been storing up a lifetime of heart-ache, she forced her numb legs into supporting her and prepared to make a dignified exit.

She watched as his grey gaze ran lazily over her rather crumpled uniform and found her lacking. How she wished she dared to slap the suggestion of a smile from his handsome face. Spoilt and silly Miss Alethea Hardy would have fallen headlong for such a dangerous, damn-your-eyes rogue, but prosaic Hetty Smith was surely immune to his dubious charm.

'Tiresome heavy these great books, ain't they, your lordship?'

'So you sat down and waited for that one to jump back onto the shelf?' he asked quietly, a hint of laughter vanished from his grey eyes as if it had never been and she shivered, despite the growing heat of the day.

His deep voice sounded as if he had permanently rasped it barking orders on the battlefield, she mused, feeling for one shocking moment as if his baritone rumble had found an echo in her very bones. She caught herself remembering how seductive it was when he pitched it low and lover-like and rapidly slammed the door on such idiotic memories.

'No, my lord, and now I must be about my work again,' she said, meeting his sceptical gaze with a blankness she hoped would signal her indifference.

Too well acquainted with her own features to find them in any way remarkable, she could make nothing of his frozen stillness as his grey eyes met hers. Yet a whisper of that forbidden longing brushed down her tingling spine like a lover's touch once again. He turned to gaze at the Wiltshire countryside through the long windows. His grey eyes were so wintry when he fixed them on her again that she had to control an urge to shrink away.

'I need to get on,' she said truthfully.

'Then stop treating me like a flat and tell me what you're up to.'

Heaven forbid! 'Her ladyship will need me any minute,' she told him with a perplexed expression that should have told him she was innocent.

Lord Strensham's reflexes were so good that her wrist was caught in an iron grip before she had time to take evasive action. She held as still as a statue and refused to struggle with him like a country maid in a bad play. Yet the touch of his warm fingers on her bare flesh sent an insidious streak of warmth jagging up her arm to earth itself in the most unwelcome places, and she shivered with superstitious dread before bravely meeting his eyes again. If only she was as indifferent to his touch as she had been to Nick Prestbury's, she thought hazily, but it seemed there was no point wishing for the moon.

'I don't think my cousins will be downstairs betimes if the lady you refer to has been running the household round as you say. Since you don't look like any ladies' maid I ever came across, I rather doubt Lyddie will need you either,' he said silkily as he ran his mocking gaze over the housemaid's uniform no self-respecting dresser would be seen dead in.

Feeling the hot colour stain her cheeks, Thea could not govern her reaction to his touch. Lately she had shrunk from any contact with the male sex, managing to avoid the roving eyes of both visiting masters and their servants by keeping her head down and disappearing into her ill-fitting, hand-me-down clothes. Lord Strensham's less than lover-like grasp on her wrist sent her wayward heartbeat dancing as if performing a waltz at Almack's.

It was perfectly ridiculous, this terrible need to have him kiss her again, she told herself. Secretly longing for him to draw her nearer and satisfy this feral desire was folly. She controlled a warm shiver as his strong hand gentled on her slender wrist and sparked those ridiculous curls of heat into life. They were worse than strangers and must remain so. There was an unbridgeable gulf between them, and she ordered herself brusquely to stop staring up at him like a mooncalf.

'And to think I was warned about *gentlemen* like you,' she snapped.

He dropped her hand as if it burnt him and jerked backwards so violently he was in danger of being overset for a moment. His dark brows snapped together, his eyes fierce as a hawk's and his firm mouth set in a hard line. At least he was himself again; the drawling fop banished by the raw reality of what lay between them, however he tried to deny it, and she tried not to exult at the transformation.

No, she was ruined in the eyes of the world and he didn't want her even as Hetty Smith, foundling! Thea gasped at the bitter memory of that day at the crossroads and almost shrank away from him, shocked at her own stupidity in laying herself open to such hurt a second time. She stood and faced him, raising her chin to spark dumb defiance at him; set on defying him even if it cost her the place she needed so badly.

'You know I don't trifle with innocents,' he ground out, as if the very idea outraged his peculiar notions of honour. 'But if you trap any more unwary gentlemen in otherwise empty rooms you won't be one of those for very much longer, you foolish child.'

Child—how dare he? Thea gritted her teeth and managed to remember why she had to stay here undetected for at least two more months. By dint of promising herself that she would seek him out the moment she came of age—and give him her unvarnished opinion of his dubious morals and scurvy manners—she somehow mastered her fury. Unfortunately a mental picture of him, faced with a vaguely familiar female haranguing him over the breakfast table, presented itself to her inner eye, and an appreciative chuckle escaped her before she could check it.

For a second his remote façade seemed about to crack and his chilly grey eyes warmed, as if he too realised how ridiculous they must look, facing one another across Sir Edward Darraine's library like duellists. Then his expression became bleak and unreadable again, even as all manner of forbidden questions trembled on her unruly tongue. She blinked to rid her mind of a ridiculous image of those grey eyes hot with passion, a smile of infinite promise on a firm mouth that had suddenly become sensual rather than hard and angry, as he moved ever nearer to her own waiting one and…and nothing!

'I ain't got all day to waste gossiping, even if you have, m'lord.'

'No, I dare say you have work to catch up on.'

'Most likely I have at that.'

'Just make sure you don't get caught next time, Hetty.'

'There won't be a next time,' she assured him emphatically, and swore privately that it was true.

Some risks were not worth taking twice, and my Lord Strensham was one of them.

'If I catch you out in one more misdeed, your mistress will hear of it,' he warned and his mistrust hurt.

'Maybe she'll wonder why you care,' she was stung into replying pertly, wondering why that threat tormented her so much she had to blink back tears.

They could never be more than master and housemaid after all, the Winfordes had seen to that.

'Try that tack and you'll soon find out your mistake, my enterprising little doxy, and maybe I was mistaken about that innocence after all,' he ground out harshly, and she was helpless in his powerful embrace before she had even registered the fact that he had moved closer.

Lost for words and even breath as the potent reality of being locked in his arms once more hit her, she forced air into her protesting lungs. Breathing in the scent of clean linen, warm male and fine broadcloth, she forgot all else. Strength so certain it knew nothing about force wrapped her round and she had the most absurd desire to nuzzle deeper into his arms and forget all her troubles, even as common sense was vainly ordering her to drag herself out of them by whatever means needed, fair or foul.

His touch was gentle and sure, and she felt as if she alone knew the breadth and depths that made up Marcus Ashfield, the person under the lordly cynicism. Even that foolish notion flew out of her head as he stroked down her cheek to her chin in a caress that had her obediently raising her head before her brain managed to inform her she was making life too easy for a practised seducer.

Even as her wiser self was ordering her to struggle, to kick or bite if that was what it took to get him to let go, the fool in charge angled her mouth to meet his descending one and determinedly shut her eyes to reality. His lips were gentle on hers and her eyelids fluttered open again so her dazzled eyes could meet stormy grey ones. She gasped in a breath that carried his unique scent and an echo of his latent power right to the heart of her. Then, as the blue faded from her turquoise eyes and they became green under such extreme emotion, his own need burnt hotter, and his kiss seemed about to draw the very essence of her into his powerful protection.

'Sea-witch,' he murmured, his lips so reluctant

to leave hers that she felt his words as much as heard them.

Then he ran his tongue along the softening gap between her lips and they parted for him on a sigh, as if she spent her entire life waiting around for his kisses. Sensible Thea was screaming at the willing and needy creature who seemed to have been born fully formed and defiantly wanton in his arms that morning in the woods, but the thunder of his heartbeat where her wondering fingers rested against his powerful chest all but drowned her out.

She was putting the few dreams she had left at risk, for a few moments of enchantment in the arms of a philanderer. Yet his mouth firmed and demanded on hers, and he explored her lips with a wholehearted pleasure that was a seduction all on its own. Despite everything, she longed to explore this heady passion with this unique man. Stern Thea snapped something very rude at melting, desiring Thea, who just murmured something foolish and felt Marcus's tongue explore her all-too-willing mouth with irrepressible delight as he asked more than her pride should grant him. A request she unhesitatingly allowed as her mouth opened under his, and the feel of him dipping between her lips and flirting with her tongue sent shivers of longing down her spine.

'No,' sensible Thea murmured a protest that she knew was half at losing his warmth as he raised his head.

She saw a blaze of emotion light his grey gaze to silver, and knew all that heated desire was for her. Then he put his hands on her upper arms and set her at a distance as she realised just what she had done.

'Oh, no!' she whispered and it sounded like a parade-ground bellow in the sunny room she had previously found so peaceful.

'Oh, no, indeed,' he murmured softly.

Wasn't it just like him to act as if he had just discovered her committing some trifling misdeed? Especially when she felt as if caught by such wonder she was surprised the world had not changed by more than seconds since he shook the foundations of it again. It had never occurred to her that he might be as amazed by that tumultuous kiss as she was herself, so she took his light tone for mockery and her temper lashed the hurt aside to blaze at him.

'I hope you marry the high-nosed bitch who runs us all ragged from dawn to dusk with her demands and her megrims!' she raged, what had to be hot fury stinging her eyes. 'You richly deserve one another, and at least then you won't inflict yourselves on better people,' she finished triumphantly and stamped a sensibly shod foot so there could be no mistake about her outrage.

'Indeed,' he replied blandly, all expression vanishing from his face as he stepped back from her, looking as if he had just encountered a flying artillery shell and was unsure where it might explode.

'Oh, get out of the way, you, you…*man,* you,' she demanded in reply to such blatant provocation and could have kicked him when he obligingly did so. 'Somehow I'll make you pay, my lord, if it's the last thing I do,' she threatened, once she was so far out of his reach that even he had no hope of catching her.

Thea marched out of the library with a seething mass of confused emotions powering her about her neglected duties so effectively that she had finished them in record time, despite that shocking interlude in Sir Edward Darraine's well-stocked library.

'No doubt you will, you little shrew,' the rueful gentleman she left behind her murmured as the echoes of the door slamming still resounded.

Marcus had never intended to touch the girl again, let alone kiss her. Now he was half-willing to sell his soul to the devil for a night of insanity in her arms. It could not happen, he informed himself sternly. It must not happen. He hadn't spent so long battling his inner demons to succumb within minutes of setting eyes on her again. Even such fiery passion faded, he reassured himself, and she would hate him for ruining her if he gave in to it.

So why did he constantly have this uneasy feeling that he was wilfully turning his back on something unique? Because he was an idiot, and, even if love existed, he still had nothing. Nothing to offer Hetty Smith, housemaid and enigma at any rate. Miss Rashton, heiress, wanted his title and a well-bred son and heir, so at least he had something to give her in return, even if the thought of bedding her left him cold. He shivered as he contrasted his molten feelings for Hetty with his indifference to the strident heiress.

Yet the lovely Mrs Fall would want affection at the very least. Timid little Sophronia Willet would sooner be locked in a cage with a hungry bear than marry him, so Miss Rashton it must be, and at least there would be no nonsense about love. No nonsense at all and the thought of carrying out his marital duties under his bride's stern gaze made his toes curl.

A few minutes alone with Lyddie's humblest housemaid was all it took for passion to make a fool of him. His loins quickened at the thought of her lips under his and the delicious friction of her curves fitting themselves to his angles. It always felt as if they had been formed to meld with such right-ness, when the time inevitably came to do so. Not so, Major Ashfield sternly informed his traitorous body. He had to marry money, or let his dependants starve and reduce his brother to penury along with himself. No impulse to forget the world in a runaway wench's arms could stand in his way.

Years of military discipline made him sit at Ned's desk to write his letter, fighting the inclination to lounge there and muse over a stolen kiss, as well as Virgil's *Aeneid* in the original Latin Hetty had left there. It was on that renegade thought that the peculiar nature of her reading sank in.

Marcus put aside the letter he couldn't give half his attention to stare intently at the book, trying to make sense out of Hetty Smith. A female of birth and education who read Virgil's *Aeneid* in the original Latin would be an eccentric, so surely a maidservant could not con such a text? Although this particular maid might pretend she was no more capable of reading it than she was of rowing to the Antipodes, he was far from convinced.

The wench was hiding something, besides sea-changing eyes a man might happily drown in and the softest, most tempting mouth he had ever kissed. Perhaps she had been waiting for her lover in that shack in the woods that night? The very thought made his long fingers tighten into fists and his mouth hard. She felt like the most innocent female he had ever kissed when she took fire in his arms, but was she acting a part?

If she could play the housemaid to Lady Lydia's satisfaction, she might as easily fool an ex-soldier who had spent years fighting for his country rather than dealing with duplicitous females. Disillusion set another layer of ice about what he assured himself was a cold and indifferent heart, and he tried to consider the Darraines' third housemaid dispassionately.

The cunning minx could earn a fortune on her back if that naiveté was an act. Marcus was well aware of the dangers of taking liars at face value, even if a less disillusioned man might forget discretion and common sense under Hetty Smith's potent spell. It was clearly his duty to find out if she presented a threat to his cousin's household after introducing her to it so blindly. Passion was a snare that could bring down the best of men, let alone a fortune hunter with nothing a year to support his obligations on, but he didn't have to give in to it.

Picking up the calf-bound volume, he shook it and, when nothing fell out, assumed she had been looking in the wrong place. Yet Ned was a respectable country gentleman nowadays—and what fool would risk hiding anything in here, when his cousin was commonly known to be bookish? Maybe *he* had read too many improbable tales for his own good.

Of course the wench *could* have been taking a wistful look at the mysteries of the written word and not know English or Latin from Double Dutch. Despite this comfortable notion, he was left with a lingering impression of her remarkable eyes, full of native wit and wary as a cat's. Someone must keep an eye on her, and, if a gang of felons were targeting the house, he would frustrate them, short of putting the under-housemaid's slender neck in the hangman's noose.

An icy shudder ran down his spine at the thought of such an outcome, but the idea of any woman suffering such an untimely end would disturb him, he hastily reassured himself. Yet never before had Marcus experienced such an insane compulsion to seduce one of the servants, and how he wished he had only ever known her as such.

To compound his sins by continuing her downfall would be despicable, and he prided himself on carrying on his *amours* with women who knew the rules. Somehow he had managed to convince himself she was an innocent after all and, picturing her looking as confused and confounded as he had felt just now, he could not believe her the hard-eyed seductress he half wanted her to be. If only she were that siren, he could take her and be damned, but somehow he must slam the door on that heady notion if he was to be fit for company any time soon.

Could the wench's eyes be best described as sea-green, aquamarine or turquoise? he mused. Without the abundant life behind them, they could be any of those fanciful colours. With it they were extraordinarily her own and then there was her mouth, so soft and yielding under his that he felt the rogue she thought him as his body clenched with need. He shook his head in an effort to gain control over his baser self. No sooner had he resolved to forget all idea of succumbing to Hetty's artless charm that the memory of her tripped him up once more.

Well, it had to stop—the little witch was quite right to wish him on Miss Rashton. He lacked the funds to keep his vagrant waif in anything but penury, if he ruined her for the sake of his pleasure and made it impossible for her to stay under his cousin's roof. Anyway, it would inevitably be more than that—once he lost the self-control he had once prided himself on, he knew he could never stop his obsession ruining her in more ways than one.

Hetty Smith was an ingenue with hard edges who could not possibly understand Virgil, he reassured himself, and marched from the room as if he was back on parade. He even managed to look delighted at the sight of the heiresses gathered in the drawing room, despite what fate and Miss Rashton had in store for him. At least he could not dwell on the third housemaid's hidden depths in their presence, for fear of saying or doing something so idiotic even Miss Rashton gave him up as a lost cause.

Chapter Six

Thea climbed the back stairs to her attic, angrily muttering some satisfyingly unladylike oaths as she trudged up the seemingly endless flights of narrow wooden steps. His lordship's practised kisses were not wondrous at all, obviously. Meanwhile every step taught her a salutary lesson in the many differences between an unimportant maid and the noble Viscount Strensham.

She must move about the house like some sort of undesirable beetle emerging from the very walls, while for such as my lord there were elegant marble stairs gently rising to the heights of elegance. Which suited her very well. She was much safer here than she would have been as an unsuspecting guest. She sincerely hoped the ignoble viscount was enjoying his Pyrrhic victory though, because soon she would walk away from his cousin's house with her fortune *and* her freedom intact, while he bore off a much lesser heiress, and serve him right too.

Yet even after washing with the rough soap thought fit to keep servants clean and decent, and changing into her afternoon uniform, she was still haunted by the memory of Lord Strensham's steely gaze softening for the open-mouthed idiot she became in his presence. She supposed he must think her an over-eager trollop now. How could he do otherwise when she just stood round like a hypnotised rabbit waiting to be seduced whenever he felt amorously inclined? And why let him kiss her, when she knew he was an embittered cynic who meant nothing by it?

Well, if she was nothing to him, she would make sure he meant less to her. If he chose to kiss half a dozen maids every morning, it wouldn't matter tuppence to Hetty Smith. The thought of a bevy of starry-eyed females lining up before breakfast to receive such a dubious honour, appealed to her sense of the ridiculous and rapidly banished her frown. She had survived worse things, she told herself, and ran down the back stairs to help serve the refreshments Lady Lydia ordered *al fresco* on such a beautiful afternoon.

Whisking unobtrusively into line, Thea recalled meals at Hardy House with a wry smile. Determined to do things right, Giles Hardy had sat at the head of a table long enough to seat a regiment, while his granddaughter sat at the foot and each had their own footman, with the butler orbiting between them like a satellite moon.

'Earywigs in the cake and wapses in the lemonade again,' whispered Carrie and Thea chuckled softly, but refused to join the second housemaid's muttered litany on the lack of state kept at Rosecombe Park nowadays.

Jane often complained about the family's insistence on saving tax by employing maids rather than footmen, but Thea had given up pointing out that if they did not, Jane might not be here to flirt with those stalwart specimens of young manhood she yearned for so badly.

'More lemonade from the house, Hetty, and be quick about it,' ordered the Darraines' stately butler, sparing the least significant foot soldier from a line he directed with the aplomb of a field marshal.

Feeling her humble position under Lord Strensham's steady gaze, Thea departed. She waited while one minion was spared to squeeze lemons and crush sugar and another fetched ice from the depleted store in the icehouse. Fifteen minutes spent in that sweltering kitchen fetching and carrying, and she could understand Cook's bad temper and was beginning to share it.

'Not before time,' said the butler, sounding like an archbishop sorely tried by a minor cannon when she finally reappeared, hot and flustered from the kitchens.

She waited for further orders and wondered if she was fated to play the lowly housemaid for the rest of her life. It occurred to her that, once upon a time, she would have formed part of Lady Lydia's bevy of ladies with large moneybags and doubtful pedigrees eager to wed a lord. The appalling prospect of competing with Miss Rashton in the Viscount Stakes grated on her wounded pride—at least that must be what sent a stab of dark pain shooting through her.

How the mighty are fallen, she thought ruefully, before diligently attending to her duties once again. The rightful heiress to one of the largest fortunes in the British Isles, she spent the evening carrying cans of hot water for the quality and closing curtains and attending to crumbs and spills.

If she couldn't sleep for thinking of a particularly annoying nobleman, slumbering in comfort and solitude a floor below and half a world away, that was because he was so infuriating. All three housemaids made do with one old bed in their stuffy attic under the leads, so to feel resentment of the privilege he so undeservedly enjoyed was perfectly natural, she assured herself. Thea set about counting sheep with grim determination and at last fell into an uneasy slumber.

'Oh, Marcus, thank heavens it's only you,' Lady Lydia greeted her husband's cousin as he sought sanctuary late the following afternoon. 'There's no need to look at me like that, for I didn't mean to be rude,' her ladyship said with a smile.

'I didn't realise how frightening I could be, until
your youngest guest took one look at me and bolted
for the less-threatening company of the schoolroom.
If you ask me, she should never have been allowed
out of it so soon. Did I send you to earth as well?'

'I just need to regroup my forces before going
into battle again, Major.'

The pretty little cottage by the lake had been re-
decorated for her on Sir Edward's orders, and
Marcus knew his hostess resorted to it when her
duties threatened to overwhelm her. It was so much
more in Lydia's style than the grand Grecian temple
he could see across the lake and the household
would leave her in peace here. He sincerely hoped
Miss Rashton did not even know of its existence.

'Who can blame you? I'm sorry to inflict this on
you both,' he said stiffly, all too conscious of what
he asked of her and Ned in hosting this house party.

'Nonsense, we would have been sadly flat without
company this summer,' she said bracingly and he
gave her the smile she remembered so well from her
days as an army wife, before Ned succeeded to the
family baronetcy and had to come home, and Major
Ashfield found himself in urgent need of a rich wife.

'Sadly flat can sometimes be a desirable state,' he
said ruefully and she shot him a speculative look.

'Have you grown weary of doing the polite
already?' she asked with apparent carelessness.

'More than I dare admit, Lyddie, but needs must

when the devil drives. If you find this business so tedious, why did you not tell me so at the outset? My stepmama would have introduced me to some unfortunate female with plenty of money and a sickly constitution—in the hope she would fail to provide me with an heir and Colin could inherit my obligations in due course.'

'That wretched woman would do anything to dis-oblige you, and I am a better friend than to leave you to her untender mercies.'

'You are the best of women and, if you were not so unfashionably in love with Ned, I might carry you off across my saddle-bow—debts or no debts.'

'I should not come—you would break my heart inside a month if I was foolish enough to succumb to your dubious charms, Marcus Ashfield.'

'Never, I like you far too well to break your heart, Lyddie, even if I didn't know how surely it wasn't already given to my unworthy cousin.'

'Just as well. Your lordly indifference would rapidly do for me I fear. I suffer from a ridiculous need to be loved back, you see? You consider such emotion a sad weakness.'

'More of an eventuality to be avoided.'

'Have you never been in love then, Marcus? And pray don't fob me off with the tale of your more out-rageous misdeeds, for I witnessed a fair few of them don't forget.'

Her wicked smile at the memory of some of his

more outrageous *affaires de coeur* lifted her face from attractive to nigh irresistible and Marcus wondered why he had never fallen in love with her. Surely the fact that he had not meant that he was right and love was not for him, even if he heartily disliked hunting a wife solely for her money?

'There's nothing wrong with good old-fashioned lust,' he replied uneasily.

There was something very wrong with yearning to bed a girl he should not even dream of insulting with dishonourable attentions, but he was not about to admit his state of near-constant arousal since he kissed the third housemaid again to himself, let alone Lady Lydia. Such ridiculous passions burnt out as quickly as they sparked to misbegotten life, he told himself sternly.

'I grew up knowing that love was an obsession best avoided,' he continued truthfully, as he considered the effect of it on his early life.

'Surely your father could not have been so very deep in love? After all, he remarried six months after your mama died.'

'Considering she never stopped pining for another man the whole time they were married, I can only be surprised he waited that long. He was not a patient man and had long got over whatever obsession led him to marry her in the first place, against all sensible advice. My mother and her sisters believed in loving unwisely and all too well, Lyddie.

That will cover the family quota of ungovernable passion for a few generations.'

'I never hear your mother's sorry tale without wondering why someone didn't give her a fine dressing down and a dose of cooling mixture.'

'Much might have been avoided if they had,' he admitted with a grin.

'As for your aunt Prestbury, running off with her footman was bad enough, but to drown—in the Mediterranean of all places! What a feather-headed bungler.'

Marcus roared with laughter at the disgusted expression on her face. 'There's really nobody like you, Lyddie. Please don't ever change.'

'I can safely promise not to do that. I always got into trouble for saying what I should only think.'

'Which makes this house party such a heroic effort that I can only admire your self-restraint.'

'I can't tell you what an effort it has been to keep my tongue between my teeth this last week.'

'Believe me, Lyddie, there isn't the least need— your expression often says it for you.'

'Oh, dear, does it?'

'Only to those of us who know you. Miss Rashton thinks you as charmed by her opinions as she is herself.'

'There, you see? You can't possibly marry the wretched creature when you don't even like her!'

'And therefore will be less likely to hurt her.

Admit it, Lyddie, she loves Miss Rashton nearly as sincerely as my late and unlamented papa did the Honourable Julius Ashfield. That qualification alone makes her ideally suited to become Lady Strensham, when I can only offer her the title she seems to want so badly.'

'If there is not even respect between you, you will be offering her nothing worth having—be you prince or pauper.'

'Definitely pauper.'

'Does that mean you have to settle for such a cynical alliance?'

'A marriage of convenience, Lyddie. Most of our kind enter those.'

'A marriage of inconvenience when you are doomed to end hating each other. You have less in common than two strangers passing in the street!'

'Would you have me seek out a paragon with a fortune, Lyddie? I might search for a lifetime and still have nothing to offer her.'

Lydia felt that at last she had reached the crux of the problem. Marcus was not the cynic he would have them all believe, but he *was* in grave danger of trapping himself in a deeply unhappy marriage, just because he thought he must avoid anything better as he was poor and his mother had been a fool.

'I would have accepted Ned if he had been a beggar,' she said gently.

'Which proves what a rare creature you are.'

'Any female would rather be loved than acquired—except perhaps the one you are considering.'

'Which is why she will suit me so very well,' he assured her, forcing a mental picture of a very different female indeed to the outer reaches of his mind and silently ordering her to stay there.

'That cold-blooded creature will make you both miserable. She lacks any gift for contentment so far as I can see. Yet you are as stubborn as a whole string of pack-mules and will not be convinced, whatever I say.'

'While you are as pacific as a diplomatic corps?'

'No, for I could not stomach all the lying.'

'Neither could I, my dear, neither could I,' he said softly.

Lady Lydia didn't know whether to cry or throw something at him. Aside from putting frogs in Miss Rashton's bed, or drugging her favourite relative by marriage, then kidnapping him until he came to his senses, she could think of no way to stop him. Reluctantly rejecting both ideas, she let Marcus divert her into a discussion of the victory celebrations currently obsessing the capital, and fervently hoped his guardian angel was feeling more resourceful than she was herself.

Fifty miles away, in the sitting room Lady Winforde had made her own since she took up residence at Hardy House, Sir Granby Winforde was peering incredulously through his quizzing glass at the wiry looking individual he had hired to track down his errant bride.

'You find no trace of the chit in all this time, then demand payment?'

Joshua Carter thought his latest employer a fat rogue with a nasty glint in his pale, prominent eyes. As he was also a fat rogue with a vast fortune at his disposal, he would not dream of saying so unless his bill for a month's expenses went unpaid. Then he would repeat his suspicions to the nearest magistrate.

'The girl was very clever, Sir Granby,' he said with what he considered remarkable restraint, since he had spent so long trying to follow the trail of a female more elusive than a will o' the wisp.

'Lucky,' the third member of the company argued with a distinctly unladylike snort. 'The stupid wench has less sense than a newborn kitten.' The baronet's formidable mama reached out for another sugarplum and consumed it with the fastidious air of a connoisseur.

'Whatever my ward's intelligence,' her son said impatiently, 'she must be found. I was told you were the best man to do it.'

His eyes were suddenly hard and Carter had to fight a shiver. He had faced down far more enterprising rogues than the unhandsome baronet in his time and wasn't about to show any weakness— Even if the pair of them did make his flesh creep.

'I always get my man in the end,' he assured them.

Carter had a reputation as a hard man with no scruples about turning over his quarry to the hangman, so even the former runner himself could not quite understand why he felt so uneasy about returning the errant heiress to her rightful guardian. Winforde might be more like the villains he was accustomed to tracking down than a gentleman of birth, but he was offering a rich reward and Carter had his professional pride. If word got about that a mere female had out-witted him, and a spoilt one of little account at that, his hard-earned reputation would be in tatters.

'Maybe a false sense of gallantry has got in your way,' the lady observed as coolly as if she was dis-cussing a matter of no personal concern whatever.

In truth the lady was a more formidable character than her blustering windbag of a son and he felt sorry for anyone who crossed her, let alone a wench not long out of the schoolroom. Still, the girl would probably be safer in the care of her relatives than wandering the countryside unprotected he told himself doubtfully, and remembered the fat fee he would receive when she was back where she belonged.

'I helped send Fancy Payne to Tyburn in the year nine, so I can't say as her being a female would stop me doing my duty.'

'It is to be hoped not. We pay for results, Carter, and so far there have been precious few of them,' Sir Granby informed him quite unnecessarily.

'That last lead seemed a good one,' he offered in his own defence.

'The one that yielded nothing more than a silly schoolgirl on her way home from Bath? You were lucky not to be arrested for abduction after that fiasco. I have no intention of lying for you a second time, Carter.'

'There will be no occasion for you to do so, my lady,' he replied, shifting uncomfortably under her indifferent scrutiny.

'Exactly. Fail again and I will leave you to your fate.'

'I will find her this time,' Carter promised with an even more determined set to his mouth than usual.

Failure was not to be countenanced when half the West Country would be laughing at him. After reconsidering the weak leads he had managed to find over the last few weeks, he had already decided there was one sighting that would bear closer scrutiny.

'It is to be hoped so,' Lady Winforde replied indifferently. 'Pay the creature, my son,' she ordered grandly and they parted company with a distinct coldness on both sides.

Having grudgingly handed over some of his errant ward's guineas—money better spent on the kind of buxom, knowing female he preferred to sharp-tongued little viragos who were a great deal more trouble than they were worth—Sir Granby was inclined to be sullen.

'Why should he succeed this time, when he has failed time and again, Mama?' he asked petulantly as soon as the door shut behind their visitor.

'My son, that man's precious reputation is all in all to him. He will never let himself be beaten by a chit not long out of the schoolroom when he has brought down some of the most notorious villains this country has ever seen. And if you were less inept, she would never have got away in the first place.'

'I never liked her,' he replied sulkily. 'And I don't want to marry her.'

'Fool! All you need to do is get the wench to the altar. A few months later she can have a tragic accident and all our troubles will be over.'

'Murder, Mama?' he said with a certain amount of awed admiration mixed in with squeamish horror.

He couldn't help admiring the frigid ruthlessness underlying her apparently indolence, when it was not being directed at him.

'Practicality. You just said you never liked her.'

'That's not the same as doing away with her!'

'Keep your voice down. If you are too big a coward to be sensible, then you will just have to keep her, even if she is an ungrateful shrew.'

'Yes, she is, isn't she?' he asked as he mused on some of his ward's freely expressed opinions of his habits, person and character. 'And even if a wife can't testify against her husband, someone might listen to her prattle about her precious grandfather and ask questions we would rather not answer. You're right, Mama, getting rid of her would be for the best.'

'Granby, when you have spent a little longer in this world, you will doubtless realise that I am always right,' Lady Winforde informed him majestically and went back to her sugarplums.

Thea began to sleep poorly as she struggled with contrary urges to confide in Lord Strensham, or run harder than she had from Granby. The memory of what she was running from haunted her, and the weeks until her birthday still seemed to stretch endlessly away as all she could do was wait.

One night she tumbled into bed after a gruelling day and fell instantly asleep for once, uncaring of the sullen heat of the attic room and the restless whispering of her fellow maids. Tiredness soon overcame Carrie and Jane, and the entire household was lost in slumbers of varying degrees of innocence when a series of terrified screams tore through the hothouse silence. If it had been cooler, the fuss might have been confined to the top floor, but the noise floated in through windows open to catch a breath of air, despite warnings that night vapours were potentially deadly to the sleeper.

Marcus was roused from an uneasy sleep and started from his bed, convinced for a moment that the sounds coming through his open window were the herald of a night skirmish and he was back in the Peninsula. Then he shook his head and remembered how far from Spain he actually was. Hastily donning a shirt and breeches, he went to find the source of the outcry.

Miss Rashton, hair in curl papers and a shawl of violent clashing colours about her ample shoulders, was glaring accusingly at Hetty's averted face. The girl who occupied far too many of his thoughts was sitting on the side of the dilapidated old bed, looking deeply shocked. Marcus decided Miss Rashton should be in bed and ignored her, knowing any hint she should go back there would fall on deaf ears. He was family of course and didn't count.

At first sight of Lord Strensham looming in the doorway, Thea averted her face, but he forced his way into the room to get a closer look. Too weary to guard herself against his sharp-eyed scrutiny, she looked blindly back. She even found an odd sort of comfort as his watchful eyes flicked over her with apparent concern, and she told herself even his mistrust was a relief after the dream she had just suffered.

She had no way of knowing that her face was white as her nightgown, her eyes vividly green as the blue tones leeched out of them from the strength of her emotions. Marcus had to fight a nigh-overwhelming impulse to take her in his arms and offer what comfort he could—whatever the assembled company might make of such an extraordinary spectacle.

For an endless moment Thea held his gaze, then

looked away, feeling as if something precious had been offered and rejected in that fleeting contact, which was patently ridiculous when he had absolutely nothing to give. He had made that abundantly clear the day she became Rosecombe's third housemaid. Shivering at the thought of his rejection, she let the scene in the attic play out round her and struggled with overwrought tears she assured herself were nothing to do with his lordly lordship.

'I believe Hetty has a summer fever,' Mrs Meldon declared at last.

'Then she's a selfish hussy to rob her betters of their rest,' Miss Rashton said grumpily, evidently in sore need of her beauty sleep.

'Indeed?' replied his lordship coldly. 'I thought she was crying out in her sleep.'

For a long moment there was a heavy silence in the stuffy room as his intervention was fitted into a variety of stories, none of them precisely true.

'Ah, Carrie, you are a good girl.' The housekeeper rushed into the breach, as the head housemaid appeared at her side with a glass of water and an ominous blue bottle. 'Just a few drops of laudanum to calm her I think, or Hetty will never be fit to work tomorrow.'

She carefully measured out a Spartan dose, under Marcus's frowning scrutiny, then held the glass to the sufferer's lips and obliged her to drink.

'Quite right, Meldon. I told Lady Lydia you

would deal with whatever was to do,' approved her employer, his face flushed with sleep and temper at its interruption. 'The rest of you go back to bed.'

He spared Thea a condemning look, but mercifully said nothing. Aware a good servant should be seen and not heard, she shuddered. Doubtless she had fallen even further in Lord Strensham's estimation for waking her weary colleagues, and infuriating the master of the house. Not quite sure why that fact mattered more than Sir Edward's displeasure, she meekly swallowed the laudanum and wished they would all go away.

The wretched stuff weakened her control over her wayward thoughts, though. When his lordship came into the room she had felt the grip of terror ease. Now she thought vaguely that it would be wonderful to relax into his powerful arms and let the world fade away. She fought the dizzying embrace of the opiate for a few moments while she tried to remember why that was impossible. As the drug finally sapped her will, she held out a hand as if reaching for something only he could offer, then slipped into unconsciousness between one breath and the next.

Chapter Seven

Seeing no more entertainment was on offer, most of the spectators had obediently returned to their beds, but Marcus stayed to watch the opiate take effect. His waif had been cursed and drugged, when even meddling Miss Rashton would have been petted and consoled in similar circumstances—if she possessed a single nerve to give her the night terrors in the first place.

He wasn't quite sure if he was silently railing against a common inequality, or her treatment in particular. Either way, he could not espouse the cause of a girl who should be invisible to him. Yet when she seemed to appeal for his protection he had stayed where he was only by exercising the fearsome self-control he had learnt in the face of battle. He reminded himself that she had been avoiding him like the plague since he last lost his head, so even in dire need of comfort she would not accept it from him.

Then her dark head drooped onto the meagre

pillow, her thick plait of glossy nut-brown hair snaking across the patched sheet and her face pale and unguarded. It shook him to discover how badly he wanted to see that silky mane loose about her shoulders again, and have the right to slip into that rickety old bed beside her, so she could sleep in his arms, safe from whatever demons drove her. Startled by his own wayward longings, he frowned fiercely at the remaining occupants of the attic room.

Luckily the housekeeper clucked over Miss Rashton, before he ordered her to her bed with less ceremony than he might have a subaltern under his command. With a nod to his cousin, and a murmured 'goodnight' as Sir Edward mentally went back to sleep on his feet, Marcus had nothing else to do but seek his bed once more.

He asked himself if a libidinous master would really haunt the troublesome chit so deeply that he pursued her into her dreams? He had heard of thief lords who terrified their cohorts as much as their victims. Could she be the victim of such a man? He pictured her standing in the library spitting defiance as if they were equals and shook his head in the darkness. The little vixen would doubtless put a knife into any robber baron foolish enough to try to put his hands on her. So if all she wanted here was a refuge, what right had he to force her out of it?

None at all, but he should warn his cousin he supposed. No, the chit would be turned off and his curiosity for ever unsatisfied, and that, he told himself cynically, would never do.

The idea that he could be besotted with a maid-servant was as ridiculous as his aunt running off with her footman. Maybe he should set the little firebrand up in discreet comfort after all though, and visit her whenever the demands of his interfering viscountess and encumbered acres became too much to endure. He fought a picture of Hetty Smith, her astonishing turquoise eyes disillusioned with the littleness of it all, and punched his pillow with frustrated fury.

Since he could not have the wench with any honour remaining to either of them, somehow he would overcome this damnably inconvenient urge to carry her off and keep her in his ramshackle lair in defiance of the world. A less likely gallant she would go a long way to find, but the idea of Hetty turning to any other man for comfort and heroics nearly made him throw his abused pillow out of the window and himself after it!

The next morning Thea cursed all carelessly handsome noblemen long and bitterly under her breath, as Jane spent the morning daydreaming instead of doing her share of the work. Thea was having enough trouble with her aching head and heavy limbs, without hearing eulogies on the Viscount, rendered even more heroic by his hasty arousal from sleep!

She would have cut her tongue out before she admitted she was haunted by a vision of his interfering lordship as well, dressed as he had been only in shirt and breeches and handsome as the devil. His bare throat had been as brown as a farmhand's, she mused in a careless moment, then caught herself speculating whether the smoothly muscled chest just visible in the open neck of his shirt was tanned all over as well. Her fingers flexed of their own accord, as if they could actually feel his golden skin and steely sinews under them, and she berated herself for being such an idiot.

Lord Strensham was as distant from her as the stars. Contemplating a marriage of convenience with one of the seedy adventurers Grandfather brought to woo her had been bad enough. To be locked in such a bloodless affair with Lord Strensham would be a living nightmare. Far better to stay a humble skivvy for the rest of her life than descend to that, she assured herself, and tried to concentrate on her work before she broke something.

Just as they finished the bedchambers and she was about to slip out for five minutes' illicit fresh air, the butler appeared like a portly harbinger of doom. She suppressed a groan and, resuming her false humility with even more effort than usual, curtsied and stared at the floor while she awaited his instructions.

'Jane, you are needed in the dining room,' he

informed the flighty second housemaid and she meekly departed. 'Nobody will notice if you slip outside and take a tray to her ladyship who has the headache, Hetty. Just don't drop anything,' he concluded severely, his frown leaving her in no doubt that Lady Lydia's affliction could be laid at her door.

She bobbed him a deferential curtsy, but her heart lifted despite her worries as she stepped out into the golden afternoon with her burden.

'Oh, thank you, Hetty,' her mistress murmured when Thea reached the summerhouse.

'I'm very sorry, my lady,' she said with a humble curtsy after she had placed her tray on the wrought-iron table.

Lady Lydia poured a cup of fragrant China tea and sipped it with apparent enjoyment, but ignored the tempting array of delicacies.

'Whatever for?' she asked absently.

'Waking the household and causing your headache.'

'I think we can safely blame the next generation of Darraines for that,' Lady Lydia told her with a rueful smile and suddenly much was clear that should have puzzled Thea, if she had been less preoccupied with her woes.

Of course her ladyship could not go to Brighton, or stay in hot and stuffy London when the longed-for heir might be on the way. She wondered what Marcus Ashfield was thinking of, drawing his relatives into his self-serving schemes at such a time.

Then she remembered how fiercely loyal he was to his family, and knew he would never have accepted the Darraines' help if he had the slightest idea Lady Lydia was *enceinte.*

'I can't hide it for much longer I suppose.'

'Nobody will hear of it from me, my lady.'

'You're a good girl, Hetty.'

'Thank you, my lady, you're very kind.'

'Am I? Sometimes I wonder. At any rate I enjoyed my tea, but pray take the rest away now before I turn queasy again.'

'Very good, my lady, and if anyone asks me I haven't seen you.'

'Unless Sir Edward has escaped his duties as well.'

'Of course, Lady Lydia,' Thea agreed, knowing too well how it felt to long for one man's company above all others.

She tried not to envy her mistress the certainty that she was loved in return, that was something she would never have and there was no point in yearning for the unattainable. Seeking escape from such idiotic thoughts, she took time to appreciate the fine walks Sir Edward's ancestors had planted on her way back to the house. What his forebears would have said about a scruffy maidservant enjoying their handiwork, she shuddered to think. Yet she dawdled along one of the meandering paths and nearly walked into Lord Strensham coming the other way.

'Good, I've been wanting a word with you.'

So have not I, she thought despairingly, and eyed him with wary mistrust.

'Have you recovered?' he disconcerted her by asking abruptly.

'I am perfectly well, my lord,' she lied.

'Then what was that brouhaha all about last night?' he asked in what she always thought of as his officer's voice.

'It were plaguey hot, weren't it, my lord?'

'Indeed it was, nearly as hot as the night before, or possibly the one before that, wouldn't you say?'

'Maybe I would at that.'

'Then what happened last night and none of the other hot nights?'

You did, she just stopped herself from saying.

'Bad luck, or ill wishing,' she told him instead, and made a show of making the horns as she had sometimes seen the other servants do when nobody in authority was looking.

'Who abused you, Hetty?' he asked gruffly and stilled the lies on Thea's tongue.

The rough note in his voice reminded her of her grandfather's brusque anxiety when she had been so ill of the scarlet fever that her life was almost despaired of, and she battled an absurd urge to pour out her woes.

'Cat got your ready tongue?' he asked with a rather twisted smile and she opened her mouth to lie and found nothing would come out.

'Seems so,' she managed eventually, stifling a pang of longing for the comfort of his strong arms that was quite ridiculous.

'I'm not sure if that's a blessing or a curse.'

'Me neither, m'lord.'

Silence again, but this time it felt charged with unspoken possibilities and she shifted restlessly under his watchful scrutiny. On the edge of something momentous she hesitated, and told herself that confiding in him would be folly.

She told herself to be glad when Miss Rashton strode towards them with far too much purpose to be out for a casual stroll and very sure of *her* welcome. 'There you are, Strensham.'

'Here I am, Miss Rashton,' he replied smoothly and waited blandly for her next truism.

'And whatever is one of Lady Lydia's servants doing, strolling about bold as brass?'

'I have no idea, perhaps you should ask her?'

Thea tried to look as if being discussed like a piece of faulty furniture meant nothing to her, at the same time as she tried to sidle past his lordship's stubbornly unmoving figure.

'Well, what brings you here, girl? And why are you accosting his lordship in such an impudent fashion?'

Thea curtsied as humbly as she could while burdened with a tray full of tea things and wondered for a fraught moment if she would be able to get up again without disaster. Lord Strensham put a weary hand under her elbow and assisted her to her feet, then just as languidly let her go again. How could he look so cool and collected when just that simple contact had sent a wave of heat through her that threatened to take her breath away?

'If you refrain from bobbing up and down whilst you enlighten us as to your mission, Hetty, it might be better for Lady Lydia's china,' he advised laconically and Thea decided his heiress was welcome to him after all.

'Yes, m'lord, happen you're right.'

'Of course he is, you ignorant fool. Explain yourself and don't answer back to your betters.'

'I was told to see if I could find her ladyship, miss.'

'And did you?'

'Oh, no, miss,' she replied, all wide-eyed innocence.

'Yet that cup has been used and I dare say you have hardly bothered to look for your mistress at all,' the lady said.

'Saves wasting all that tea,' his lordship asserted lazily.

Thea observed the amount of self-restraint it took Miss Rashton not to snap back a scathing reply with cynical eyes. The Viscount would certainly not have everything his own lordly way if he wed the heiress, she realised, with no satisfaction whatsoever.

'Your mistress will hear of this, but now you may go back to work,' Miss Rashton informed her regally.

'After you have sought out my cousin and

informed him we are bound for the lake,' Lord Strensham added as Thea humbly squashed herself into the hedge so the two of them could pass.

Since his lordship had come here to wed a fortune, he seemed to be wriggling rather oddly on Miss Rashton's hook. It was almost as if he was hoping for a third in what the lady intended as a tête-à-tête, disguised as a search for her hostess. Remembering Lady Lydia's need of solitude, she sped off for those reinforcements.

Running the baronet to earth in the drawing room where he was gallantly keeping the vivacious widow and the schoolroom miss busy, Thea was glad he could take the hint and stride to his lady's rescue.

'His lordship asked me to tell you as he and Miss Rashton are heading for the lake, Sir Edward,' she told him, meeting his eyes boldly for once in an effort to remind him where his lady was.

'Are they, by gad,' Sir Edward snapped, and stormed to the rescue under an amused Mrs Fall's sparkling eyes. Thea thought she would have liked the merry widow a great deal if she had met her under different circumstances, curtsied humbly and went back to her duties.

Out by the lake, Marcus met one of Miss Rashton's simpering looks with bland incomprehension, and ruthlessly bore her off to inspect the temple on the opposite side of the lake from Lydia's refuge. Luckily for him the widow trumped her rival's ace. Before Miss Rashton could feign the vapours or stumble into his lordship's arms, Mrs Fall and her pale little shadow strolled up to join them. Marcus tried hard not to think why he had passed up a golden opportunity to propose to his heiress, and remembering his pressing obligations, cursed himself for a weak fool.

Lydia was restored to her usual high spirits by afternoon, and Marcus slipped away to join Ned in his library, the one place Miss Rashton did not dare intrude. Yet Marcus found no peace there; the place reminded him too vividly of a very different female indeed.

'For heaven's sake, sit down and stop pacing before you wear out my carpet,' Ned finally snapped, after his cousin had picked up and put down half a dozen books, then spent ten minutes marching up and down the room like a drill sergeant. 'You're a resty devil at the best of times, Marcus, and anyone can see this ain't one of 'em.'

'Find me a way out of this damnable coil and I promise to sit still as long as you like.'

'You and Nick always came up with the ideas when we were young,' Sir Edward replied acerbically, 'even if most of them were ludicrous.'

'Not as daft as this latest one,' Marcus said gloomily and resumed pacing.

'Hate to say I told you so, but in your case I might manage it.'

'Why is it so hard to bite the bullet, Ned?' Marcus asked, thinking out loud rather than expecting enlightenment.

'That Rashton female could probably stop Boney and the Imperial Guard in their tracks. I hope you don't expect us to visit if you wed her.'

'One heiress is much the same as another.'

'Think you'll find that's not quite true.'

'Are you suggesting I ask that child Lydia was misguided enough to invite here to marry me instead?'

'No, my money's on the widow.'

'She expects to make a love match. I can't offer her that.'

'You think you'll make the Rashton chit ecstatically happy, then?'

'I doubt if anyone could, but I'll do her no harm.'

'Shame you can't get yourself to sticking point then ain't it?' Ned said with a guilty feeling that he was taking out his temper on his unlucky cousin.

'It's her or ruin. Colin's future prospects and my pensioners' well-being depend on finding a way out of this mess.'

'She's a bit of an extreme one, though, Marcus,' Ned said mildly, his own temper fading as he was reminded how serious his cousin's situation was. 'There has to be another way.'

'If you can think of it, you're a better man than I.'

'What about the land? Coke of Norfolk turned round a failing estate and made a fortune.'

'You haven't seen the state of my acres.'

'You have good soil and that's half the battle.'

For a few minutes they discussed the steps that would need to be taken to bring the land back into good heart and the farms into profit, but in the end Marcus had to face reality.

'Don't you think I went through this when I came home, Ned? Colin's other grandfather will pay his way through Oxford, but I doubt he wants his grandson to take up farm labouring afterwards, or horse dealing.'

'I dare say he would enjoy either more than a political career or the law.'

'True,' Marcus said with a rueful smile as he recalled his half brother's freely expressed feelings on the subject. 'But what if he wants to marry, Ned?'

'There's enough room for half a dozen families at Chimmerton.'

'Amongst the dust and fifty years' worth of neglect I lack the funds to remedy? No rational female would live in such a way while we pulled the place round, even if I promised faithfully never to wed myself so he could inherit.'

'I think you underestimate the fairer sex, cousin,' Sir Edward informed him with a reminiscent smile as he considered his lady's likely response to such a challenge.

'Lady Lydia is unique,' Marcus replied, his hard expression softening.

'Here, you're not in love with her too, are you? I was for ever falling over besotted poets and smitten sprigs of the nobility in town and I won't put up with it in my own home, even from you.'

'If there was the least risk of me tumbling into a headlong passion, I would pick a female who wasn't in love with another man.'

Ned looked rather satisfied with life for a moment, then eyed his cousin warily. 'You can't control love like a brigade of infantrymen, Marcus,' he cautioned.

'It only exists in novels and the minds of woolly-minded débutantes.'

'I ain't got that much imagination, and Lydia wouldn't thank you for such a description either.'

'I grant you the odd exception then, but only to prove the rule.'

'Kind of you, Marcus.'

'Yes, isn't it?'

He would not let himself be lured off course by a ridiculous infatuation with a girl outside his sphere. It was not even to be thought of, he decided, unaware he was pacing again. Yet such an unwary seductress might land in the most appalling mess if she let passion rule her with a less scrupulous man. His hands clenched as something perilously close to anguish shot through him, followed by a surge of fury that set his mouth in a hard line and made him long to hit something.

'If you can't keep still, for goodness' sake take that rogue of a stallion I offered you for a ride. I can't get my legs across the brute and you will either kill one another or come back half-civilised,' Sir Edward said, with a thoughtful look at his cousin's stormy countenance.

'It would solve at least one problem, I suppose,' Marcus said rather bitterly and went to do as Ned suggested.

With any other man, Sir Edward might have wondered if he was suffering from unrequited love. As this was Marcus, his dire situation must be grating on the fiery temperament that lay under the starch my lord Strensham used to keep the world at bay.

On Sunday morning there was a stranger at church to distract Thea from watching Lord Strensham court his heiress. She concentrated on the respectable-looking man greeting the vicar, instead of his lordship's dark head bending attentively to listen to Miss Rashton.

The newcomer was dark, too, but there the resemblance ended. He was of middling height and spare looking with rather an expressionless face, but he smiled amiably enough at the vicar, then quietly took his seat. As he dutifully bowed his head in prayer she told herself to stop turning every stranger into her enemy. In three months she had heard nothing of her enemies and could only hope they had given up.

'Staying at the Crown, he is. That upset at losing his wife the doctors ordered him into the country,' Carrie whispered as she noticed the direction of Thea's gaze. 'His name's Carter. Jane's probably in love with him already.'

'She changes with the weather,' she murmured back, wondering how Jane could dream of transferring her affections so easily.

Luckily the service began before she could look too hard at her impatience with the flighty second housemaid. After church, the servants had no time for the leisurely gossip indulged in by the better off, so Thea had no idea if Miss Rashton triumphed over her rivals again.

At least it was her monthly afternoon off, so she was spared the nauseating spectacle of a fortune hunter chasing down his quarry for a few precious hours. As Nurse Turner had gone to stay with one of her many relatives, Thea begged a hunk of bread and cheese and an apple from the cook-maid, stole a book from the deserted library and ghosted away to enjoy them in peace.

The Home Wood was within Rosecombe's parkland, but just in case it invited anyone else into its green-and-gold shades on such a lovely day, she went far enough in to avoid casual explorers. She

finally sat down under a stately oak tree to eat her
lunch, then opened her book with a satisfied sigh.
Absorbed in the sayings and doings of the Bennet
sisters, she was transported to a world where choosing
a husband was the most taxing activity demanded of
a young lady, with happy endings all round.

Marcus was prowling his cousin's acres, trying to
come to terms with his own folly. Twice now he had
been on the brink of offering for Miss Rashton and
drawn back at the last minute. Once he had
imagined her horror when confronted by his house
in its present state. Then he decided such hurdles
would have to be got over, only to see Hetty scurry
past the open sitting-room door as if she had been
scalded. Absently wandering off to find out what
she was up to this time he turned back, cursing
himself under his breath, and found the lady so
furious and distant even his nerve failed him.

His obligations were still enormous and his means
non-existent, but the solution that seemed sensible
once upon a time now looked impossible. He strode
on until he was nearly out the other side of Ned's
carefully managed woods. Taking a deep breath, he
finally became aware of a glorious golden afternoon. Just the sort of day Major Ashfield had dreamt
of when the ragtag Peninsular army tramped the
boiling Spanish plains in high summer, or went over
the Pyrenees, bone weary and racked with fever

and hunger, he mused. Then any day in England, with the sun mild on his back and good food in his belly, had seemed like the promise of heaven to him. Life had been simpler when they had often had no food, no money and no baggage, and still survived to fight another day.

Finding Hetty asleep at the foot of the largest oak tree seemed almost the work of fate. He told himself to steal away, before she opened those remarkable eyes and he found the wrong answers in them, yet he watched her like a greedy lover. Without that wretched mobcap he could see her heavy nut-brown tresses, bound up in a glossy mass. He so longed to feel those silky waves under his stroking hands again that he wished he could loose the heavy topknot or explore the wispy curls that softened her brow.

Not to be thought of, even if she allowed it, he told himself, and tried to turn back. His feet obeyed a deeper need and carried him over to drink in more than he should of Miss Hetty Smith. He already knew her figure was slender, but far too womanly for comfort, and managed not to torture himself by imagining the feel of her in his arms again for more than half a minute. He summoned up all those years of military discipline to divert his gaze onto her hands. Of course they were rough and reddened, but long fingered and finely made, and he noted another book in her slack grasp with a rueful smile.

Cautiously leaning over to read a few words, he

wondered whatever his enigma was doing with the second part of a three-decker novel, whose humour and sure touch he had thoroughly enjoyed. Wondering once more who and what she might be, he stepped back unwarily and a twig snapped under his booted foot with a crack that could have awoken far heavier sleepers than Miss Hetty Smith.

Chapter Eight

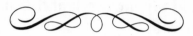

'Spying, my lord?' Thea asked sleepily, trying to fight the heady idea that he had sought her in preference to his heiresses.

The reality of her situation came back with more than the usual sting, and she could have kicked herself for such arrant nonsense. She sounded defensive, but at least he could not know what effort it cost to renounce the fantasy of waking to see love in his cool grey eyes instead of scepticism.

'Should I be?'

His deep voice did strange things to her insides as she scrambled to her feet. 'Er, no... You just startled me, my lord.'

'Did I? Your nerves are not what they were, are they, Miss Smith?'

Why did he have to be the only one in the household to doubt she was anything other than a silly maidservant who ate too many pickles with her supper and had nightmares as a consequence? It really was most inconsiderate of him.

'There's nothing wrong with my nerves,' she informed him shortly. There was nothing wrong with them when he was absent, so it wasn't that big a lie.

'I beg to differ.'

'You would be wrong.'

'Would I? Did you never hear that a trouble shared is a trouble halved.'

'I did, but I never believed it.'

'Try, you might feel better,' he said softly and gently lifted her chin so she must pull away or look him in the eyes.

They were as complex as he was, she decided, heartbeat accelerating as she studied the fathomless depths she suspected very few were permitted to plumb, and wondered what he was looking so intently for in her own.

'I doubt it,' she replied huskily, not knowing whether to be pleased or desperately disappointed when his gaze iced over and he stepped back from her as if he couldn't understand why he had let himself to get so close in the first place. 'Better ask no questions, my lord.'

'What of my incurable curiosity,' he said, his knowing smile and the rasp in his deep voice catching on her sensitised nerves.

'Give it a holiday.'

He chuckled and the sound sent a warm shiver to

her tingling toes. Then he sat down on a venerable oak root and wilfully ignored her embargo.

'There's no point trying to persuade me you're not educated now.'

Thea felt the full power of his presence as the sun found unexpected chestnut lights in his dark hair. He was a gentleman of such sensual appeal she almost forgot she had been brought up a lady. Even the fugitive scent of him posed a threat to her hard-won composure, made up as it was of clean male, sandalwood soap, fresh air—and Marcus Ashfield.

She tried to reorder her insubordinate thoughts. What had he just asked her? She reconstructed her barriers once more and marshalled her lies.

'I told you that my last mistress taught me to read and speak well, my lord,' she reminded him earnestly.

'Housework must be a come down.'

'What other trade can a respectable girl take to?'

He glanced at her mass of rich brown hair, her fine-cut features and neat figure, then nodded as if he considered it a fair answer.

'In a better world there would be many openings for one of your talents, but not in this one. Respectable marriage to an equal might serve, but you have been educated beyond the common run.'

Thea considered this statement then smiled hesitantly.

'Will you not sit down?' he asked politely.

Thea decided he was more dangerous in this mood

than when he was examining her like a raw recruit, but she sat before she could tell herself it was not fitting for a nobleman to hobnob with a drudge.

'I'm an honest maid and you're an honourable man, so what could be amiss in that?' she replied, with an airy indifference she did not quite feel.

'A good many things, but the gossips would be disappointed if they could see us being so proper. So, what *can* we talk about, Miss Smith?'

'Perhaps you would tell me about life in the army, my lord?'

He looked very grim for a few seconds, and Thea thought of the hardship of those who had fought so gallantly for the freedom that Europe now enjoyed.

'It was often tedious and sometimes terrifying and bloody. War is a brutal business, Miss Smith, and now the men are home their country has no place for their heroes. However, the lot of a former officer is easy enough, we are of little use and less ornament, but seldom starve.'

Thea thought of the reports of great losses in some of the Peninsular battles, and realised soldiering must have been close to intolerable to a sensitive man at times. It was so much easier to think of him as a shallow fortune hunter, but under the indolent cynicism of Lord Strensham, the brusque, dashing Major Ashfield continued to intrigue her.

If Miss Rashton took the trouble to know the man she was pursuing, would she chase him down all the harder, or run in the opposite direction? The answer was she would not care, Thea concluded—the woman had his title in her sights and anything else was a bonus. The urge to strangle Miss Rashton made her slender dark brows knit in a frown, until she noted his acute gaze and smoothed it away with a conscious effort. She really must study indifference if she was to leave Rosecombe with her heart intact.

Silence fell as she thought that lowering conclusion through and it contained an ease she had never expected to feel in the company of the infuriating and domineering viscount.

Even the normal sounds of the wood were reduced to a sleepy indolence by the warmth of the afternoon and she listened appreciatively, trying not to long for this stolen hour to go on for ever. Working so hard had sharpened her ears and eyes to the world around her, and she had come to recognise the fact that she was a privileged being. This state of humility might not last, she decided ruefully, but if ever she regained her former position in life, she must not forget the hard lessons learnt in this one.

Marcus considered how his friends would laugh if he told them that a snatched hour, spent sitting on an uncomfortable perch in supposedly humble company, gave him more peace than he had experienced in years. They would be even more sceptical if he went on to claim the extraordinary chit's quick wits and acerbic tongue intrigued him more than her looks. Darting a glance at her, he decided they would be right. Hetty was far too lovely to wander the world unprotected.

He had never been bored in her infuriating, exhilarating and damnably intriguing company. It certainly wasn't altruism that made him imagine her dressed in the most expensive finery, and looking at him with adoration instead of her usual scepticism. Far more base emotions were making his body take light, as that wretched fantasy of her slender curves, warm and welcoming under him, suddenly afflicted him like a blow again. He had to slew away from the sight of her just to calm himself, body and mind, before he dared so much as breathe deeply in her company.

Made clumsy by this internal war between scruples and the drive of fierce desire she alone seemed to provoke, he jumped to his feet to establish a distance between them that was social as much as factual. He would be leaving in a week or so, with or without an affianced wife and a dowry large enough to fill Chimmerton's empty coffers, and he must do so without a backward glance at Hetty Smith—for her sake as much as his.

If he couldn't stomach Miss Rashton, he would just have to find an heiress whose company he *could* stand for the next thirty or forty years. If he didn't, he might find himself becoming a contemptible satyr who seduced the maids for want of passion in the marriage bed, and that would be intolerable.

'Lady Lydia will be furious at me for deserting my post, and I dare say the house will not clean itself.'

Thea was amused rather than annoyed by this masculine piece of chopped logic. One minute they were democratically sharing a tree stump, the next he was lording it like the Grand Turk.

'Yes,' she agreed solemnly, 'I have so many agreeable tasks ahead of me, this delightful novel and my precious afternoon off must pall.'

'I can see how desperate you must be to get back,' he said, with an attempt at lightness that sounded hollow in his own ears.

When Lord Strensham forgot to be so present and correct, he was more dangerous than the most hardened seducer. Eager heiresses would mob him if he ever set foot in London as an unwed nobleman in need of a fortune. In a few months' time his eyes might even light upon a certain Miss Hardy, a subversive voice whispered seductively. Remembering the unsavoury stories circulating about that ignoble heiress, she sternly renounced her fantasy.

'Yet I shall stay a little longer,' she attempted to say lightly.

He frowned, no doubt believing she had an assignation with one of the grooms or some such nonsense. She told herself that he was a man of small mind and limited imagination after all, and Miss Rashton was welcome to him.

'Ned says a couple of ruffians have been seen about. You should not be alone until they have been moved on by the constables,' he told her stiffly.

Thea reproached herself for jumping to conclusions yet again, and accepted his offer to accompany her at least to the lake. He strolled at her side in preoccupied silence, and became more and more the sardonic gentleman of fashion the closer they got to Rosecombe.

'I will be safe here,' she told him when they reached the path where the woods ran down to the lake.

'It would take a bold rogue to venture so close to the house I suppose.'

'Then I shall make use of yonder bench to hide from everyone and read in peace. Thank you for your escort, my lord, you are very kind.'

He bowed politely in acknowledgement, and she recalled their easy silence in that woodland grove with regret. Now that they were gentleman and servant again and never the twain shall meet, it felt as if someone had stolen the warmth from this golden day and turned it into bleak midwinter.

'That is something to be grateful for, is it not?' he remarked enigmatically and kissed one of her work-worn hands as if he really meant it, before turning away as if he had already forgotten who she was.

She must have made some small sound of dissent, because he turned back as if she had laid a hand on his arm to protest his departure. Shocked at even so small a betrayal of her deepest feelings, she gazed questioningly into his silvered eyes.

'You should have let me go,' he said softly, as he closed the gap between them as if this was as inevitable as the sun rising on the morrow.

'I know,' she breathed as she raised her mouth to meet his.

'Now there's this…' he said, as if that explained everything.

Heat blossomed between them so fiercely it might consume them and their mouths met in a kiss that just was—the overmastering reality of a forbidden 'us' spelled out by the exquisite, intimate contact.

Last time her lips had still been soft and untutored, surprised by such incredible intimacy, half-afraid of the promise of him, so intimately demanding too much of her. Now she met him fire for fire. Hungry, she thought muzzily, she was so incredibly hungry for this that she would go through far worse than she had already to hear his moan of need, as she parted her lips to welcome his questing tongue.

'And this,' he murmured as his mouth teased hers.

'Yet there's this too,' she whispered as she shamelessly stood on tiptoe and fitted her parted mouth over his and their kiss erupted into urgency the like of which Marcus had never known and she had not dreamt could exist.

'Steady, love,' he heard himself say and the tiny

remnant of sanity that was all he could hold on to groaned a protest at that dangerous, extreme endearment.

If it were true they were both done for, so he fogged his thoughts with the luxury of her mouth. Awed, he returned the generosity of her kiss, the strength of her response shaking him. This was so different from what he had known with any other woman he wished it could have another language.

Thea was too wrapped up in the now to worry about anything but Marcus's mouth gentling on hers in a long, sweet caress that acknowledged their equality. Then her breath hitched and her heart thumped a counter-rhythm, as he fitted her more closely to his leanly muscled form. With a gasp of delight she breathed him in, the scent of him, the taste of him and, most exquisite of all, the touch of him wherever she sent her mind to inquire.

Then tenderness was overcome with something more urgent as he ran an unsteady hand over the smooth column of her back and up to the tender line of her neck and jaw. Every nerve on end with anticipation for she knew not what, she drew in a shaky breath full of their intimacy and felt his long-fingered hand trail a blaze down her slender neck so that it tingled with heat. He lingered to kiss the gentle hollows at the base of her throat, and she gasped with heavy longing as his questing fingers at last found her breasts, shamelessly rounding with demand for his touch. She spared a fleeting thought for instincts that led her where she had no idea they could go, then dismissed them as she felt the soft reality of summer air on her bare skin.

He was so sure, so unerring in his pursuit of her pleasure that she almost fell back to earth, then lost herself again as he lowered his head to follow his touch with a kiss. She gasped and shot into another level of unreality, the gentle tug of his wickedly knowing mouth on her longing nipple blocking out everything but the terrible, wonderful fire that shot through her. She revelled in the unaccustomed luxury of running wondering fingers through his rebellious dark hair as he feasted so hungrily on her. His tongue flicked across the coral-crowned breast that pressed toward his teasing mouth of its own accord, then such a wave of heavy longing shot through her that Thea gave a soft gasp of protest.

'Kiss,' she demanded in a husky whisper she hardly recognised as her own.

'Hussy,' he responded with a rumble of masculine amusement she felt through the fine lawn of his lawn shirt.

Luckily for this wanton Thea, he obeyed her before a spark of unease could blaze into humiliation at her wild response to him. His lips on hers were like water to a parched man, and she opened for him as easily and sweetly as if she were wild, ardent young Juliet to his demanding and impassioned Romeo. His tongue took up a new rhythm that made her heart leap in response, as the blaze they had summoned up between them seemed to take up residence in the most intimate heart of her. She groaned and he brought their bodies urgently up against each other so that she felt the awesome arousal of him and watched his heated features with hectic eyes and a hammering heartbeat that matched his.

'Yes,' she breathed, unable to withhold anything from this man who had altered her for ever in her own eyes.

For a long, luscious moment it seemed as if he would be unable to keep any part of himself from her, then his mouth gentled on hers, his hands soothed instead of inflaming and she felt a sob building somewhere in the outer darkness her most tender desires had suddenly fallen into. He was about to say something kind, she decided, something designed to make his withdrawal a light thing and not the darkest pain she had ever experienced.

'I believe that you have other fish to fry, Lord Strensham,' she said, in a voice that she had a hard time recognising, so cold and withdrawn as it sounded in her own ears.

'No!' The protest in his deep tones resounded against those still-aroused breasts of hers, where their bodies were locked together like lovers.

Even so, she strove to harden herself against the very intimacy part of her craved, while the wonder of his deep voice echoing in her own torso nearly made her break down and beg for the impossible.

'You kiss much better than your cousin does, my lord,' she told him in a brittle voice, her gaze cooling to turquoise again as she eased away from him.

'I'll kill Ned,' he vowed, shock and a lingering heat still silvering his eyes as they met hers with dazed fury.

'Not the master,' she protested, 'the Captain.'

'Then I'll find Nick and kill *him,* after I strangle you.'

She somehow fumbled her buttons back into place and stiffened her wobbling legs as she tried hard to meet his hotly furious eyes. Her heart hitched a fevered beat as she took in the blaze of rage and implacable purpose there, but it was the hastily hidden hurt there that made her recover her growing feelings for him in one painful jolt. She could love him, if he let her. She finally acknowledged that disaster as she stood there and looked the truth full on.

'It's not true,' she admitted painfully.

'No,' he acknowledged with a heavy sigh, 'Nick has his own peculiar code of honour.' The noises of late afternoon settled round them like a curative to passion as they stood in silence. 'You should have let me leave the first time,' he finally said with a humourless smile.

'Yes, please go now,' she said in a thin voice she hoped only she knew was wobbling on the edge of hysteria.

'And put the clock back as if it never happened? You might be able to manage such conjuring feats, Miss Smith, but they are beyond me.'

'It didn't happen, you refused to let it.'

'How could I? It would have taken you into a world you cannot dream of. I can't marry you, you little fool, and lack the funds to support the dependants I already have, so I can't keep you either.'

'Dependants?' How dare he categorise her so? Her chin shot up and a martial gleam entered eyes that were already shading to emerald fury under his fascinated gaze.

'I should wait until you are asked if I were you, my lord,' she spat out with a toss of her head that would have done credit to the finest lady in the land, before she swept out of the little clearing as if she was royalty at the very lowest.

'And that's telling me,' Marcus murmured as he watched the unconsciously seductive sway of her hips under her plain gown as she walked straight-backed down the path.

Need sprang to life, complete and demanding as memory joined observation. She was not just the most unusual housemaid he had ever encountered, he knew with a sinking heart she was also the one woman who might have breached his splendid isolation. Now he must turn his back on her and walk away, as if she meant nothing to him. He was too experienced to doubt that she wanted him just as badly as he did her, but they would both get over it, in time.

When she was safely out of sight, Thea put a hand to lips that were still stubbornly sensitive from his kisses, as if to protect the lingering taste of him from chilly reality. She was torn between obsessively watching for his straight-backed figure to walk by her hiding place, and wishing him a thousand miles away. Still the feel of his warm touch lingered on her skin, and she smiled at nothing like a lovelorn schoolgirl.

The thought of his mouth on hers again made her pull in a great breath of air, as her body tightened with too vividly remembered promise and her legs felt wobbly. Wishing she could erase his kiss by effort of will, she set about forgetting his lordship was anything other than the cause of more work for a harassed housemaid.

Unfortunately a lingering image of his handsome face, dominated by laughing grey eyes and a wry smile, intruded every time she tried to immerse herself in Mr Darcy's iniquities. How very much she sympathised with Eliza Bennet's tribulations with an equally impossible male she decided militantly, and tried not to consider that both the fictional gentleman and the real one had a rock-bottom integrity that drew women to them in a disastrous fashion.

Even as she tried so hard to be rational, irrational

Thea was at work. Today, she recalled with a besotted smile, his lordship's hair had shown a distinct tendency to curl rebelliously, once it was released from battle order. She had been allowed a glimpse of the carefree gentleman nature formed him to be. Adversity had made that wicked, slow smile of his a rare gift. She hugged it to her like a miser, even as she cursed her own need to feel it form against her most tender places as he gloated over every one. Where she had got this wanton imagination from she had no idea, but it would not seem to go back to respectable slumber.

She was just drawn to him because the fates had not been particularly kind to either of them, she re-assured herself. He too had grown up with all the privileges of wealth, only to have them summarily taken away from him by those who should have guarded his future. In some ways their lives held astonishing parallels, in others they were as distant as if a vast ocean stretched between them.

Despite all her resolutions, and all the reasons she could come up with why Lord Strensham and Miss Hardy must never meet, she still found it impossible to dismiss him from her thoughts. She sighed impatiently as she realised she had left the fictional lovers suspended in mid-quarrel once again. If it took her the rest of her time here, she would learn to think of Lord Strensham as an aloof stranger once more. She refused to nurture an unrequited passion for a man who regarded her as a mild diversion for a day when no cards or sport could be considered, when he could be bothered to think about her at all!

By dint of fierce concentration, she lost herself in her novel so successfully that she missed dinner and had to go to bed supperless. Just one more reason to avoid the peerage like a noxious disease in future, she decided crossly, as her stomach rumbled like distant thunder and still failed to wake Carrie or Jane. She tossed and turned restlessly for what felt like hours, telling herself that it was because the heat of the day still lingered unpleasantly, despite the open window. At last she was convinced their encounter had been fired by a heady combination of his desire and her fear that he might smoke her out, and went to sleep to avoid the disappointment.

Lady Lydia had watched gleefully all evening while Miss Rashton eyed her distracted suitor with disfavour. That was much more like it, she thought, smiling sweetly at her domineering guest as if she hadn't noticed the heiress's repeated failure to hold Marcus's wandering attention. If the daughter of an earl ignored such blatant bad manners, Miss Rashton could hardly challenge him, so the heiress had gone to bed thoroughly out of sorts with the so-called lords of creation.

'I always had my doubts about this cold-blooded

idea of Marcus's, but now I've seen him with his heiresses I can't help thinking it quite ridiculous,' Lady Lydia informed her husband as they too sought their bed.

'Which idea would that be?' asked her spouse, distracted by the sight of his lady with her silky blonde hair flowing free, and arrayed in an insubstantial nightgown that he was particularly fond of.

'Marcus's marriage of inconvenience, of course,' she told him sternly. 'I do wish you would concentrate.'

'I'm doing so, quite avidly,' he informed his lady, who had little difficulty deciding just what he was intent on from the wolfish glint in his eyes.

'Then kindly attend to what I'm saying instead, husband. We can spare your cousin a few moments when we have the whole night ahead of us.'

'Not so, for I intend to get some sleep before that wretched female screams the house down again.'

'She wouldn't dare, Miss Rashton and Marcus would have her court-martialled for a second offence.'

'Nice to know they have something in common, then.'

'Hah! So you do agree that they would make the most ill-matched couple you ever came across?'

'Of course they would. Marcus would be compelled to strangle the woman before the ink was dry on the register, and no juryman who ever met her would convict him for it.'

'Then, money or no money, we have to make sure he abandons this absurd scheme.'

'If it's so absurd, why did you invite those peculiar females here for him to inspect as if we were competing with Tattersalls?'

'Because I wanted him to see how nonsensical it was for himself of course. If I really wanted him to marry for money, I should have invited heiresses I would not mind as a cousin by marriage. When it came down to it, I liked them too well to watch them become leg-shackled to his noble indifference.'

'He's not really a cold fish,' her husband protested half-heartedly.

'Of course not. I should not go to all this trouble to show him the error of his ways if Marcus was half as cynical as he believes himself to be.'

'He is wondering if his Home Farm could be brought back into profit—if he works it himself— so maybe he's not as enamoured of fortune hunting as you think.'

'I hope you encouraged him?'

'I told him it would be grinding hard work and might not pay for years, but that I would loan him the money for new machinery and improved seed and not take his usual stiff-necked no for an answer.'

'That must have rankled.'

'Aye, he hates owing money and is obstinate as an ass.'

'How fortunate he doesn't share such dreadful

faults with his cousin,' his wife said solemnly, and was quite content to abandoned the subject of Lord Strensham for the time being, as her husband retaliated with actions rather than words and she found *his* faults far more intriguing.

Chapter Nine

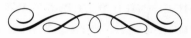

Marcus lay wakeful long after the rest of the household was fast asleep, trying to make sense of the impossible. This ridiculous preoccupation with Hetty Smith had to stop, he told himself sternly. Yet, even if he could dismiss his primitive need for the least likely siren he had ever encountered, she was a puzzle. Since he couldn't shrug their latest encounter off as the irrelevance it must be, he might as well think rationally about the wretched girl, instead of dwelling on the fathomless mysteries in her lovely eyes and the innocent ardour of her fiery responses.

As even Hetty acknowledged she could read, the little devil must have been doing so when he caught her in the library. It occurred to him at last that the Darraines' humblest housemaid must really read Latin well enough to be halfway through Virgil's *Aeneid*. Which brought him to the conclusion that no elderly mistress, however kind or lonely, would trouble to teach a foundling the classical languages, in the unlikely event that she knew them herself!

He sat up in bed to glare out at the indifferent darkness, cursing his slow wits when it came to 'Miss Hetty Smith.' Without her incendiary presence to distract him, he suddenly knew she was no more born to toil than he had been himself, and had been feeding him a parcel of lies since that first night in the woods. All he need do now, he decided grimly, was discover what induced a lady of birth and education to embark on a life of hard work and reluctant humility, then he could leave her to her amateur theatricals.

She had assured him she meant no harm, and something about the steady clarity in her eyes told him she was telling the truth in her own limited fashion. So, she was masquerading as a humble drudge for her own peculiar reasons. All he had to do now was work out what made such a hard lot appeal to her, then perhaps he could get a decent night's sleep for a change.

'The most shocking thing has occurred, Marcus, or have you already heard?' her ladyship asked her cousin the following morning as he failed in his intention of leaving the house unobserved for his morning ride.

'Prinny has paid his debts, perhaps, or maybe Liverpool has resigned?'

'Of course not, you idiot. Pigs would fly first.'

'Then whatever could be exercising you so, you are out of bed before ten, Lyddie? You know perfectly well that nothing exciting *ever* happens in the country—Miss Rashton told us so last night and she is always right.'

'Maybe that's why she annoys me so much, although this time she is quite wrong.'

'Then hurry up and tell me what *has* happened, Lyddie? I'm supposed to meet Ned and Birkin for a tour around the Home Farm this morning, and we should like to begin before dark.'

'They will talk you to death, and you'll be gone hours,' she replied, trying to hide her glee that he was more serious about rescuing Chimmerton by his own efforts than he was admitting.

'I dare say, but are you prepared for a day of exclusively feminine company?'

'I shall weather it, but don't you wish to know what has occurred?'

'You certainly wish to tell me, so why not do so and let me go?'

'You're not very polite, Marcus, but the Squire's niece was carried off by kidnappers last night. As if the poor creature hadn't enough to try her already, with losing her husband and child to typhus fever.'

Marcus considered all he knew about the grief-stricken little widow and wondered what on earth she had done to deserve such attention. Not only was Mrs Townley as poor as a church mouse, and a surprising quarry for an extortionist, but she hardly ever left her uncle's manor, even to go to church. How she could have set herself up as a target was a mystery to him.

'What ransom is demanded?'

'That's the oddest thing of all. She was taken from Squire Banks's garden last night, then left wandering on Comerbourne Common half an hour later in hysterics. That strange man at the Crown found her—Carter, I think he's called. Maybe they'll make a match of it, for he seems quite as grief-stricken and nervous as she is, but I must not make a joke of it. The Squire fears the poor woman will take a brain fever.'

'Have they had the constables out?'

'Of course, but they found no clues and they can get little out of her, apart from the fact that they wore masks and didn't speak. Squire Banks worried at first that they had taken her for more sinister purposes, but she denied it furiously and I doubt she was in a fit state to lie.'

'That's something to be thankful for, then,' Marcus replied grimly as he considered the unlikelihood of it all.

There was something more than an ill-planned attempt at blackmail behind this business. It had the hallmarks of a well-planned attack, not a wild scheme thought up on the spur of the moment. Well-honed instincts were warning him this hit closer to home than he liked.

'What's being done?' he rapped out, and Lydia was forcibly reminded of Major Ashfield of the 95th, tersely in command and ready for action.

'Everything you would expect, but Ned ordered me not to go about the grounds without half the staff and most of the stable-yard in attendance.'

'Then do as you are bid for once, Lydia. You would make a fine quarry for such villains.'

'Not as fine as your heiresses, Marcus.'

'Ned and I had best not go out today,' he said stiffly and Lydia could have kicked herself for pointing out that possibility.

Now he would feel responsible for them, and take some bull-headed notion into his head that he must ensure their safety, probably by marrying one of them and escorting the others back to town with half his old regiment in attendance.

'No kidnapper would dare carry your Miss Rashton off,' she told him waspishly, thoroughly out of sorts with fate for dealing her such a poor hand to play. 'If they did, they would be paying us to take her back after half a day.'

'Lydia, you are the most outrageous female I ever came across,' he informed her with a mix of exasperation and affection. 'How Ned keeps from strangling you I shall never know.'

'If you ever find a woman of character to marry, I will get him to give you a few hints. Until then you may strangle Miss Rashton with my blessing.'

'Thank you, my dear, I will tell the judge you said so. Now kindly tell me where I can find Ned and go and attend to your guests, if you can spare the time from traducing them.'

'Yes, if I leave them alone with Miss Rashton much longer they are like to murder one another and save you the trouble.'

'Then nothing should keep you from so necessary a task.'

'Maybe this will frighten them into leaving,' the doting hostess said hopefully and Marcus left her looking so thoughtful he half expected to find the hall full of maids and luggage when he came downstairs again.

After a day when everyone's nerves were so stretched her pale face and shadowed eyes had gone unremarked, Thea rested even less easily that night. Mrs Townley's abduction had stirred up a hive full of bees in her bonnet, and nothing would stop them buzzing as she lay courting sleep in vain. The sad little widow was much the same height as Thea, and her enemies would remember her as the dumpy female she had been before misadventure had fined down her face and figure.

So far the kidnappers had confined their attentions to the gentry, but if Granby had tracked her to Wiltshire she would not be safe for long. Yet she was strangely reluctant to relinquish her hard new life. That was clearly because she liked Sir Edward and his irrepressible wife so much, not because she felt empty at the idea of never seeing Marcus Ashfield again. Finding no comfort in such gloomy thoughts, she tossed and turned as she mulled over her latest dilemma.

If Lord Strensham lost a wink of sleep, it could only be because he had an uneasy conscience, she thought crossly, and if he hadn't one of those, he should. A wolfish glint had lit his grey eyes when she served him in the drawing room tonight. His hot glance had made her blush, and feel certain the temperature had gone up by several degrees.

He was no better than other so-called gentlemen who preyed on the maids and should be ashamed of himself. Working herself up into a temper might make her forget the effect that heated look had wrought on her ridiculously susceptible senses, but was unlikely to lull her to sleep.

She dare not examine the idea that the biggest sin she held his lordship guilty of was not being in Devon a year ago to court *her*. If she stood in Miss Rashton's shoes, she would swear black was white to persuade Lord Strensham to offer for her. Miss Alethea Hardy, her good name gone and no more than a few pounds to her name, could not serve him such a backhanded turn, even if he was chivalrous, or desperate, enough to ask her.

Of course, if he gave one of the heiresses a look such as he had sent her tonight, he would be turned off the fortune-hunting circuit for good. Evidently Hetty Smith was a convenient outlet for his lordship's baser impulses, but she was better off at Rosecombe Park than making a hasty bolt for freedom, and loneliness. Her thoughts became inextricably tangled at last and she fell into an uneasy sleep. As Carrie and Jane wanted no repeat of her last nightmare, when she began to toss and turn in her sleep one of them would stir and half wake her with a nudge, sharp or gentle depending upon who it was.

Thea had misread the blaze of emotions turning Marcus's grey gaze silver. As the truth finally dawned he cursed himself for a slowtop and her for the devious little devil she undoubtedly was. He was furious that she did not trust him, and shocked at his own idiocy. He finally worked out who the lying minx really was and couldn't believe it had taken so long. He wanted to shake her until her teeth rattled, or ride off with her across his saddle-bow so her wretched guardian never got near her again.

Several hours later he was awake and brooding. The duplicitous female must have been laughing up her sleeve at him for weeks, he fumed, as he silently paced his bedchamber. However much he might want to stamp up the stairs to the attics and drag her out of bed to give an account of herself, he was at least partly civilised and knew he could not cause such uproar without courting disaster.

A brief smile softened his grim face as he wondered if it might cause Miss Rashton to depart forthwith. It faded as he remembered how much he still needed her money. Of course the Hardy fortune put her dowry into the shade, but he would sooner wed a budding harridan than the lying little witch who had led him around by the nose for the last four months. Not that she would have him, he reminded himself. If she had the slightest intention of doing so, she would have told him who she was that first day in the woods.

Only a desire-fogged fool would fall for the story she had spun him then, and realising she was the kidnappers' true target finally made him see it. The unlucky Mrs Townley was small and brunette and, when he caught sight of a rebellious curl escaping from under 'Hetty's' mobcap in the drawing room, all became clear, at last. A case of mistaken identity, he finally realised, as all that was out of kilter about a supposedly humble maid slotted neatly into place.

The widow had been taken in the mistaken belief that the Squire was concealing the Hardy heiress. The ruthlessness of that abduction made him pause and glare into the darkness beyond his window. His hands tightened into fists at the very thought of his duplicitous maidservant being coerced into marriage with her guardian, but the law was against her. If only she had confided in him, perhaps he could have kept her safe until she came of age.

He found it hard to decide if he was more furious with her for deceiving him, or himself for being taken in. She had certainly played him beautifully that day in the wood, when he had sat and wished he was a humble clerk, a man who could make an honourable offer to an over-educated maidservant. How Miss Hardy, heiress to riches beyond a fortune hunter's wildest dreams of avarice, must have laughed at a fool who declared himself too poor to keep her.

It was just as well that he remembered his many obligations in time to still his tongue. To offer his hand and a joint berth on the next ship to Canada would have been folly of the highest order. The temptation to tug Miss Rashton into the nearest empty room and propose to her had nearly overmastered him tonight. Yet offering for one heiress because he was furious with another was insane, even to a fortune hunter in a towering rage.

He then struggled with an urge to drag Hetty Smith out of the servants' hall and teach her what she risked with her farrago of lies. Eventually he admitted to himself that she had not instigated those incendiary kisses, however heady her response. Yet the suspicion she would rather have his indifference than his ardent attentions put the seal on another day of heiress chasing, and he had retired to his bedchamber with the brandy bottle.

He tossed down another glass and waited in vain for it to take the edge off this furious hurt. He told himself it was just frustrated desire for a lying hoyden, not lacerated feelings at all. Whatever it was, it seemed resistant to Ned's fine cognac, so he flung the glass into the hearth and seized the boots his cousin's valet had cared for so lovingly with impatient fingers. With the care of long experience he ghosted out of the room and stole downstairs to let himself silently out of the house, then pulled on his mistreated boots and strode off into the night. At least now he could walk off some of his fury and, with any luck, exhaust himself enough to get a few hours' sleep after all.

The following morning he left Rosecombe Park before any of the quality were up and set out for a punishing ride on Ned's tricky stallion out onto Salisbury Plain and up to the Downs. He returned with barely time to change for dinner, which he faced with a fine appetite and a cynical determination to take no further part in Miss Hardy's melodrama. Yet that steely resolution lasted mere hours.

The next morning he spared Ned's stable and took a walk instead of his customary ride, and came upon the supposedly timid Carter surveying Rosecombe through a spyglass.

'The classical style, ain't nothing to beat it,' the man offered uneasily, finally noting the soft-footed gentleman watching him. ''Tis a noble sight, ain't it, Lord Strensham?'

'Very fine, but I dare say you have more impressive in London.'

'But the setting, my lord,' said Carter with pained ingenuity. 'Ain't got the like o' that in London, not even Carlton House.'

'Indeed,' Marcus agreed blandly, 'it only lacks a pair of nymphs and shepherds to become a very Arcadia, does it not?'

'I wouldn't know, sir, never having bin there.' Carter looked uncomfortable, until inspiration struck him. 'I needs to go for me breakfuss, your lordship, before it's ruined and the lady of the house fit to be tied.'

'Far be it from me to keep a man from his food, but you really must ask my cousin's housekeeper to give you the tour of the house some time, Carter. It would be a crying shame to keep such a gem from a man who admires the Palladian style so much.'

Marcus was grimly amused by the man's retreat on a tide of gratitude, all of it spurious if he was not mistaken. He didn't think Carter had the least desire to experience Rosecombe's delights, at least during daylight hours. Reminded of the wilder tales doing the rounds about Miss Hardy's venal guardian, he decided he could not leave her to fate after all.

Indeed, over the last few days she had grown so pale and anxious he almost forgave her that endless tangle of lies, and fought an urge to persuade her to confide in him.

The girl was a devilish nuisance, he thought later, then frowned at the assembled heiresses when he should have smiled. Then he sank into such a profound reverie that even Lydia found herself cravenly wishing something would lighten the brooding atmosphere of her drawing room. Yet she was smugly conscious Marcus wouldn't stand a chance of winning her guests over with his recent performance, and decided sitting through a dozen nights like this one would be worth it for such an excellent outcome.

'Well,' her husband finally remarked into the brooding silence, 'it's high time we all sought our beds, I dare say, if we are to meet my cousin Prestbury with suitable fortitude tomorrow.'

Eyeing the fine gilt clock on the mantel, Lydia sent her husband a laughing look, eyebrows raised in surprise as she recalled nights when they had danced half the darkness away in Spain, before setting out on the march the next day as if they had rested righteously all night long. Still, Ned had suffered manfully throughout a day made hideous by Miss Rashton's pettish demands.

First she wanted an ice pack from the exhausted

icehouse, then late strawberries might appeal to her
jaded palate, but when they came somehow they did
not. Lydia knew she was trying to get Marcus's attention, for all the good it did her. Somehow Ned
had restrained himself from telling the woman to
pack her boxes and depart at the double. In the face
of such fortitude, she gave her husband an alluring
smile and obligingly rose to her feet.

'Indeed, husband, I hope Captain Prestbury is recovered from his journey in time for the party I
have arranged tomorrow night.'

'Ooh, a party!' the youngest heiress exclaimed
with the first signs of animation she had shown
since she had arrived. 'How delightful, will all your
neighbours be attending?' she asked, then blushed
like the schoolgirl she so very nearly was.

'Most of them,' Lydia told her kindly and ignored
Miss Rashton's icy disdain of such country
company, then guided the ladies inexorably towards
the stairs and the candles set ready for them.

Thea helped light them, handing out one after the
other under the butler's stern eye, thankful Miss
Rashton would not dare play her usual spiteful tricks.
Yet her hand wobbled as Lord Strensham stepped
forward and she dripped hot wax on her wrist.

'Oh, you poor child!' Lady Lydia commiser-
ated and Thea could have wept from the kindness
in her voice.

Hearing of Carter's curiosity about Rosecombe's

inhabitants from Jane, who thought it a great joke that he was interested in everyone from the bootboy to the mistress of the house, Thea knew she must leave. Suddenly everything about the place was inexplicably dear to her. She was a goose, she chided herself silently, as she smiled a wan reassurance at her ladyship.

'It just stung for a minute, my lady,' she murmured and forced her hand to remain steady as she finally handed a candle to the man she would never see again after tonight.

Somehow she managed to avoid his eyes, and permitted herself one glance of farewell as he walked slowly up the stairs, straight backed and preoccupied. This was the last time she would set eyes on his reassuringly broad shoulders and proudly held head, and she would not show regret as he walked out of her life for good. She fleetingly considered telling Sir Edward and Lady Lydia the truth, but knew that in the unlikely event they believed her, they would still be obliged to return her to Granby, as the law demanded.

She could never wed Granby after learning what marriage could have been in Marcus's arms, if only everything had been different. Thea fought off a weak desire to picture him as husband and protector. The notion that, even if she managed to evade her enemies, her future was meaningless without him was best not even considered.

Later that night she cautiously slipped out of bed, hardly daring to breathe in case she woke Carrie or Jane. Stealing carefully down the back stairs and out into the hall, she fought an urge to run back and burrow into the safety of the lumpy old bed by Carrie and Jane's side, as full night made everything strange and the lonely future terrifying.

If Marcus had been asleep, even his sharp ears would not have detected enough noise to wake him. He had left his bedchamber without thinking of undressing, and let himself out of the garden door to brood on the terrace in blessed solitude. The moonlit garden seemed reassuringly silent, so he sat on a convenient bench and stared into the night, not seeing anything in the stars but a plain miracle of nature, and getting no closer to finding a solution to his problems.

He now knew that he couldn't ask Miss Rashton to marry him. An inner voice always whispered it would be a travesty whenever the words trembled on his tongue. He only had to think of the wretched life their unfortunate children would have, torn between parents who had no affection for each other, to wonder why he had ever thought he could make such a cynical bargain in the first place.

The Hardy heiress seemed unlikely to accept a shabby viscount's offer when he had no heart to offer with it, even if he did want her almost beyond reason. No, the chit was clearly a romantic—or she would have wed Sir Granby Winforde and waited for him to predecease her, before marrying again to please herself. All he asked of marriage was a bond of friendship and mutual respect, and if he must go to London for the Little Season to find such a paragon, so be it.

He was gloomily contemplating marriage à la mode when he caught a hint of movement out of the corner of his eye. He blinked, wondering if tiredness and the black mood he couldn't shake off were making spectres out of barn owls. No, he was too experienced at nightwork to doubt the evidence of his senses when they screamed this night owl was human.

He forgot his woes as he slipped into the friendly darkness underneath the trees. No use wishing for the dark green uniform of the 95th now, although the evening attire of a gentleman, with its scrupulously clean linen shining white in any available light, could easily warn his quarry that he was in determined pursuit. Knowing that he had the advantage of surprise, and a good many years' experience of creeping about in the dark, he didn't think that likely and, if it were only a night creature after all, at least nobody would know his folly but him.

Thea reached the cottage by the lake without the least inkling Marcus was on her tail. She breathed a sigh and made sure the shutters were closed, then

lit her candle stub with a flint and tinderbox pur-
loined from the lamp room. Shivering nervously,
despite the soft warmth of the summer night, she
hastily stripped off her nightgown and dressed in the
boy's raiment she had taken from a bundle collected
for the poor, and hidden under one of the window
seats earlier in the day. Thank goodness she had not
needed to spend much at Rosecombe so at least she
had some money left.

Just as she was about to hack off her thick plait
with the sharp knife she had stolen from the
kitchens, Thea sensed as much as heard the door
open very softly. As a familiar figure ghosted
through and shut it silently behind him, she cursed
her own carelessness at not locking it, then nearly
sat down on the floor and wept.

Chapter Ten

She had got so close to freedom and, if she couldn't convince him to let her go, she would very soon be back in Granby's toils. Carter had struck her as an intelligent man who would not let her escape now he had tracked her down. When Granby arrived, there would be no hope of evading him.

Despite her terror, Thea felt uneasy in her borrowed raiment. There could be no doubt his lordship had noticed it, when he was eyeing her slender legs in the boldest manner. She felt a fiery blush spread over every inch of exposed skin under his insolent scrutiny.

First he had seen her guyed up in the most deplorable set of clothes a desperate female could steal off various washing lines, then a humble maid's uniform, and now she was dressed in a fashion most young ladies would avoid if their lives depended on it. Somehow she couldn't convince herself it didn't matter a jot if he thought her a scarecrow. Some vain part of her wanted him to think well of her, not remember her looking deplorable!

Part of her flinched, another wanted to lift her chin and meet his contemptuous grey eyes with the pride she had been forced to swallow these last months. She settled for a defiant toss of the head and studied her bare feet as if she had never seen them before. It *could* have been worse of course, she concluded gloomily. He could have been Granby Winforde, complete with special licence and a well-paid priest with an accommodating conscience. Oddly enough, she had no thought of sticking her knife into his lordship's inconvenient hide, until he strode over and wrenched her wrist down with a grip so ruthless she could almost feel the bruises forming.

Now it was too late to dodge him and run, she heartily wished she had possessed the wit to do so when he first came in. She released the knife only to wrench at his gripping hand with her free one but, try as she might to wriggle free, he anticipated her every move and weathered every kick. She thought wistfully of the stout pair of boots waiting just yards away, and went still in his imprisoning grip. There was little point fighting the inevitable, so she glared up at him with helpless fury, which grew hotter when her anger seemed to amuse rather than humble him.

'Well, well, a vixen in sheep's clothing,' he drawled with a lazy grin that didn't reach his hard grey eyes.

She wondered briefly whether to abandon decorum altogether and bite the long-fingered hand that held hers so easily, but he seemed to sense her intention almost before she knew it.

'I shouldn't if I were you. I shall not hesitate to retaliate, whatever you are contemplating doing to me.'

'I always knew you were no gentleman,' she informed him coldly.

'And I knew you were no simple maid, so we're quits, are we not? I, however, could bring a troop of relatives and a division of infantry to prove my credentials, gentleman or no. Can you produce one person of integrity to swear you are Hetty Smith, my dear?'

'You know I cannot, and I'm not your dear,' she snapped crossly and, reminded of her alias, added defiantly, 'Anyway, I told you I was a foundling.'

'I never said I believed a single word of that tarradiddle though,' he said and Thea saw a gleam in his eyes. Surely it couldn't be admiration?

'Believe what you please. It's of no importance to me,' she told him untruthfully, then shrugged her shoulders, trying to look as if she found this whole wretched business tedious in the extreme.

He was so close she could feel the unhurried rise and fall of the breath in his chest, while doubtless he could hear the light hurry of hers and perhaps even the loud thud her quickened heartbeat was making in her ears. Oh, why couldn't she be as cool and in command of herself as he was in a crisis?

'It should be,' he replied to her disclaimer. 'I hold your fate in my hands at the moment.'

He looked down at her and Thea suddenly saw a wicked gleam light his grey eyes as he impudently surveyed her from top to toe again. He slowly worked his way from her white face down over her bosom, outlined by the much-washed white shirt and clumsily tied cravat, on to the curve of her hips then down her slender legs, exposed to his bold gaze by her scandalous attire. She flushed with mortification and anger, and cursed her lack of inches under her breath. How she longed for the height and strength to smack that wolfish grin off his insufferable face!

'Nobody has the right to dictate another's destiny, and I will be no man's doxy. Indeed, I would starve to death rather than become yours,' she raged at him.

'I should wait to be asked if I were you, my dear.'

Marcus looked her up and down again with a dismissive lift of his eyebrows and finally met her furious green eyes, fascinated to see that under the stress of deep emotions they had changed colour once again. He swiftly dismissed the memory of them doing so from emotions of a very different kind, before it inflamed his senses beyond control.

It would be far too easy to let thought proceed to action, he decided, and released her as hastily as if the contact of her body against his had actually burnt him. By dwelling on his duty to protect a girl who had been raised a lady, even if she had learnt a few tricks from the gutter during her adventures, he eventually fought his body into submission and managed to face her angry glare impassively.

'Enough of this folly, child. Tell me the truth, unless you wish to find yourself brought up before my cousin in his official capacity come morning.'

'Whatever for?' she asked scornfully. Child, indeed! She would give him child once and for all if he wasn't careful, although quite how was currently beyond her.

'Deception, fraud, theft—what matter? I expect I'll think of something.'

'You'll have to, for I have stolen nothing.'

When he surveyed her scandalously clad person and quirked one of his eyebrows derisively, she tried hard to look down her nose at him from her disadvantage in height.

'I left payment for what I took,' she informed him crossly.

'Then *you* were robbed.'

'Oh, I could kill you!' she told him between gritted teeth.

'You had me at knifepoint just now, and it never occurred to you. You are no murderess, my dear, whatever else you're guilty of.'

'I'm not your dear, and I'm guilty of nothing.'

Thea caught his sceptical look and suddenly all that invigorating anger disappeared and she felt weak, tired tears gather behind her eyes. She steadfastly avoided his eyes until she had her emotions under control.

'All I want is to be left in peace. Is that so very much to ask, my lord?' she asked wearily.

'If you insist on running about the countryside engaged in a series of ever more unlikely masquerades, I fear it probably is.'

He sounded sincerely regretful for an unlikely moment, before his attention suddenly shifted from her wilting person to the world outside the wavering circle of light cast by her candle she had forgotten all about. He listened avidly for a moment, then pulled her close and murmured softly in her ear. She was so shocked to find intimate contact with his warm, muscular body was still incendiary rather than objectionable, that his words did not register until she recovered some sense and recalled the warning note in his voice, if not his actual words.

'Keep talking, as if I'm still beside you,' he repeated impatiently. 'I can hear someone moving outside.'

Fear blocked that ridiculous impulse to nestle into his arms as if she belonged there; she nodded mutely while her heart lurched at the danger he was probably courting all unknowing. In the heat of the moment, it felt as if any blow that damaged him might put a period to her existence as well. Having the vapours would help nobody, however, and he had the advantage of surprise, if he didn't squander it by being too much of a gentleman.

'I can't see why it's too much to ask to be let alone,' she said pettishly for the benefit of their audience, then inspiration hit her at last. 'Yet I seem to be for ever pursued by ruthless men, intent on exploiting me at any cost.'

She hoped he would listen to her implied warning, and not dismiss it as the sort of idle prattle produced by overstretched feminine nerves. She kept up her litany of complaints as she watched him move swiftly across the room, and some of her tension eased as he did so as silently as a stalking cat. He would be a formidable opponent in a fight, if he didn't make the mistake of acting like a gentleman when Granby's methods belonged in the gutter, for all his so-called breeding.

Then there was a swift blur of movement and the door was open, the wiry rogue outside helpless in a hold his struggles could not break, and it had all been done with no hint of a fracas to alert a waking soul in the house. She need not have worried, she decided as she shut the door and bolted it behind them at a terse order from his lordship. There was no trace of the urbane gentleman of leisure left in this dangerously hard-eyed man. No wonder he had survived so long in his deadly profession, for in action Major Ashfield was all merciless efficiency.

'Hand me your belt,' he ordered briefly, and Thea found herself obeying as meekly as a raw recruit under his command.

She ran to find something to bind the man's wrists, blessing the fact that Sir Edward had installed curtains as well as shutters in his beloved wife's favourite refuge, as their silken tie-backs were coming in very handy. For a moment her resolve faltered as her confederate handed her the wickedly sharp knife he had been holding at the man's throat to keep him still and quiet. Then she remembered the many humiliations she had endured at the Winfordes' hands, and held it with such ruthless purpose that Carter was mighty relieved when that cold fish Lord Strensham took it back again.

Once he was tethered, and his captors stood back to survey their prisoner, Carter gulped convulsively as he finally dared swallow again. He had been bitterly deceived by Lord Strensham's indolent good nature and the wench's rumoured timidity. There was no sign of the die-away, silly creature his principal had described so contemptuously when he set his hound on the girl's track. The shameless hussy in front of him looked as if she was up to every rig and row in town, aye, and a few even he didn't know about.

Maybe the worthy company he had been keeping lately had left its mark on him, because he found that he was deeply shocked to see a wench standing there bold as brass in borrowed breeches. Nor was his lordship the suave gentleman he pretended. Sharp enough to cut himself more like, and anyone else daft enough to get close, the enterprising Mr Carter decided, sizing up the coolest gentry cove he had yet come across with a jaded eye.

'Good evening, Carter,' Marcus greeted him mildly enough, 'if, of course, that is your real name?'

Carter risked a cautious nod; there were enough of his name in London to make confessing that one fact easy enough.

'I really must insist that your sightseeing trips be confined to the hours of daylight in future, Carter,' his lordship informed him with an inexorable coolness that made his captive shudder. 'You would find it so much more instructive to take the house-keeper's tour as I suggested, don't you think?'

Carter had learnt during a varied career when to stay silent in the face of provocation from the gentry. He doubted whether his lordship, or his scandal-ously dressed doxy would wish it known what they were up to, and his thoughts were there to be read on his weather-beaten face.

Marcus regarded the sullen sneer on the man's face with apparent amusement. 'Neither my wife nor myself would flinch from our duty, Carter, even if I deplore her habit of playing practical jokes on my family.'

Fortunately Carter was too shocked by this statement to look to the supposed Viscountess Strensham
for corroboration. Just as well, considering Thea
was more startled by her elevation to the ranks of
the peeresses than Marcus had bargained for and
was staring open-mouthed at him. Suddenly realising it, she gathered her senses and snapped it into a
resolute line, wondering whatever he might say next
to overset his audience.

'Wife, is it? Now, that'll put his nibs in a fine taking.'

For a moment Carter looked rather gratified by the
knock back his employer would shortly receive,
then he became suspicious again.

'If you're wed, how come you let your wife come
here pretending to be no more than a common
maidservant?'

'Common? D'you really think so, Carter? I
always thought her the most uncommon wench I
ever had the misfortune to meet, but I'm sure your
experience of them is much wider than mine.
Anyway, you're deceived in thinking I let my wife
go anywhere. The truth of the matter is that her
ladyship ran away from me, just as she earlier
eloped *with* me. That really is getting to be a habit,
my dear, and I wish you would make up your mind
once and for all to stop at home and do as you're
bid. My lovely wife doesn't care for the curb you
see, Carter. Being a man of the world, no doubt you
know how tricky a female can be if she's accus-

tomed to having her head. Spare the rod and spoil the wife and all that.'

Carter nodded sagely. His own wife would be disgusted with him if he went home with nothing to show for a fortnight's work—and not slow to express her feelings either.

'Quite so,' Marcus said and nodded resignedly at his captive's unspoken agreement. 'My lady is devilish hot at hand, but this time I have decided to forgive her, have I not, Claudia my love?'

Thea bared her teeth and sent him a furious look. As she had been given the part of shrewish wife, she might as well play it to the hilt. She only had to imagine her outraged feelings if she really was this unscrupulous adventurer's unfortunate wife, being addressed in such a cynical fashion, and then let them show for once.

Carter would expect fury from a woman forced to watch her husband woo three other women when he was married to her, and far be it from her to disappoint him. She was working up such a fine spurt of indignation that she had to remind herself she was no more Lady Strensham than she had been Hetty the housemaid, before she slapped the cynical smile off her supposed lord's handsome face.

'Claudia?' asked Carter, obviously all at sea. 'But that ain't the name as I was given.'

'Dear me, you don't mean to say there are more ungovernable wives running about the place, do you? We may well need to call out the militia to suppress such a monstrous regiment of women.'

It seemed to Thea that his lordship was enjoying his mythical role far too much, so she glared realistically and clenched her fists until her knuckles showed white even by the fitful light of the flickering candle.

'Call out the Duke himself for all I care. I'm not coming home to be bullied, slighted and neglected while you pay court to any other woman who takes your fancy in front of my very eyes. I should have known you would come up with such harebrained nonsense when you swore you would mend our fortunes by fair means or foul!'

'Since you like spending the readies so much, you can hardly blame me for trying anything out of desperation to provide them, now can you?'

'Bah, you waste far more than I do on your fine clothes and those silly great horses you spend so much time with!'

This apparent play for Carter's sympathy fell on deaf ears; indeed it seemed to clinch matters rather than winning him to her side.

'Aye, you're wed all right. Women always think the daftest rubbish once a man's simple enough to marry one. You take her home and beat her, my lord. If she were mine, I'd get lots of little 'uns on her and keep her short of the blunt. That's the only way to tame these high-tempered ones, and you can take the word of a man who knows it from experience.'

He sounded as if he might well offer to take her off Lord Strensham's hands at any moment, from sheer fellow feeling. Thea was so furious with the male sex in general, and one member of it in particular, that it was only half an act when she picked up the knife from the table and rushed at her supposed husband with it.

'You damnable wildcat!' he exclaimed, grasping her firmly by the waist and forcing her to drop the knife once again with the other hand.

She rubbed her maltreated wrist, and glared defiance at her supposed spouse. Seeing the genuine fury in her eyes, Carter dismissed his last suspicion that this was an act put on for his benefit. The little wildcat was truly mad as fire. Nobody could have faked the temper that whitened her cheeks and sparked out of her eyes, any more than a man could mistake how much his lordship relished their fight and its inevitable ending.

Then there were those eyes of hers—green as grass and nothing like the description he had been given of Sir Granby's errant ward. This wench wasn't plump, she certainly wasn't soft and she didn't have the 'sort of blue' eyes Sir Granby had listed. He might be deceived on one count, but nobody could put all three discrepancies past a man of his age and wide experience. He finally admitted his error to himself and the important part of his audience, as he saw it.

'Sorry, m'lord, but you can't blame me for doing me job. Now I'll have to start all over again and ain't that enough for you, without you murdering me or turning me over to the magistrate?'

'Maybe, but the question is, can I rely on your discretion, Carter? My darling wife doesn't care a snap of her fingers for the proprieties, but I've no mind to have my good name dragged through the mud, thanks to her wanton stupidity. It's been hard enough keeping her identity from my cousin, while pretending to court his guests. My creditors will be most unhappy when they find out I'm already wed to a very different article from the one they guilelessly believe I'm in a position to offer for.'

'I knows which way is up. My gentleman won't be too bobbish about me going down another pudding-bag alley, your honour, so I'll say naught about all this. I like peace and quiet and nobody ever accused me of being a gabber, never you fear.'

'Good, then I'll leave the door unbolted for you,' Lord Strensham offered blandly and undid the belt that tied the man's ankles together. 'I think you'd best have this back, m'dear. I don't want the stableboy's breeches falling down round your ankles *before* I get you to my bedchamber.'

Carter was torn between salacious amusement at Thea's supposed fate at the hands of her forceful 'husband,' and righteous indignation about his own.

'What about these 'ere ropes, your lordship?'

'Really, Carter,' replied that gentleman wearily, 'you must expect some punishment for interfering in my affairs. I'm sure you have the ingenuity to relieve yourself of them before morning. Meanwhile, I have a burden of my own. So, are you coming quietly, m'dear? Or would you rather I bound you with the other cord? I must admit such a scenario has a certain allure, and I've been a patient husband up to now. A man has his needs, and mine will be denied no longer.'

'I hate you!' Thea ground out convincingly, between set lips.

'Hate away,' he said. 'I won't be refused my dues again, wife, and I find I prefer your hatred to any other woman's submission.'

With that he picked her up and threw her over his shoulder, as if she was no more than a bundle of old clothes, or a sack of straw. Leaving Carter the candle, he strode off into the night with his struggling, cursing burden wriggling frantically, as she attempted to escape his far-from-gentle hold by beating her fists against his broad back.

'Aye, got your hands full there, ain't you, my fine buck?' murmured Carter and started to edge his chair towards the table where his lordship had left the knife with apparent carelessness.

He recalled the finer details of the little virago's face and figure, and fleetingly envied his lordship the task of taming her, but he had no time for such fantasies when he had to get out of here before morning. Not only would it ill accord with his pride to be found here trussed up like a chicken, but he had to be about his business again as soon as possible.

In six months he had not found a more promising trail than this one, but it was time to cut his losses. For once in his dogged career, Josiah Carter found himself tempted to give up and bolt for London. He was heartily sick of Sir Granby Winforde and his demanding mother, tired of the country and weary of small, dark-haired young women who didn't seem to know when they were well off.

From her undignified position across Lord Strensham's shoulder, Thea decided she had had quite enough of domineering, interfering viscounts. He had rescued her from capture, but why? And what came next? She began to struggle again as a few unpalatable answers occurred to her.

'Do you want to bring the whole household down on us, woman?'

'No,' she replied breathlessly.

'Then keep still and be quiet, at least until we get inside the house.' He sounded almost amused, but the truth came in a low and abrupt whisper. 'He has confederates and we may yet be watched.'

Suddenly Thea was as still as that inanimate bundle she had likened herself to when he threw her over his shoulder so easily. She held her breath and waited apprehensively for a word or blow to come out of the darkness, but there was nothing and, at last, Lord Strensham reached the terrace and comparative safety. Once they were inside the conservatory and even closer to temporary sanctuary, he turned to softly lock the door behind them while she fought to regain her composure.

'An interesting evening by anyone's standards except your own, Miss Smith,' he murmured as he set her gently back on her feet.

The unmistakable emphasis on the last word told Thea that a trying night was not over. He might have rescued her, but now he expected an explanation, and how much of her story could she bear to tell him?

'The library I think. We should be private there at this time of night.'

'I have no wish to be private with you, my lord,' she whispered fiercely.

She needed the time before dawn to think up another escape plan, not suffer interrogation from a gentleman with nothing better to do than interfere in her affairs. Anyway, even if she told him the half of it, he would look down his aristocratic nose at such a shop-soiled adventuress for ever afterwards.

'Unfortunately, your wishes do not weigh heavily with me at the moment. Until I have heard the whole story, neither of us is going to bed, so unless you indeed wish to continue our discussion in my bed-chamber, the library it must be.'

Realising that she had left her night rail in the summerhouse, Thea was in a fine predicament. She could hardly try to dodge past him and creep back to bed dressed as she was, nor could she return to the folly to retrieve her very respectable nightgown. Even if she had a spare one, Jane and Carrie would wonder how she managed to go to bed in one and get up in another, so, with ill grace, she followed Lord Strensham's powerful figure through the gloom to the library, and prayed for inspiration.

Chapter Eleven

Once the door was locked after them and the key in his pocket, Marcus lit a branch of candles and took a proper look at his captive. Inspecting her for sign of injury, he was annoyed at how glad he was to have stopped her cutting off that thick plait of hair. It didn't matter if she looked like a scarecrow or a princess in disguise, she was calamity on two legs and he would do well to remember it. Yet part of him stubbornly wanted to see those glossy curls loose about her shoulders once more, and Major Ashfield seemed unable to silence the reprobate.

'I beg pardon for mishandling you, Miss Hardy. I only recall hearing your name once before I met you, so I hope I have it right,' he observed smoothly enough.

Thea was convinced that if he possessed a quizzing glass, she would have received the full benefit of it.

'You are mistaken, my lord, my name is Smith,'

she replied, with as much airy composure as a woman dressed in such a disgraceful fashion could summon.

'Absconding heiresses are not exactly commonplace, you know, so don't waste your breath trying convincing me you're not the Winfordes' ward, there's a good girl.'

Thea decided she set being a 'good girl' somewhat lower than being constantly referred to as 'child'. Repressing an urge to stick her tongue out to prove the classification wrong, she tried for a look of queenly indifference as she met his sceptical grey gaze.

'I admit nothing, but what interest can my affairs possibly be to you, even if I were this Miss Hardy you seem to have mistaken me for?'

'Since you obviously don't want to marry your cousin—'

'Sir Granby Winforde is no cousin of mine,' she protested impulsively, then had to suppress a groan as she realised how totally she had just given herself away. 'Five years ago my grandfather's brother married his mother, a folly he very soon regretted, before dying of it shortly afterwards,' she admitted, realising all attempts at denying her heritage were useless now.

Anyway, for some strange reason she needed him to know that she didn't share a single drop of blood with Granby. Her grandfather might or might not have had noble blood in his veins, as he fondly imagined, but he had been far more honourable than most of the titled fops she encountered.

'Such subtleties do nothing to solve your problem, Miss Hardy. Winforde is your guardian and can dispose of you as he thinks fit until you reach your majority, have you by the by?'

'Have I what?' Thea asked absently, too deep in despair at the first part of his statement to take much note of the rest of it.

Perhaps he was right and marriage to Granby was inevitable. Without being unduly melodramatic, she knew she would not long survive it and she could not help but shiver in the warm night air.

'Your age?' he asked with exaggerated patience.

'Oh, that—I turn twenty-one in six weeks' time.'

'Then you have no hope of staying here safely. If Carter doesn't see through that rigmarole we spun him tonight, your guardian soon will.'

'If Granby ever possessed an original mind, he long ago drowned it in brandy. Unfortunately his mother certainly won't give up when my fortune is twenty times as large as Uncle Miles's. Much good it did them when his money is spent and they are hunting for more. Which is why I must get away as soon as possible, my lord,' she pointed out wearily.

'Where to?'

'My father's family live in the north.'

'And Winforde does not know of this connection?'

'Even if he does, my aunt has six burly sons. He

will not challenge them, for all they have not much more money than I at present.'

'He will find you nevertheless, and the law will force them to part with you.'

'Unless Lady Kilvane bullocks me into marrying my cousin. Then I suppose Granby will be faced with a dilemma, as possession is commonly held to be nine tenths of the law.' The distaste she felt for the whole business rang in her voice now and, try as she might, she could not make it sound disinterested. She really would never have made a proper lady, she decided ruefully. 'I could always go to London, I suppose. It should be easy to find work as a maid in such a vast city and no simple matter to track one down.'

'No!' he barked loudly, then moderated his voice in deference to the night. 'You would do better to marry a common fortune hunter than take such a ridiculous risk. Do you have any idea how many innocent young maids from the country end up on the streets of the capital, selling themselves for the price of a meal and a bed for the night?' She paled, which didn't seem to placate him very much, as his frown only became more thunderous. 'You would be better off leg-shackled to a poor, desperate man like me rather than sink to that!'

'Very well, I accept, and thank you for your kind offer,' Thea said sweetly, which should teach the interfering wretch not to involve himself in other people's private business and then look down his patrician nose at them at two o'clock in the morning.

'What offer?' he said, all lordly impatience.

'You said I would be better off marrying a common fortune hunter, although I must say you seem rather an uncommon one to me. After all you're not very good at humbling your pride to charm ladies of expectation like myself, are you, my lord? But beggars can't be choosers I suppose, so you'll just have to do.'

'Do?' he barked, caught on the raw if the blaze of swiftly controlled fury that flashed across his stern face was anything to go by. 'I cannot honourably offer you that choice, madam,' he went on coolly enough. 'You would do better to find a man of character and fortune who has the means to protect you, rather than taunting a fool like me with his poverty.'

'Nonsense, I suspect what sticks in your throat is my plebeian breeding, although I suppose my unfashionable looks and sad want of inches must be weighed in the balance as well. Would you kindly tell me where I am to meet this paragon by the way, my lord? There are few enough perfect gentle knights to be found in society nowadays, let alone in the servants' hall.'

'I wasn't serious, and well you know it. I must sell up and bear the consequences, for I refuse to be named in the same sentence as Winforde. I will not take a wife purely for the size of her dowry.'

'Then you give up too easily, my lord. I hear you have a great many obligations—should you not think of them?'

'I do, all the time,' he told her in a clipped voice.

Thea knew she had gone too far by lashing out at him because she wished his offer was a real one. Her own pain was no excuse for hurting him and her temper died as she realised taunting him until he lashed back at her felt like a very Pyrrhic victory.

'I'm sorry. It's not fair to cut up at you when you just saved me from unholy wedlock again. My misfortunes are not of your making.'

He gave her a rather weary smile. 'Will I risk being thought interfering if I wonder why your grandfather left you in such hands?'

'He thought he was invincible, I suspect, and that the question would not arise. He certainly had every intention of dandling some future lordling of mine on his knee before he went to his reward.'

The disgust in her voice at this piece of shameless social climbing made him smile, despite his own lacerated pride.

'Is that what he stipulated? In that case I'm surprised Winforde put himself forward—like myself he's too humble to sire lordlings.'

'My grandfather's will merely stipulated that I must marry a gentleman of established title, or forfeit his fortune. His mistake I feel, as Granby has a very old title.'

'How useful for him to be named your guardian, as he then had it in his power to ensure you met no other titled men.'

'The ones I met when Grandpapa was alive didn't leave me wild to encounter more, but I would marry an incurable lunatic rather than Granby!'

'No wonder I appeal to you as a husband then,' he said painfully and, Thea was about to put a consoling hand on his arm when a revolutionary idea struck her.

'But why not do it after all?' she said impulsively and, when he looked at her as if she had finally run mad, explained, 'Marry one another, I mean. You need a fortune, and I need a husband. When I come of age we can get an annulment, then I would be free and you could wed a lady of your choice.'

She could hear herself sounding less and less certain as this speech went on, and tried not to examine his thunderstruck expression too closely. Suddenly convinced that he was her only way out of a terrible situation, she persisted, however. 'It would cause a fuss of course, but I dare say we could endure it.'

'And how would this scheme benefit me, when you are to up sticks and leave me within weeks of the wedding?' he asked cynically, so obviously unwilling to give her scheme consideration that she stamped her bare foot in impatience.

'You can keep my fortune for all I care! It has only

caused evil deeds and misery up until now. I dare say I would be well rid of it.'

'I am not cut from the same cloth as your guardian, madam, and I just told you that I refuse to marry for money alone,' he replied tersely.

'You are an intelligent man. It would not take long to set your estate to rights and put your house in order, once you had my fortune to draw upon. After a year or two, I warrant you would have no need of my money at all, and it would give us a chance, you see? We could both escape from intolerable situations with no hurt on either side.'

'Two years of celibacy might prove a far greater strain for me than it evidently would for you, Miss Hardy. You know very well I'm no saint, but I still don't see mutual self-interest as an honourable reason for marriage.'

'Believe me, my lord, becoming the new Lady Winforde is not the sort of honour any sane female would wish for. After contemplating it, I think maybe my notion of what is acceptable is not as nice as yours seems to have become.'

Let him think her a vulgar cit for her offered bargain, but let him see his nobility for what it was.

'I'm not the perfect gentleman you appear to think me, Miss Hardy, and can quite see the logic of your idea, but you leave human nature out of your calculations. What if either of us falls in love after we enter this rackety arrangement?'

'What matter, when we will annul the marriage anyway?'

'And what a high opinion you do have of my honour. Do you honestly believe you could marry me and stay untouched for so long?'

He sounded as if he would be subject to the greatest of temptation, but of course he was just being gallant. After all, he would find it easy enough to stay away from a wife of such limited charm and low connections. He had ignored her as often as he could these last few days after all.

'You don't love me, so why not?' she insisted, determined to dismiss his silly scruples and her own doubts in her eagerness to escape Granby.

'Why not indeed?' Marcus replied, remembering his earlier resolution to find a wife he could respect with faint disquiet.

He certainly honoured this extraordinary girl for her steadfast courage and steely determination to escape what so many would have accepted as inevitable. Then he silently acknowledged her intelligence. As she had managed to evade her guardian, maintain a disguise totally alien to a lady, and become a scholar in the teeth of a society that required bare literacy of girls, how could he do otherwise? And yet a cautious part of him whispered that she would never conform to that picture of serene wedded harmony he had drawn himself on the terrace such a short time ago.

'Surely you don't expect to marry for love when you don't believe in it?' Thea persisted. 'Even after you are rid of me that seems a most unlikely outcome, my lord, and most of your kind don't look for such strong passions within marriage.'

'No, indeed, a vastly overrated emotion,' he replied so swiftly it killed a fantasy Thea had not known she still held.

Well, once upon a time Thea Hardy had possessed a head full of them, but Hetty Smith could not afford such luxuries.

'Yes indeed, it sounds highly uncomfortable,' she stoutly agreed.

'And I suppose you would be safe as my wife, if a wedding could be accomplished in the teeth of your guardian's opposition. Earlier tonight I decided I could not marry without being sure that mutual respect and friendship would grow up between myself and my bride.'

'Then we are at *point non plus,* are we not?' she declared bravely, refusing to acknowledge a sharp sting of tears behind her indifference. She had never thought he would love her, but she doubted he felt respect and friendship for a female who had set out to mislead him—and then fallen headlong into his arms like the sort of female a wise gentleman relegated to the mere fringes of his life. 'If you will just unlock the door, I shall have a great deal to do if I am to leave for the north before the house begins to stir.'

She was so intent on not giving in to despair that she had no idea that her face whitened and her mouth gave a betraying wobble that wrenched at Marcus's heart.

'You misunderstand me,' he objected softly. 'I admire your stalwart determination, Miss Hardy, even if you *have* deceived me and mine to the top of your bent. It can hardly have escaped your notice that I'm attracted to you on a more personal level.'

Thea's eyes widened as she took in that last statement. The idea of him being deeply drawn to her and still holding off, despite her apparently lowly status or sullied reputation, warmed her so that she was in danger of missing the rest of his careful speech.

'I believe we could build a worthwhile marriage together,' he went on blithely, evidently not seeing the tears she was blinking back. 'I would not demand my rights until you are ready to grant them to me willingly, although I should very much like to dandle those little honourables on my knee one day. So, if we can find a way of arranging it, would you do me the honour of becoming my wife, Miss Hardy?'

'It sounds as if this would be a true marriage in time?' she asked cautiously.

His offer was painfully unambiguous, but still she had to ask. The alternative seemed to be to seize eagerly on his proposal and fall at his feet, weeping with gratitude.

'That is the only arrangement I could propose

while retaining any vestige of honour, and I find I am more enamoured of that notion than I had thought. After all, I have little else to offer.'

The bitterness of that last sentence reached through her defensive barriers as no false protestations of undying affection could have done.

'What about my sullied name?' she asked, wavering in the face of almost irresistible temptation.

'Once you are my wife I will be entitled to look more closely at the Winfordes' affairs than I suspect they will like. After all, your uncle and grandfather were carried off very suddenly, and that precious pair benefited substantially both times. They will be too busy avoiding me to talk scandal, and then everything about them will be suspect. If for no other reason than that, my offer should look tempting by now, so will you marry me, my dear Miss Hardy?' he added softly, looking for all the world as if he cared very much about her reply.

If only she was his dear anyone, but she had refused to believe that careless endearment right from the start. Anyway, he wasn't offering her undying love, just a polite and friendly alliance that seemed much easier to accept. His conscience might prove a thorny growth for them both to live with in future, but she would be a fool to turn down the promise that had suddenly opened in front of her.

Instead of facing a few months of misery as Granby's short-lived lady, she could begin a new life with a man she already respected, and hankered after in the most ridiculous manner. Indeed there seemed a distinct risk she would be a fonder wife than Lord Strensham wanted. But if she managed to behave more like a lady from now on and conceal her own feelings from him, who was to say that admiration could not become affection in time? She really should not yield to temptation, but nobility would not protect her from the Winfordes and he was offering too much. If she married him she would always have someone on her side, and after so many months of being alone that was a lure beyond resisting.

Eyeing the handsome gentleman in front of her, still unfairly immaculate after tonight's adventures in dark evening coat, elegant cream pantaloons and the whitest of white linen, she saw him shift under her assessing gaze as if he was nervous. The thought of the mighty Viscount Strensham being eager to hear anything she had to say nearly brought her to the edge of hysteria, so unlikely as it seemed after tonight's adventures. She realised that tonight she had seen the arrogantly assured man of action he had been that night in the woods, before the full weight of his father's profligacy hit him and ruin stared him in the face.

Command had sat on his shoulders as if it was bone deep; quick thinking and abrupt action were as easy as breathing to him. She contemplated the

man who had existed just those few short months
ago—a natural leader and a strong man with very
definite notions of right and wrong, and thought he
must have made a very fine officer. Even so she
wondered if the Thea of six months ago would have
found Major Ashfield insufferably sure of himself,
so perhaps mutual hardship would help their
marriage work. Anyway, the alternative rendered
him irresistible, and she very much liked the thought
of those little Ashfields as well.

'I would be honoured to become your wife, my
lord,' she told him, meeting his grey eyes with her
own unclouded by distrust for the first time, and
making his heart miss a beat in the process if she
did but know it.

'Then might I not know your first name, so we can
be less formal while we plan how to carry such a
scheme out, considering you are still a minor? It
would certainly add spice to the tale if we were
forced to flee for the Border with your unlovely
guardian hot on our heels, but I am a little too old
and cynical to be playing brave young Lochinvar.'

Thea chuckled, feeling ridiculously contented
with the novel new life opening up before her and
unutterably weary at the same time.

'I'm sure you'll think of something, my lord,' she
told him sleepily, and wondered where on earth she
would find a bed for the night.

'How I wish I had your faith in my abilities,'

Marcus told her, as he watched his betrothed's eyelids grow inexorably heavier.

Only her stalwart spirit had been keeping her on her feet for so long; now reaction had finally set in, he must get her to bed before she finally collapsed. He eyed her unconventional garb, and dismissed the idea of somehow insinuating her back into her attic. He needed to find a safe place for her to sleep before she succumbed to exhaustion in Ned's comfortable chair as he picked up his newly affianced bride before she fell down.

'What are you about now, my lord?' Thea demanded crossly, as she was swept into his arms without so much as a by your leave.

If the truth were known, and it would be much better not, she liked being held safely against Lord Strensham's powerful chest very much indeed. Unvarnished truth was a luxury that must go out of the window if their bargain was to stand any chance of success, so she refused to admit the sudden acceleration of her silly heartbeat even to herself.

'Be quiet and stop asking silly questions.'

'Not a silly question,' she mumbled and Marcus looked down at the dark head drooping against his shoulder with bemused admiration.

He had never come across a lady quite like his Miss Hardy, he decided, as she gallantly fought sleep in his arms. She relaxed completely once she gave in and his body threatened to respond eagerly to the feel of her warm curves nestled so trustingly against him. He willed himself to forget that he held a potential enchantress in his arms, and foresaw a great many cold baths in the immediate future, if he was not to prove himself a liar before the ink was dry on the wedding licence.

'Alethea,' she told him drowsily, stirring briefly as he carried her up the stairs. 'It means truth.'

'How singularly inappropriate!'

She frowned sleepily at his mocking reply. 'I have never liked it, so you may call me Thea.'

'Very well, your highness, now go to sleep,' he told her softly, and prayed nobody was waking in the silent house for both their sakes.

To keep Thea out of the Winfordes' clutches until she reached her twenty-first birthday, Nick Prestbury spirited her off to Bath when he returned there, while Marcus went off to London until the day before their wedding. It would take a brave, or reckless, man to challenge the Dowager Lady Prestbury. Thea was declared an invalid not fit to leave her room, so at least she had a good rest and could spend as many hours reading as she once wished to. Yet even a new wardrobe of such exquisite creations as met her ladyship's demanding standards failed to interest her much when she longed for Marcus to reach Bath safe and sound. Still the weeks passed uneventfully, even if they did so on leaden feet, and at last her birthday and wedding arrived on the same day.

'I knew Cassie Snodsbury's sins would find her out one day,' the Dowager asserted after Thea and Marcus had used the special licence burning a hole in his pocket and they were sharing a celebratory bottle of champagne.

'Did you, ma'am?' Marcus replied blandly as he looked down at their entwined hands and the gold wedding band on Thea's finger.

'I know what you're thinking, you ungrateful boy,' her ladyship replied, 'but my sins harmed nobody. Some of the parties concerned enjoyed 'em far too much, if the truth be known.'

'No doubt they did,' Marcus replied with an elegant bow and a sly glance at the fine portrait of her ladyship in the full bloom of her youth and scandalous glory over the mantelpiece.

Wondering if her wedding breakfast was to be enlivened by an account of her hostess's more spectacular misdeeds, Thea's laughter faded the instant the sound of Lady Winforde's strident voice was heard below. Nick stepped forward as a red-faced Sir Granby Winforde and his puffing mama barged into the room.

Chapter Twelve

'Let them come,' Marcus ordered, and Thea shivered at the quiet menace in his voice. 'Two more glasses to toast this happy occasion, if you please,' he ordered the startled butler.

'Not the Waterford,' the Dowager put in irrepressibly. 'I don't want the good stuff broken.'

'I would sooner drink poison,' Lady Winforde declared dramatically, subsiding onto the nearest sofa, a lace handkerchief to her scarlet face.

'Would you, my lady? A tincture of belladonna then, or shall we be strictly classical and call it a cup of hemlock? See to it, Munby.'

'Certainly, my lord,' replied the butler with such panache Thea almost hugged him.

'You know that's not what I meant,' Lady Winforde snapped furiously.

'Do I? Being a literal minded ex-soldier, I need certain things spelled out to me, Lady Winforde,'

Marcus replied smoothly. 'Just the glasses, please, Munby.'

'Very good, my lord,' the man replied and left the room as if such goings on were commonplace.

'We came here to reclaim my son's ward,' Lady Winforde announced.

'My wife prefers my protection for some odd reason.'

'His wife? Did you hear, Mama? She's gone and married him!'

Lady Winforde waved a plump hand. 'Miss Hardy is your ward, despite her blatant ingratitude, and you did not give consent.' Her ladyship's cold eyes lighted on Thea and took on an icy glitter.

Glad of the warm contact with Marcus's hand in hers, Thea raised her chin proudly. Although her new rank sat uneasily on her slender shoulders, she was quite happy to look down her nose at the Winfordes.

'I am most ungrateful for being treated like nothing and nobody in my own home, which you are required to quit as of today by the way. Our lawyers are waiting on yours at this very moment. Or was that to be tomorrow, Lord Strensham?'

'You are quite right, Lady Strensham. Tomorrow will be the accounting of every penny spent for your comfort since the day your grandfather died.'

'Since I found it acutely uncomfortable to live in the attics before I risked my life leaving it, that should not take long.'

'You were lucky Granby agreed to wed you, you were ruined.'

'I shall have this so-called marriage dissolved and your paramour thrown into prison for abducting a minor,' Granby blustered. 'You are nothing but a counter-jumper, miss, and the whole world knows it.'

'Sir Thomas Kilvane will take such aspersions amiss, I fear, but if you're not afraid of one of the finest shots in England...' Marcus said silkily.

Granby looked as if he might faint at the thought of fighting a duel with such a man. Thea privately believed the Kilvanes more likely to agree with his opinion of her breeding, having refused her a home when she was orphaned.

Not that she had wanted one; indeed, she had been perfectly happy with Giles Hardy. Tears threatened, as they had when the vicar pronounced her and Marcus man and wife, and Grandfather was not there to hear him. She refused to show weakness in front of her enemies, though, and stood proud as an offended Greek goddess.

'Wanted to marry her, didn't I?' Granby mumbled, with what might have passed for a conciliatory smile in a poor light.

'But my wife didn't return the favour. In the best circles that is regarded as enough, you know?' Marcus drawled and Thea's hand tightened on his when she realised he intended to provoke Granby into a duel.

'Missish,' mumbled the sweating baronet, casting a longing glance at the decanters.

'Never mind all that, without our consent you are not legally married. Alethea, you will come with me,' Lady Winforde asserted loudly.

'Not if the Lord Chancellor ordered it personally.'

'*I* order it!' her ladyship barked, all trace of self-restraint gone. 'That should be enough, you ungrateful doxy!'

Seeing her steely enemy's icy mask slip and the raging harridan beneath show herself, Thea would have felt better if a lingering, shaming shiver of fear had not run through her. She hated to think what Lady Winforde might be capable of in defeat, but there was no question of going back to her brutal custody. Anyway it was time she fought her own battles, instead of leaving them to Marcus.

'Your wishes are irrelevant. I suggest you leave before you are put out.'

'You'll do as you're bid after a few weeks in that attic you claim to despise, my girl.'

Marcus saw Thea's colour drain away, even as she raised her chin and stared defiance back at the creature who had caused her so much suffering, and her gallantry clutched at his heart. Despite his instincts and training, he wanted to strike a woman for the first time in his life. His free hand clenched until the knuckles showed white. Reason told him that depriving the unappealing pair of everything they had taken from Thea would punish them enough, as he didn't want her good name traduced by the gossips again. He smiled reassuringly at his new wife and tucked her ringed hand in the crook of his elbow to show she truly was his lady, before facing the Winfordes with implacable purpose.

'Not while I have breath in my body,' he assured them in so soft and deadly a tone that Granby looked sick with terror. 'Can it be that you don't know my wife's birthdate, Lady Winforde? Your staff work really leaves a great deal to be desired. Have I wished you a happy birthday, my darling, or am I remiss too?' he said in a very different tone, turning to smile down at Thea as if they were alone.

This time her knees wobbled for a very different reason as she smiled back, unable to help herself when he seemed so sincere. 'You have, and at least I shall never forget our anniversary.'

'With two such important days combined, I shall never dare to,' he assured her tenderly, and Thea wondered if she needed a pinch to remind her it was an act.

'You damned fool, you never told me,' Lady Winforde spat at her open-mouthed son.

'Never knew.'

'You realise what you have done?' Lady Winforde demanded of Marcus, who raised his eyebrows and looked as lordly and indifferent as Thea could wish, now he was no longer doing it to her. 'We are ruined.'

'You tried to ruin my wife's good name and threatened and abused her, and I find that very hard to forgive. Reluctant as I am to threaten a lady, even one so unworthy of the title, you will never hurt Lady Strensham again, in word or deed, if you value your skin.'

'You are a penniless fortune hunter, you can't bully me.'

'Oh, but I can, and your son's account at Coutts has been suspended by the way. Since the money in it was illegally come by, any attempt to access it will lead to him residing in Newgate until brought to trial for fraud and attempted murder.'

Granby's usual high colour drained from his face, leaving it more moonlike than ever as a sweat of panic beaded it unhealthily. 'I'll have nothing!' he spluttered.

'Really? Then perhaps you will gain insight into Lady Strensham's life these last months.'

'The sly little nobody was born to the gutter— what matter if she went back to it?' Lady Winforde screamed, her voice harsh and her mouth working as if her fury was a physical thing that must somehow force its way out.

'Enough!' Lady Prestbury ordered regally and even Granby stood to attention. 'I will not tolerate such vulgarity under my roof. You never were good *ton,* Cassandra Snodsbury, and time has done nothing to improve a very commonplace mind.'

High sticklers might have frowned at Lady Prestbury's more scandalous liaisons, but she was at the heart of society and her words affected Lady Winforde as no others could have. To be thought unscrupulous and inhuman was nothing, resorting to outright criminality perfectly acceptable, but being declared bad *ton* made the bottom drop out of her world.

Nick advanced on the sweating baronet and prodded him in his ample middle. 'I should get out while you still can if I were you,' he told him with a hard look that told Granby how much he would like to punch him on the jaw, sore arm or no.

'Don't know where to go,' he protested.

'How many weeks did you wander the south country without proper food or shelter, my lady?' Marcus asked Thea softly, his gaze steady and re-assuring on hers, as if he was telling her it would soon be all over.

'Six, until I became a housemaid and earned my bread for many more.'

'You see, Winforde? There are ways and means of surviving on nothing, if you have the courage.'

Granby gave Thea the look of pure hatred he dared not send Marcus and shuffled out of the room muttering threats of revenge, but under his breath so Nick would not knock him downstairs after all.

'Madam?' Marcus said significantly as Nick held the door open expectantly.

Not so easily vanquished as her sottish son, she made a regal exit. 'You have not heard the last of us,' she threatened.

'I shall study the Newgate Calendar with interest,' Marcus assured her and signalled Nick to shut the door on her heels.

'Munby will make sure she leaves without my best spoons,' the Dowager observed as if she had just seen off a minor annoyance and Thea gave a shaky laugh.

'Is it not dangerous to leave them with nothing?' she asked Marcus.

'Would you have me hand over half your fortune?'

'No, just a small allowance to insure they do not starve.'

'They would see it as weakness and demand more every time they outran the constable, and I couldn't let them think they were free to blackmail you with promises of silence.'

'Very wise,' the Dowager put in with a sage nod at her still-fluttering companion. 'We shall spread the true tale, so they have no chance of benefiting from their lies.'

'Will that not do my cause as much damage as theirs?'

'Not when we tell the world about your long-standing attachment, my dear. After all poor Strensham has been impatiently waiting since Giles Hardy refused to let his precious granddaughter marry a serving soldier. It is a very affecting tale of constancy and hardship in the face of a young man's unswerving duty to his country.'

'It is isn't it?' Marcus said interestedly. 'Why were we so poor spirited as not to elope to Gretna long ago, ma'am?'

'Not even in the face of undying passion would you commit an act of such bad taste, Romeo,' Nick informed him with a wry smile. 'After all, you thought your Juliet safe at home with a man who doted on her, so all that was required was the patience of Job, until Boney and his *Grande Armée* were defeated, or Miss Hardy came of age and could marry to please herself.'

'Yes, imagine my anguish when I returned to England *ventre à terre* to find my true love flown, and a pair of unscrupulous rogues determined to destroy our long-delayed happiness.'

'Just imagine,' Thea agreed faintly, one eye on the eagerly listening companion.

'Still, all's well that ends well,' he asserted with a smug smile that made her wonder if he could not have made his fortune on the stage.

The companion gave a soft sigh and put on her bonnet before sallying forth to spread her story with all the gusto of a frustrated romantic.

'We should be ashamed of ourselves, imposing on that poor woman in such a disgraceful fashion,' Thea chided.

'She hasn't had so much fun in years,' the Dowager insisted.

'True, and it's high time Thea and I set out if we are to be home before dark,' Marcus said as calmly as if they had been quietly toasting their nuptials, rather than seeing off two determined foes.

Thea agreed, wondering when she would get used to calling a vast mansion home, but it had been the only way. If she had not wed Marcus, the Winfordes would have won, of age or not. She felt guilty that Marcus had thrown away his liberty to secure hers, but could not bring herself to regret their marriage all the same.

'I can't believe we actually did it,' she murmured once they were alone in the hired coach.

'I don't want to go through the last six weeks again, so I sincerely hope we did,' her newly made lord replied with the wry smile that always threatened to turn her treacherous bones to jelly.

'No, everyone has been rendered acutely uncomfortable.'

'Nonsense, they had a rare old time.'

'Your lawyer looked like an offended bishop at a bacchanal when he set off for Devon.'

'Clatmore enjoyed himself even more than Ned and Lyddie did running rings around your so-called guardian, while I rode off to London as if the devil was on my tail. Confounding another lawyer, threatening suits for this and caveats to that. Clatmore hasn't had so much fun since his schooldays.'

'I still can't believe we're husband and wife.'

'Would you rather not?' he asked rather coolly and Thea wondered if she had hurt her invincible new husband.

'Of course not,' she said impulsively, then gave an inward groan as his eyes began to resemble the steely sky of a January day. 'I mean, of course I wanted to wed you.'

'Given the alternative.'

No, she nearly assured him impulsively, out of all the alternatives. Luckily she managed to put a curb on her unruly tongue just in time. 'Well, you're a decided improvement on Granby,' she teased and watched the thaw set in with relief.

'I can't tell you how much better that makes me feel.'

'I dare say I can't. You don't think he can do anything about it, do you?'

'You are of age and wed me of your own free will, so what can he do?'

'I don't know, but I doubt they will give up. You knew they would come today, didn't you, Marcus?' she asked coolly.

'Having learnt from Wellington that a wise general chooses his ground for a battle, I left enough clues to lead even an idiot like Winforde to us,' he agreed, and Thea wasn't sure if she was more awed by his cool nerve or furious at the risks he had taken.

'Granby might be an idiot, but his mother is no fool.'

'Maybe not, but she's nowhere near as clever as she thinks.'

'She will do whatever she can to ruin me.'

'And you cannot trust me to stop her?'

'Not when you fight fair, my lord.'

'You underestimate me, my dear.'

She would not turn and stare up at him like a besotted bride, or tell him he was her hero. Theirs was not that kind of relationship and there were lines she could not cross.

'Anyway, Granby might marry another heiress and forget me,' she rattled on brightly. 'Lady Winforde couldn't intimidate your Miss Rashton, and she does want a title.'

'I would never wish that on her, although I thank my stars hourly she is not my Miss Rashton.'

'Something I shall remind you of whenever we are at outs, my lord.'

'Yet the benefits of this alliance seem to be all on my side, the debits on yours,' Marcus said with a seriousness she had to deplore.

Marriage had put a barrier between them she dare not examine, and suddenly she longed to be Hetty again, if only to scout his scruples with one of those passionate kisses she now remembered with such nostalgia.

'May I remind you that possession is nine-tenths of the law, my lord?' she again attempted to tease, but he was having none of it.

'You are no possession, Thea.'

'Maybe not, but the Winfordes thought I was, irrespective of my age, and I'm in debt to you for rescuing my ruined reputation.'

'You did no wrong.'

Serious now, she turned and faced him with conviction in her lovely eyes. 'Mud sticks, Marcus, especially when those throwing it hate you. I would be a social outcast without you; it is you who have struck a poor bargain.'

'Rubbish!' he replied, the expression Thea mentally categorised as his Major Ashfield look hardening his leanly handsome face to sternness. 'But if you are content with today's work, I am a happy man.'

'You could try and look a little more as if you meant it,' she informed him solemnly, and had to hide a smile as he cast aside his fashionable top hat and ran a long-fingered hand through his dark hair.

'Perhaps it would be as well if I amended that statement, madam wife. I look forward to *becoming* a happy man, when you decide to make me so.'

The look he then cast her made her forget convenience, caught in his grey gaze as it silvered with the anticipation of pleasure. Could she really make him happy? If he let her, she would certainly try, but first there was the spectre of Miss Rashton to banish from her mind.

He had been ready, if not willing, to wed the woman. Pride demanded that Alethea Hardy must mean more to him than his strident heiress. Then she remembered some encounters between viscount and housemaid with heated cheeks and a stuttering skip of her heart, but she must hold back if they were to build a marriage. He didn't want love, she reminded herself, and tried to pretend it didn't matter.

'You have gone quiet, Thea.'

'Today has been exhausting even by my standards, my lord.'

'Persist in addressing me so and I shall retaliate, Lady Strensham.'

'It's too grand a name for a dab like me.'

'Rid yourself of false humility, Thea, or we'll very soon be at outs.'

'I was never good *ton*. Maybe you should have married Miss Rashton after all,' she finally admitted rather mournfully.

'I swore off the lady before we made our bargain, and I'm very happy with my bride,' he reassured her abruptly, looking as if he was holding on to his patience with difficulty.

'You have impeccable manners.'

'You certainly didn't think so when we first met, but I'm not an untried boy who changes his coat with every wind that blows, Thea, just as you're no shrinking débutante. We shall do very well together, once you get over this attack of missishness. So if you want time to grow accustomed to your husband, don't provoke me to show you how I like my viscountess.'

Wondering at her own seesawing emotions, she managed a wobbly smile at this veiled declaration of desire, but still suspected his manners were a great deal better than he claimed. How could he be content when she was too public a butt of scandal to make him a comfortable wife?

'You're very kind,' she said, and a frown she remembered from the early days of their acquaintance straightened his dark brows into a stern line.

'You will shortly find out how ill mannered and short tempered I can be, if you don't stop traducing yourself.'

'I'm saying what the world will whisper behind our backs.'

'The uncharitable might call me a cynical fortune hunter and Winforde a buffoon, but our true friends know the facts?'

'Which aren't palatable, Marcus.'

'In what way did you encourage what happened to you?'

There was a challenge in his grey eyes now, a dare for her to take the burden on her own shoulders. It felt both wonderful and terrible, as if a new Thea must grow out of the old one—and she didn't know if she was up to the challenge.

'I was arrogant and spoilt,' she reluctantly admitted.

'Then you grew out of it. What else?'

'I was a fool!' she snapped, remembering the chances of escape she had missed, before the collapse of her safe little world finally became real to her—when it was nearly too late.

'You were human, that's not a crime in any calendar I know of.'

She met his intent gaze with a question in her own and he smiled a warm slow smile that made her knees feel shaky.

'You think I make too much of it all, then?' she managed, trying not to grin fatuously in return.

'By taking the blame on yourself, you're letting them have a moral victory, even if they would rather have your money.'

'That will never do, so I shall play the heroine after all. Remember you insisted on it when I trumpet my greatness to your friends and neighbours.'

'I'll be too busy holding forth on my own glorious deeds, after slaying your dragons and nobly carrying the day in the face of enormous odds.'

'What a well-matched pair of braggarts we shall be.'

'My thoughts exactly, my lady,' he said, with such heat behind his silvered gaze that she lacked the courage to meet like for like.

Gasping in an unsteady breath, she searched for another topic of conversation and latched on to one she had been curious about for hours.

'When Lady Prestbury helped me dress for the wedding I told her I would bring scandal on you, and she said I was an amateur compared to the Bellamon sisters. Whatever did she mean, Marcus?'

The warmth died out of his eyes and Thea shivered. In her need to protect her vulnerable heart, she had struck on a question she dearly wished unasked, now it was too late.

'She is right,' he said at last. 'They were called the Three Graces when they made their come-out. Some wag renamed them the Three Disgraces when they fell off their pedestals. Even my aunt Darraine eloped, despite her engagement to an elderly duke. She was the respectable sister. My mother was found in a compromising position with another woman's husband at some grand ball or other, and declared her undying love for him as if it was something to be proud of.'

Thea wondered if she could have resisted kissing Marcus, even if he had wed Miss Rashton. Temptation was easy to fight, until the devil found a sufficiently compelling reason to succumb. Thank heavens for Carter, and Lord Strensham's prickly conscience, even if she now had to live with the infamous bargain they had struck that night.

'She was extraordinarily beautiful and half the men in society were mad for her, which was probably why my father wanted to possess her, despite the scandal. He made her live in the country and had her watched to make sure her lover made no contact with her. By the time I first remember any feeling he had for her was gone and she hated him. Their arguments are legendary in Chimmerton village to this day, and I always wondered if her fall was deliberate.'

'Poor creature,' she ventured rather lamely, wondering how any woman could wilfully desert her son in such a selfish way.

'Yes, I'm afraid she was,' he replied ruefully. 'You're as different as chalk and cheese.'

'Thank you.'

If his mama had been a fabled beauty, that was a certainty she thought ruefully.

'She hated me for being my father's child, and after she died he disliked me for reminding him he had failed to win the most beautiful woman of her generation, despite marrying her.'

'Thank heaven for grandfathers, then, but you said there were three sisters?' she prompted, appalled by his parents' selfishness toward him.

Although she could not remember her mother and father very clearly, she recalled being deeply loved. Marcus had not had that luxury. It explained his cynical attitude to love, but perhaps nothing would ever convince him it could flourish between man and wife after such a start? Trying not to despair too soon, she made herself listen to his tale of Nick's mama.

'Aunt Kitty ran off with her footman, taking Nick

and the Prestbury jewels with her. Lyddie thinks her a complete widgeon, but I can't help admiring her magnificent cheek.' And her devotion to her son, Thea suspected. 'She drowned in a squall on the Venetian lagoon when Nick was twelve. His father had divorced her, of course, and he favours his second son. Little wonder when Nick insisted on speaking only Italian and gloried in being the finest pickpocket outside St Giles. I can't tell you how I envied his skill.'

'He must have given up the habit, since he is welcome in society.'

'Aye, he walks just this side the line now.'

'He makes a dangerous foe, I suspect.'

'And one Winforde would do well to beware of. Nick likes you.'

'We quarrelled all the way from Rosecombe to Bath.'

'He hates adoring misses. That's probably why he took to you.'

'No doubt he said so for your benefit, but how will the rest of your family like having a notorious woman as a relative by marriage?'

'Lyddie already loves you for rescuing me from her heiresses.'

Thea knew he was avoiding the subject of his more starchy relatives, but she was tired now and let him.

'You tried me almost beyond reason on occasions with them.'

'And you came close to feeling the flat of my hand on your delightful derriere more than once.' He laughed at the look of dignified disgust she cast him. 'You'll need all your strength when you see the state of my home.'

'I'm not a hysterical young lady.'

'Society misses are a dead bore.'

'I'm glad to be common and exciting, rather than genteel and tedious.'

'You are very uncommon indeed, so stop fishing for compliments and tell me exactly what you and my cousin got up to when you left Rosecombe.'

Chapter Thirteen

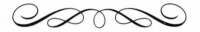

So Thea told the tale of her journey to Bath, masquerading as a fractious schoolboy travelling with her irritable tutor, and they were pulling into an inn yard at Chippenham before either thought it possible.

'Would you like to stay the night?' Marcus asked as she stumbled on leaving the carriage.

'One of my legs went to sleep, but I would rather go on.'

'Very well, but I suspect Lady Prestbury is a harder taskmaster than Lyddie ever was. The modistes and milliners of Milsom Street will have to work non-stop to restore their stock, and you must be worn out.'

'I begged her to stop, but it was like arguing with a stone wall.'

Marcus regarded his new wife wryly. Most women in her shoes would angle for compliments on their transformed appearance. His lady was just as likely to consign her fine muslins, silks and satins to a dark corner and walk about the countryside in the old gown she had once worn to clean the grates at Rosecombe. He was suddenly grateful that garment had been left behind, although he doubted Hetty's replacement would be quite so appreciative.

'Then we'll go on, if you're sure?' he replied with a sigh, remembering the parlous state of his home.

'I am certain,' she said, not wanting to spend her first night as a married woman in the bedchamber of an inn.

After a quick stop to refresh themselves and change the horses, Marcus handed his lady back up and gave the nod to the waiting coachman.

'Imagine my chagrin if I had been compelled to introduce Hetty to my neighbours, so I'm glad the old dragon turned you out in prime style, even if she did wear you out in the process,' he teased gently as they took their seats once more.

'I'm vain enough to agree, although the thought of meeting your friends makes me shake in my new boots.'

'You have courage enough for anything.'

'Effrontery, rather.'

'No, courage is what I said and that is what I meant. You're not turning into a managing wife already, I hope?'

Miss Rashton had 'managing' all but written across her chilly white brow, so he must have been eager indeed to avoid marrying her. Eager enough to wed a girl with a bad reputation and a cit for a grandfather, she wondered gloomily? How she wished she were his chosen wife, a woman he would take home with pride and love.

'My temper is not biddable, Major, especially when I'm given arbitrary commands as if I was a lazy recruit in your brigade.'

'I had noticed.'

Marcus gazed down into her lovely eyes for one long moment, then, by dint of pointing out some object of interest on the horizon, stopped himself kissing her temptingly parted lips. It might be as well to spend as little time alone with the little witch as he could from now on. He admired her, of course, and that was as far as matters could go for now.

Rather disappointed by a sense that some wonderful possibility had just slipped beyond reach, Thea watched the passing scene for a while before her eyes closed and she slept the late summer afternoon away.

Twilight was falling when the horses slowed to take the turn into the overgrown avenue, and, looking down at Thea's dark head resting confidingly against his shoulder, Marcus smiled with a rueful tenderness that would have amazed her had she been awake. He was reluctant to disturb her, but doubted she would thank him for carrying her into her new home. He shook her gently to no avail. Yielding to temptation, he kissed her softly, then hastily withdrew as she began to stir.

By the time Thea was properly awake, she was

sitting a demure distance from her husband, gazing into the darkening evening and wondering at the delicious dream she had experienced. She had been securely held in her lover's arms and could almost feel her lips tingling from his incendiary kiss, so vivid had it felt. Sighing, she gathered her senses, and peered at her new husband through the gathering darkness.

'I have been asleep over an hour, my lord, how very rude of me,' she said stiffly.

'Not at all, but now you are awake, I bid you welcome to your new home, Lady Strensham.'

As he spoke, the hired carriage lurched to a halt and he jumped out to hand her down. Still not fully awake, Thea looked about her, comforted by the warm clasp of his large hand engulfing hers in the chill of the autumn evening. The vast house looming over them looked more like a palace than a manor house and she quaked at the idea of being mistress of such a vast place.

Marcus tensed, sure she was noting the rotten window that had been blown in by a summer gale and covered only by a rough tarpaulin. Or perhaps the mass of weeds growing between the great slabs of local stone that paved the old courtyard the coachman had driven into, when the gravelled sweep proved too full of potholes to take them to the newer wing? He looked at his home through new eyes and despaired.

'I'll take you on to London tomorrow.'

'I would rather stay here,' she replied firmly.

Thea would not be banished to London if she could help it and now she was getting her night eyes, pity for the crumbling old place overcame awe.

'Unless you want to be alone for a while?' she conceded reluctantly.

'That I don't,' he said emphatically, and she felt equal to the challenges ahead after all.

Marcus ordered the guard to rouse the stable-yard, but the man stayed stubbornly where he was.

'We'll be goin' back now, m'lord,' the coachman replied and peered owlishly at Marcus through the gloom until his tip was forthcoming.

The guard and coachman piled luggage round Thea's chilled feet while Marcus went to rouse the household, silently fuming over the welcome his bride was enduring. Meanwhile, Thea stood like a goose-girl waiting at the castle gates, watching the carriage wheel then melt into the darkness as her doubts crept back.

'I can see my lady shivering from here, Barker, so let's move this mountain of luggage and get her in out of the cold,' Marcus said, carrying a much more efficient lantern than the one Thea had used in the woods the night they met.

A sturdy manservant and a gangling boy piled her luggage on a handcart, and Marcus handed the lamp to the wide-eyed lad before picking up his own valise and a couple of bandboxes. Following in their footsteps, Thea remembered her dread of droves of superior servants looking down their noses at her with a rueful smile. Peering through the shadows at a grand portico and the gloom beyond, she saw what splendour had once reigned, even if had become dog-eared.

At the foot of shallow marble steps, the cart was unloaded with a bustle that must echo past glories. Once the place must have been alive with activity, getting ready to host this dignitary or that celebrated beauty. Thea's imagination took flight as she added flambeaux and a blaze of candlelight to light the way of extravagantly gowned ladies with powdered heads, handed up these very steps by periwigged dandies in silk and satin.

In the present, her luggage was piled up in the cavernous hall and the handcart made its creaking exit. A staircase large enough to parade a regiment swept out of it into the darkness, and empty marble plinths at the base indicated that classical statues should have been overawing them with grace and beauty. Once inside, she gazed about her, wondering how she would fool anyone she was chatelaine of all this.

'Daunted, my lady?'

'Perhaps, but unless you show me to the nearest fire, I'll shall be found here frozen like Lot's wife before long.'

'A convenient replacement for the statue of Juno that should be standing yonder, I suppose?' Marcus replied, his smile doing something very off to her knees if he did but know it.

'Unkind creature,' she answered solemnly, placing her hand within the arm he crooked invitingly.

Thea puzzled over the distance yawning between them, despite his smile and physical closeness. One moment he was teasing and charming, the next he was the aloof and cynical man who courted heiresses at Rosecombe. If he remained her companion and protector, instead of reverting to the drawling and unreachable aristocrat, she might cherish the most unlikely hopes for this strange marriage. Dashing Major Ashfield had been arrogant and annoying, but so strong and steady that she had instinctively trusted him with a great deal more than her makeshift shelter for the night.

They had promised each other a marriage of convenience, never mind his faults or virtues, and suddenly she felt tired again. She told herself she had weathered worse, so what if he didn't love her? At least she was safe and he was solvent.

No sooner had they entered a comfortable sitting room than Barker and a cheerful-looking woman bustled into the room with tea and coffee pots, and a large array of pies, rolls and cakes. Thea decided she had a great deal to learn about the appetites of gentlemen, and used the excuse of taking off her fashionable pelisse to hide her blushes at that heady thought. She really was a wicked woman to find the idea of meeting her husband's other needs a promise of future delights, rather than an unfortunate duty. Sinking into a comfortable chair by the fire, she realised nobody had the slightest inkling she was a fast woman, so she sipped her tea and felt her toes thaw.

'Better?' Marcus asked at last.

'Much better,' she agreed, and, making gallant inroads into the plate full of food he absently piled high for her, counted her blessings.

'Do you think you will ever feel at home here?'

'Your grand house has the air of a family home.'

'Chimmerton is shabby compared with Rosecombe, but we all love it.'

'All?' she echoed faintly.

'When I left Grandfather and my sister were still living here and my half brother always spent the summers with us. Now Grandfather is dead, Emma has been wed these last four years, and Colin is at Oxford.'

'Drastic changes indeed—you must feel them.'

'Not as much as when I first came home, and with you here I see the place through new eyes.'

Thea tried to tell herself that he meant her presence was a good thing and wondered how much of her disreputable story he would tell his family. As her story was no doubt doing the rounds of Mayfair's elegant drawing rooms, he had little choice but to tell them all and she frowned at the prospect.

'You look tired, my lady,' Marcus announced. 'It might be as well if you went to bed,' he advised gently, and she felt herself blush like a schoolgirl.

Furious with herself, she refused to look at him as she waited for the housekeeper to come and guide her to her bedchamber.

'I will join you later, my love,' he said smoothly and kissed her hand as that worthy lady waited for her new mistress to precede her.

Thea was assailed by the most ridiculous urge to burst into tears at the pretence of it all and decided he was right: she was tired. Which was why these seesawing emotions were afflicting her so badly.

'Very well, my lord,' she replied steadily enough.

As Mrs Barker led the way, Thea wondered how she would have felt now if she were a normal bride. Doubtless then she would have been looking forward to her wedding night with a heady mix of excitement and apprehension. As this was just a bargain, she must spend it alone.

'Here we are, m'lady.'

Thea looked about her at the faded brocades and gilded furniture of another age. It would be like sleeping in a museum.

'Thank you,' she said, wondering how she would ever sleep among such faded splendour.

Even the housekeeper seemed to share her doubts.

'Maggie and I only had time to whisk the dust covers off and tidy it, but the sheets are fresh and the bed's aired.'

'I wonder you managed so much in a short time.'

'Thank you, my lady. I wish you and his lordship very happy on behalf of us all.'

'How kind of you, and would you show me round the house in the morning? My husband will be reluctant to spend his first day indoors.'

'Of course, my lady. Should I send Maggie to help you undress?'

'If you would just loosen these ties before you go, I can manage the rest myself.'

Mrs Barker managed to keep her face blank at the prospect of a lady managing her own *toilette*. They said a cheerful goodnight and Thea supposed she must get used to being dressed and undressed again, but tonight she wanted to be alone. Feeling so weary that Marcus's uninterest was almost a relief, she washed and brushed her teeth before sliding between warmed sheets with a grateful sigh. She was almost asleep when she heard a slight noise and sat bolt upright, seeing Marcus stand just inside the door to his suite and dressed in a splendid robe.

Thea eyed him warily, noting the oddly intimate sight of his strong, bare feet. She should have known he was not the type for slippers and a nightcap, she decided with a curious detachment, rather surprised at the presence of a robe and nightshirt. Then she saw both were short and too large, and had to stifle a near-hysterical giggle. The old lord must have been a dandy to own a splendid silk robe adorned with sinuous fire-breathing dragons.

Heart beating at a gallop, she watched her lawfully wedded husband walk towards her as if he hadn't a care in the world. Her mouth went dry and her silly heart began to beat like a drum. Did she have the resolution to turn him away? Especially when memories of his passionate kisses at Rosecombe goaded her not to. She opened her mouth to protest and found no sound would come out. No, it wouldn't, the stern voice of her conscience informed her, not when you are busy contemplating the pleasure such a handsome and masterful lover could arouse in an all-too-willing woman.

'I'm not here to ravish you, Thea. If not for Winforde, I would never enter your room without an invitation. We must spend the night together so he can't challenge our marriage.'

'How would he know?'

'Servants talk, Thea, a fact that cannot have escaped your notice over the last few months. I can hardly ask them not to drink in the local inn or stop visiting their families.'

'I don't see how they could know if we live in each other's pockets or never speak when we are private together,' she argued, finding the idea of

Marcus besotted with her more appealing than he must ever know.

'And when they discover me in my grand bed while you lie in yours three doors distant every morning, they will not suspect our marriage is in name only? No, I must share your bed for a few nights at least, but I shall behave like a very Galahad, you have my word.'

He probably would be as well, she thought in disgust, desolate at the idea of remaining an untouched bride whilst her husband slumbered untroubled by her side. She smiled stiffly and resolved not to care if he thought her an antidote.

'I was half-asleep when you came in.'

'And you may be used to alarms and excitements, but I'm not.'

'No, Major Ashfield, of course you're not,' replied Thea pertly, and tried to ignore the forbidden excitement that assailed her as Marcus slid under the covers of her great bed.

When he chose to lie between them and the sheets, she was as safe from her bridegroom's attentions as if she was sleeping in a different county, and highly dispiriting it was too.

'Go to sleep, wife, it has been a long day and I dare say we are in for another such tomorrow.'

'Very well, Goodnight, Major.'

'Goodnight, my Alethea.'

'Thea,' she argued drowsily and in an instant was fast asleep, having just decided that she would not manage to doze for five minutes together with his disturbing presence nagging at her much-tried senses all night.

'God send I don't run mad,' Marcus murmured an almost inaudible protest and turned his back on the unknowing temptress on the other side of the bed in the vain hope he would forget her presence so close he could hear her soft breathing.

If he strained his imagination to the utmost, maybe he could pretend he couldn't smell the faint scent of lavender and roses and soft, clean woman next to him, or feel the subtle warmth of her curvaceous body curled up so close to him. All it would take to wake her was one kiss, and then...

'No, Major, shut down your senses!' he ordered himself silently, 'and while you're about it, imagine yourself back in Spain or somewhere equally distant. With an imaginary continent between you and your lady, you might get through the night without embarrassing the poor girl by waking her up and begging for mercy.'

Thea had no idea where she was when she first woke from a deep sleep the next morning. Then she remembered and eyed the indentation in the pillow next to her with dislike. Her husband had lain chastely at her side all night and nothing could quite soothe the sense of desolation that swept over her. To have truly lain with her husband would have been no hardship whatsoever, and she wondered fleetingly if she was in love. If so, it was nothing like the tumultuous, adoring state described in the novels she had once consumed so eagerly.

If Marcus had exquisitely refined sensibilities, he kept them well hidden and she certainly didn't consider him perfect. He had a harsh temper and an austere way with him when faced with disobedience or insolence, but his honour went to his very soul, and she suspected that he would walk over hot coals for those he truly loved. As she would never be one of those lucky few, she braced her slender shoulders and faced the truth. She was determined she would not let herself become one of those sad wives who clung to their indifferent husbands like leeches, so it hardly mattered if she loved him or no.

With that important matter settled, she breakfasted and went outside to see what her new home looked like in daylight. In the garden a young forest grew in the disused avenues, and brambles and dog roses obscured most of the paths. It should be a sorry sight, yet the wild setting only made the house seem more beautiful. It was vast, of course, she concluded, eyeing Tudor pomp and neo-classical elegance with awe, but a far cry from the chilly splendour she had dreaded. She could even see why Marcus had been prepared to sacrifice so much to keep it and hoped he was not regretting their bargain.

'It might be best to put on an old gown, my lady,' Mrs Barker cautioned when Thea went inside and declared herself ready for her tour.

'All my old clothes were given away when I ordered my trousseau,' she replied, picturing this respectable woman's reaction if she put on one of the cut-down, worn-out garments Hetty had rejoiced in to accompany her around my lady's new domain. 'I will just have to take care of it and hope this particular cambric washes well.'

'Very good, your ladyship.'

Thea could not but notice that even the newer wing was comfortably shabby, but the old part of the house was full of dust and cobwebs. The silence there was so profound it seemed to be outside time as it dreamed of former glories.

'The last Lord Strensham ordered the Tudor wing to be closed many years ago after his wife died in childbed,' the housekeeper said apologetically.

'A sad waste.'

'I hope you'll not think I'm gossiping, my lady, but they say the old master never forgave Mr Julius for killing his wife at his birth.'

'Poor little boy. At least I had a doting grandfather to look after me when my parents died, so cannot help feeling sorry for my late father-in-law, however wild he became.'

'His old lordship was a fine man, but they say grief drove him wild and he loved her so deeply he never looked at another woman in fifty-odd years without her. Once he had begun wrong with Mr Julius, he just couldn't seem to get right with him again though. He doted on his daughter and Mr Julius's children. We feared his heart would break when Miss Lavinia was murdered in that nasty French revolution with all her family, the poor lady. My poor old master was never the same again after that. Still, he made sure Miss Emma was presented in fine style, and he used to say he'd see Mr Marcus and Master Colin right, even if Mr Julius and the French finally managed to do their worst.'

She shook her head and they silently contemplated the follies of lonely elderly gentlemen, until the sound of a vigorous young one's booted steps on the dusty flags banished past shadows.

'My lord!' Thea greeted Marcus more joyfully than her latest stern resolutions ought to permit. 'I thought you had gone for the day when I was told you were out with your bailiff.'

'I escaped, but I shall be hunted down and ordered sternly back to my duty, unless you take pity on me and grant me sanctuary.'

'Stuff! You're perfectly capable of standing up for yourself.'

Despite her brusque words, Thea's disobedient heart sang as Mrs Barker curtsied and left the newlyweds to continue alone.

Chapter Fourteen

In truth, Marcus had cut short his morning ride and his bailiff's many queries to find his wife. He had felt restless and on edge until this moment when he saw her looking peculiarly at home in his beloved home. Today everything at Chimmerton was outwardly the same, yet somehow it felt different to him. He was changed, he supposed, and perhaps that accounted for the restlessness that afflicted him. Setting up as a fortune hunter had chafed his temper and his principles, but apparently becoming a successful one had made him a stranger to himself.

It would have been selfish to declare himself too noble to marry for money, when Thea so badly needed his help. Yet until now he had felt as uncomfortable as a man who had woken up too large for his own clothes, then been forced to wear them just the same. Even as part of him wanted to get on his favourite horse and gallop away until he forgot the uncomfortable questions he could not fail to ask himself here, another had been drawn back to his bride like a compass needle to true north.

'Do you intend to ruin that very pretty gown trekking about this mausoleum?' he asked abruptly.

'Somehow I mislaid all my old ones,' she told him, mischief lighting her incredible eyes, 'but I like your house.'

Resisting an urge to mesh his gaze with hers and lure them both onto very dangerous ground, Marcus managed to tear his eyes from the very pleasing picture she made standing in a dust-moted sunbeam. Somehow her vibrant energy only made the neglect around her seem more profound.

'It's still an antiquated dust heap,' he informed her gruffly. 'It's also Mrs Barker's job to run it. You deserve some leisure after slaving away every hour God sends.'

'I have just had six weeks to rest and soon grew heartily bored with nothing to do.'

'Precious little rest you had, if I know Nick's grandmother at all. I expect she had you writing her letters and running errands, as well as standing for hours while the dressmaker pinned and prodded at you.'

'You know a scandalous amount about a fashionable lady's wardrobe, husband,' she teased.

'I have a sister don't forget.'

'How could I? She will think me a very low connection.'

'Emma and Lady Lydia are bosom bows, which

should give you some idea of her views on life. They will both welcome you with open arms.'

Thea rather doubted it, but knew better than to tell him so. Their ladyships would be polite toward her, because they knew it would upset Marcus if they were not, but they could not approve.

'Anyway Lady Prestbury's companion would have been highly insulted if I had taken over any of her duties, so I can assure you I did rest, for there was nothing else to do. It would take a lot to send me back to Hetty's life voluntarily, but I'm clearly not cut out to be a lady of leisure. So, as you drove Mrs Barker away, won't you show me your house instead, my lord?'

'Your wish is my command, even if I can't understand why you're not more than ready for some peace after the excitements of yesterday.'

'I don't pretend to a life of fashionable ennui, however much you feel it would add to your consequence.'

Marcus stared down at his wife for a timeless moment, his whole body one aching roar of desire. He felt stormy passions he did not fully understand thunder against the stern control he had imposed on himself the moment he agreed to her offered bargain. He reined them in with a mighty effort and covered his confusion by examining their dusty surroundings as if he had never seen them before.

For a fleeting moment Thea had wondered if he meant to kiss her, and a forbidden longing shot through her. She only just managed to pretend a magical interlude among the cobwebs was unthinkable when he suddenly became remote Viscount Strensham once again.

Marcus was manfully trying to divert his errant thoughts from the delightful idea of ravishing his wife with hot kisses and persuading her to seek her bedchamber in the middle of the day after all.

'Mrs Barker should never have brought you in here,' he said abruptly.

Thea followed his disgusted gaze and saw bat droppings and other unsavoury debris covering the wide hearth of his ancestors' great hall.

'Although at least Merry's terriers seem to have kept the larger vermin at bay,' he added absently.

'A blessing indeed,' she replied with a shudder. 'I loathe rats and the mere sight of one would turn me into an abject coward, I fear.'

'Nonsense, you're courageous as a lion, my dar...' He paused and said more stiffly, 'That is, you have proved yourself brave indeed, my lady.'

'I didn't feel brave that night in the summer-house at Rosecombe, if that's what you're referring to,' Thea said lightly. 'I thought you were going to beat me.'

'If you ever try running away from Chimmerton in such a guise, I shall undoubtedly do so. I refuse to countenance the idea of my wife cavorting about the countryside in such an improper fashion.'

'I'm far too comfortable here to do anything like that.' Seeing his sceptical expression and quirked eyebrows as he looked about him as if he was questioning her sanity, she grinned. 'Parts of your house may be sadly neglected, Marcus, but at least you don't expect me to get down on hands and knees and scrub them for you.'

His bark of laughter echoed in the great room and Thea sighed with relief. She had promised herself that she would make their pact work when she married him, so she must curb this wayward desire to be more to him than just a convenient wife. They would never be happy with too much feeling on one side and not enough on the other.

'Yet this could be such a beautiful room,' she remarked, gazing up at the mighty hammer beams in the roof and the massive proportions of the latticed windows that filled most of one wall. 'No, awe-inspiring would be a better description.'

'Awe-inspiringly filthy.'

'But imagine it full of warmth and laughter, Marcus. The whole family and their servants and the estate workers gathered to eat round the great fireplaces at Christmas or Easter.'

'Yes, and all the noise and the stench. I believe a new set of rushes was thrown atop the soiled ones and the whole household lived together for months on end, cheek by jowl. It must have smelt like a cow-byre when it was summer at long last and it could all be shovelled away.'

'Stop! Now that you have ruined my most cherished fantasies, you can show me the rest as a punishment.'

'Haven't you seen enough yet?'

'No, but if you are too busy…'

'Hussy,' he replied, not fooled in the least by her gently reproachful air of disappointment. 'When you're draped with cobwebs, don't blame me.'

'I wouldn't dare.'

'I doubt that, but come and survey your new domain, before it falls down.'

He held out his arm to her with all the ceremony of a knight of old conducting his lady around her new hall.

'How dashing,' she told him approvingly, laying her hand in the crook of his elbow and sweeping out of the Great Hall like a great lady.

'Where next?' he asked.

'The Great Parlour I suppose,' Thea replied absently. She found it hard to concentrate on the dilapidated grandeur around her when the feel of her hand on his arm was sending tingles up and down her spine. He didn't love her, she reminded herself harshly. In time they would share a bed and she would give him a son, or sons, then he would go his way and she would go hers. The very idea made her so deliriously happy that she almost wished herself back at Rosecombe, cleaning grates and emptying chamber pots.

'And this is, or rather was, the Crimson Suite,' Marcus announced as they ventured up another flight of stairs and into another set of grand chambers. 'Both Mary and Elizabeth Tudor slept here, my ancestors having a genius for turning their coats to fit the prevailing order.'

'I would have nightmares sleeping in such gothic splendour.'

'I suspect they had them anyway.'

Under its ancient dust covers, the stiffly luxurious room reminded Thea of her grandfather's suite at Hardy Hall. Giles Hardy had loved the richness of velvet hangings and brocaded upholstery that were so very different from his poverty-stricken youth, but Granby had appropriated his chamber after he died. Thea shivered and concern warmed Marcus's austerely handsome features. Fighting an urge to throw herself into his strong arms and pour out her troubles, she shuddered uncontrollably, despite impatience with her own weakness.

'What's wrong, Thea?'

'Just a goose walking over my grave.'

'Sooner or later I will find out exactly what those rogues did to you, my dear, so why not tell me now and save us both some trouble?'

'No, I would rather forget them.'

'Yet you will learn to trust me, in time,' he

promised softly, and looked stubbornly determined to get the whole tale out of her, the one she was just as stubbornly determined to conceal from him.

As they embarked on a tour of long undisturbed rooms, Thea wished she hadn't quite so much to hide. And it had not escaped her that, while he had succumbed to the temptation to kiss her all too often while she was pretending to be humble Hetty Smith, he had no such heady desire for his wife. He had obviously married her out of duty and not inclination. Hetty had been a fleeting diversion for a lord in dire straits, forced to find a way out of difficulties that well nigh oppressed him.

Or perhaps his amorous attentions to a vagrant servant had been part of the conundrum that was an aristocrat's life to her. She did not understand the breed, she decided, as she followed him into yet another splendid room that looked as if it had lain undisturbed since the Flood. Until recently the Ashfields had been rich, yet they had allowed this to happen, so maybe she never would understand her husband's philosophy.

A viscount stood little chance of marrying for love, so he would have grown up expecting to find passion outside the marriage bed. Yet after the heated desire that burnt so fiercely between them once upon a time, his viscountess was finding it very hard to keep her side of the bargain. In fact, if she heard Marcus had set up a mistress to deal with his more urgent needs, she would hardly know which of them she hated most. Yet she had offered him this deplorable bargain, so she could hardly complain after he accepted it that she didn't like the terms after all. In that well-tried truism, she had made her bed and now they would both have to lie in it.

'I never saw such a gloomy sight as some of these rooms present,' she offered with a smile that felt as sociably empty as their marriage.

'Then let's get back to the nineteenth century without depressing ourselves with any more. I'm dry enough to drink a young river.'

'That will be the dust I dare say.'

'Yes, I apologise for that, even if I was not the one to insist we breathe it in. Maybe one day we can have it swept away, and the ghosts along with it.'

Thea thought that must happen sooner rather than later and she badly needed something to do, lest she sit and brood on what might have been and faded away because of the disappointment. He would refuse to spend a penny piece of her fortune, over and above the sum Clatmore had been ordered to accept as her dowry after his father's debts were paid, if he got his way. It had been just enough to ensure his half brother's comfort and set the estate on the long road to prosperity, but not a farthing more. She wondered why he was so blind to *her* pride. It might not be honed by generations of misplaced nobility, but it still stung sharply when he set her fortune so firmly apart from his.

As it would never do for word to get about that the new Lady Strensham knew so much about brooms and buckets, black lead and holystone, after luncheon Thea consulted Mrs Barker about such work-a-day necessities. She was composing an enormous list of supplies needed from the nearest town when she heard voices raised and went to investigate, only to see Marcus marching toward her. She took one look at his rigidly controlled features and hard grey eyes and saw the suspicious and cynical Lord Strensham she had first encountered at Rosecombe Park once more.

'A private word with you, if you please, my lady,' he barked, then bundled her into his bookroom and shut the door before she found breath to argue.

'Mrs Barker informs me that you plan to hire half of Gloucestershire and open up my house,' he accused. 'She only just managed to disguise her shock that I was the last person to know of it.'

'What else do you expect me to do with myself all day?'

He sent her another of those hard looks. As Hetty she was used to them—as his wife she *would* not let him see how they hurt.

'Make yourself known to our neighbours and visit my tenants, while Mrs Barker keeps house as she has always done. At least she knows what she's doing, as you patently do not, my lady. My wife should not interfere in what does not concern her.'

'You can't treat me like a useless drawing-room knick-knack.'

'I suppose we could clean up this wing and tidy the gardens near the house,' he conceded gruffly.

'The ballroom will be essential if we are to entertain, as well as some rooms in the old part of the house.'

'Which ones exactly?' he asked with an ominous frown.

'The great parlour and the hall to start with, Mrs Barker thinks the floor of the ballroom too delicate for the tenants' ball we must hold at Christmas.'

'No need to ask how all this would be paid for I suppose? It must come out of your deep pockets, considering mine are to let.'

They were married, all their worldly goods supposedly bestowed on one another, but not in her husband's eyes. She wondered if there were any of the marriage vows he would have her obey and temper flashed in her eyes.

'Well, of course,' she forced herself to state blandly, as if it was a matter of indifference to her that he was watching her as if he hated her.

'My family have managed to live happily in only this wing for the past fifty years, so I see no valid reason why you should not do so as well.'

'Using my money offends your pride, my lord,' she said flatly, determined he should see his stubbornness for what it was.

'I look after my own.'

Which made her the outsider, she decided bitterly. 'Pay me back when you turn a profit then, Lord Strensham. Isn't that just the sort of bargain you expect from the granddaughter of a parvenu?' she sparked back, fighting hot tears to proudly brave his icy gaze.

'No, it is the logic I would expect among a sisterhood far less honest. We will speak of this matter no more!'

He turned his back and made for the door as if to breathe the same air as her filled him with disgust and he must escape before it choked him. That he should liken her to those rapacious females who sold themselves for less than a marriage licence was bad enough, but the fact that it bit so deeply that she was actually shaking with distress was far worse.

'You may ignore the subject if you choose to, but I shall continue with my plans,' she insisted in the face of it, and jumped when he turned away from the door, his mouth hard and angry and eyes aglow with fury.

'Then obey your husband in one thing at least,' he gritted.

Breath she had not realised she was holding was released in a shocked gasp as he seized her by the waist, and pulled her into a punishing embrace, stopping her mouth with kisses designed to punish rather than seduce.

She struggled wildly, but he just tightened his grip. For one blazing moment she felt only stinging fury and the heat of tears as his hard mouth took hers, then passion sparked into spontaneous life despite the tempest—maybe even because of it. Now his lips were coaxing hers open, as if he could not help coaxing her to match him pace for pace, despite his fury. He groaned and seemed about to step away when she murmured her dissent and raised her hands to his shoulders to keep him close.

Even as her mind was slewing between hurt and desire, Thea's body had no doubt what it wanted. It responded eagerly to the firm pressure of his mouth, and the delicious glide of his strong hands exploring her eager curves as if that was what they had been formed for. Only the feel of his mouth, open and gently questing on hers, was real now. A sensation as if she had been shot through with warm lightning shimmered through her, and her knees wobbled so weakly in its wake that she clung to him for support. Temper and everything else faded to the gentle insistence of Marcus's firm mouth on hers, and she bid the invasion of his exploring tongue welcome with a moan of sheer pleasure.

'Sweet Thea,' he murmured into the velvety skin just beneath her ear as he ghosted kisses along her jaw. 'Wife,' he whispered into her ear, making her whole skin shiveringly sensitive by letting his tongue explore with exquisite restraint.

'Yes, husband?' she just managed to gasp out an inevitable agreement long enough to spare his mouth, then shamelessly nudged his lips with hers, hating even so slight a separation.

This felt right, however it had begun, and every sense she had cried out for more. The sound of his accelerated breathing was the only music her ears wanted to hear, as he let his strong hands explore her with a touch so gentle, so erotic that the small hairs on the back of her neck stood up alert and eager for his next move. She let her dark lashes sweep up from dazed green eyes, just as he dipped his head to press urgent kisses to the base of her neck and her pulse leapt at the sweet heavy feeling that made desire weigh her eyelids half-closed again as she longed for more. The sight of his dark hair dishevelled from her touch weakened her hold on where they were and what they were at, and she sensed the control he had clung to ever since he made her leave him at Rosecombe crossroads was slipping beyond him.

Then, just as one of his hands stroked the small of her back into a fire that seemed to melt the last ounce of strength from her legs, and the other cupped one of her needy breasts with equally wicked intent, the door opened.

Appalled at his own maladroit entry to what he had

thought an empty room, Barker stood staring at the
guilty couple, still locked in a passionate embrace,
as shock held all three still as a set of statues. For all
the world, Thea thought hysterically, as if they were
a rather shocking tableau at a waxworks. Fortunately
Barker recalled himself, and waved an apologetic
hand in explanation at the brandy decanter he had obviously come to replenish.

'I beg your pardon, my lady,' he finally managed
with a dignified bow and softly closed the door
behind him.

Even so little a noise seemed to echo in the
silence, as Marcus released Thea with uncompli-
mentary haste and they steadfastly managed not to
meet each other's eyes. At last she risked a sidelong
glance that revealed streaks of red slashed across his
high cheekbones and a look of stunned disbelief
blanking his grey eyes to winter. He was obviously
aghast at her abandon, and was quite unable to think
of anything to say to the wanton he had so lately
held in his arms!

Finding the prospect of picking over that shatter-
ing interlude unendurable, Thea looked for the
quickest escape route available, even as she raged at
herself for being such a coward. She pulled her shawl
round her shivering shoulders and fumbled one of the
floor-length windows open to escape into the wilderness beyond, trying not to hear his husky protest.

Free to find solitude complete enough to lick her

wounds, she ran through the overgrown shrubbery at random, finally spotting a faint path that promised to take her deeper into the neglected gardens, and further from her horrified husband. A burning humiliation that outdid any sting life had so far launched at her pushed her blindly onward. Their passionate encounters at Rosecombe had not carried this burn of shame in their wake, and she swallowed back a betraying sob. Unfortunately, nothing could make her forget the look of frozen horror in Marcus's eyes as he stepped away from her as if he had just touched pitch.

She tore along the overgrown path and deeper into the wild gardens, refusing to sob out the hurt roiling within. Somehow the fact that she was hopelessly lost mattered very little; seeing another faint path cross the one from the house, she took it gratefully without considering the practicalities of finding her way back, or letting herself know that the blurring of her gaze was caused by anything so weak as tears.

How could she have confronted him so soon into their marriage, and lost her own temper and self-respect into the bargain? Remembering the hot, arousing feel of his lips, hard and demanding, on hers, she raised her hand to soothe the sensitised fullness with shaking fingers. As soon as she touched her mouth, her heart skipped in an echo of the passion, fury and need she knew in his arms.

Then reality barged in and reminded her he had
only kissed her in anger, and in return she had responded to him like a bee drunk on nectar, besotted
fool that she was.

Maybe she was not much better than the lightskirt
he had almost named her but, until she met my lord
Strensham's smoky gaze across that tumbledown shed
in the woods, Thea had believed she was naturally
rather cold. She had never felt much for her suitors
beyond relief at their leaving, but Marcus Ashfield had
taught her to know herself better, she decided bitterly.
Now she contemplated the humiliation of longing for
a man who could spend the night at her side as if she
were a wooden effigy, and felt that salty burn behind
her eyes again and blinked determinedly.

The last thing she had needed to know was that,
with one furious kiss, Marcus could set her desires
blazing so fiercely there was no room for self-control,
or the memory of Granby's wet mouth and greedy
eyes. She shuddered at the unwelcome idea that men
could work up to a blind kind of wanting, even when
they actively disliked the object of their desires.

No! Marcus was an honourable man who had
rescued her from Granby, whatever the finer details of
their alliance might suggest. He had probably kissed
her because he did not have it in him to hit a woman,
and she was in danger of making him sound like some
impossible knight in shining armour—inhumanly
virtuous and sternly priggish. Which was hardly a true

picture of her new husband, if only a tenth of the stories the servants at Rosecombe had whispered about his more colourful adventures were true!

By now her unwary wanderings had brought her out onto a piece of boggy land, once designed as a pretty dell to enhance the small lake and still not quite engulfed by bulrushes and flag irises. It was, however, a trap to the unwary and her lightly shod feet sank ankle deep in the boggy ground, so at least she had to forget her turbulent emotions for a time and navigate a careful course out of the quagmire she had unheedingly plunged into.

Once she finally managed to win free of the mud so cunningly disguised by all that soft, sappy grass, she inspected her ruined shoes and the muddied hem of her gown with resigned exasperation. What an unsatisfactory lady she was proving to be, she mused, her heart jumping to attention as her husband strolled out of a clump of trees ahead of her, looking exasperatingly unruffled.

Chapter Fifteen

Trust the noble viscount to discover her at a disadvantage, and for a minute Thea's memory flashed back to their first meeting. At least she had started the day better dressed than humble Hetty, but as she looked down at her muddied and dishevelled person she almost wished she had her old role back, for all its hard work and petty rules.

'How am I to prove myself worthy, when my lady insists on rescuing herself?' he finally observed, laughter lighting his grey eyes as if nothing untoward had occurred between them.

For him it probably hadn't, but a needy part of her wanted to smile right back like a besotted idiot, and it took an effort of will to stop a grubby hand reaching up to tidy her disordered curls. It was better not to know if she looked as wild as she felt, and that excited leap of her pulse would never do either.

'I thought you might not be conversant with the day-to-day hazards of life among the ruins, so I came to rescue you and beg your forgiveness, Thea,' he went on. 'I behaved appallingly and, if you will come out of that quagmire, I should go down on my knees and beg your forgiveness.'

She sniffed and gave him the benefit of her most sceptical social smile. He looked so handsome and relaxed, she only just managed to stop herself taking the hand he offered her with an infatuated smirk and a few fluttered words of acquittal. Truly her husband was dangerously charming when he chose to exert himself; when he didn't, he was just downright dangerous!

'You forget that I am very muddy,' she said stiffly.

'No, how could I do that?' he replied with a wry glance at her ruined gown that almost made her wish she were ten years younger, so she could throw some of this noxious mud at his infuriatingly unsullied person without losing the rest of her dignity.

'If you will point out the path to me, I shall endeavour to go back and change once more.'

Marcus offered her his hand again, and Thea ignored it just as pointedly, shifting for herself until her foot slipped and she was forced to put out both hands to avoid a tumble. To her added humiliation, the feel of his strong hands pulling her upright before she hit the ground made her breathless, as none of her efforts to free herself from the mud had done. She drew breath to demand he let her go, when he confounded her by doing so as speedily as if he had touched a hot coal.

'I can manage perfectly well, I thank you.'

'So I see. Now pray contain your transports at my company for just a moment longer and drink this. You have had a punishing day one way and the other, and I can see you shivering from here.'

He passed her a silver flask and, when she wrinkled her nose at the smell of brandy, he told her abruptly not to be a fool. 'For heaven's sake, drink it, Thea, before I pour the stuff down your throat myself.'

The prospect of being manhandled again made her obey him with alacrity, and her shivering stopped as the fiery stuff hit her stomach, even as she fought the choking fumes of the powerful spirit. Then he unbuttoned his coat and insisted she put it around her shoulders.

'I'm a rifleman, for heaven's sake, not a Hyde Park saunterer,' he said roughly, when she protested at the thinness of his fine linen shirt and silk waistcoat.

Thea just managed not to quiver when the warmth from his body and the faint masculine scent of him enwrapped her by proxy, but it was a close-run thing. She was tired and felt a little defeated, but how wonderful it would be if his concern were born of love rather than thorny pride. It would never do for him to lose his rich wife so soon after the wedding, a hateful, mocking voice whispered in her ear; the rumourmongers would have a field day.

Careful not to let their fingers touch, she handed the silver flask back, her eyes watering for a quite legitimate reason as he bowed to her with exaggerated gallantry. He had driven her to such extremes of passion in the last hour that she had not dreamed existed before she met him, and she might as well be a silly schoolgirl someone had carelessly misplaced for all she meant to him! She stalked along the path he indicated, with her head held so high he had to warn her to watch her step.

'You will fall head first if you bustle about like that and, small as you are, I couldn't guarantee to carry you through this wilderness without dropping you.'

'I am not small,' Thea told him through clenched teeth.

'Of course not, a veritable giantess.'

His teasing might have wrung a reluctant laugh out of her, if he hadn't chosen that moment to take her arm to guide her around the roots of a great oak. Her heart began to perform acrobatic feats at even that impersonal touch and she silently cursed him for making such a fool out of her. Doggedly watching her steps from then on, she prayed to be swiftly delivered from this ordeal. Then they reached a bridle path that cut through the wood at last, and she could hold on to her anger no longer as she stood shivering in the twilight.

'I'm sorry. I have just behaved like a spoilt brat,' she said stiffly.

'No, and it is I who should be begging forgiveness, Thea, on my knees as I said, although not just here, if you don't mind,' he said, waving a hand at the rutted bridle way.

His mix of genuine apology, and the invitation to share his amusement at their plight, wrung a reluctant smile out of her at last.

'Not here nor anywhere else, I hope, but how are we to get home?'

'Being a resourceful man, I have prepared for any eventuality, my lady.'

They rounded a bend in the path and Thea saw Hercules waiting. The prospect of sharing an outing on horseback with Marcus was to contemplate an intimacy her pride shied away from just now.

'Shall you ride for help, then?' she asked hopefully.

'You'll not overburden Hercules that easily. He has the stamina to carry us both for miles, haven't you, old friend?'

Marcus petted him fondly, the great beast nuzzling at his master's shoulder like a docile pony. She allowed herself to be boosted up in front of the saddle with resigned stoicism, as her husband lithely mounted behind her.

'Lean back and stop holding yourself like a bodkin, or you'll fall off before we've gone five yards.'

Telling herself it would accelerate their return, she sank back into his arms as per orders. Revelling in the warmth of his body and the strength of his muscled arms, despite her more cautious self screaming warnings at her, Thea was in danger of contrarily wishing this ride would go on for ever when an anxious voice rang out of the gathering darkness.

'Be that you, Master Marcus?' the elderly head groom asked.

'Indeed it is, Merry. I have my ladyship safe, but she's tired and frozen half to death, so take Hercules's reins from me, will you?'

Ignoring her protest, Marcus insisted on lifting Thea down himself and then carried her into the warm kitchen. Not for half her fortune would she have admitted her desolation when he ordered Maggie to see her mistress took a hot bath, before striding off to fuss over Hercules instead. So much for a gentleman's priorities, she thought woefully, and followed her new maid into the scullery to scrape the black mud from her feet and dispose of her ruined slippers.

Refusing to stay in bed like an invalid, Thea had dressed in a sophisticated gown of cream silk and dusky rose velvet that Lady Prestbury had assured her was just the thing for a young wife. From the glint of silver heat in Marcus's eyes when he entered the drawing room, it seemed her ladyship knew what she was talking about.

'You look thoughtful, my lady?'

Marcus sat down on the *chaise* beside her and took her hand, absently playing with her fingers until hot shivers ran through her, even as she ordered herself not to let him affect her so ridiculously.

'Maybe we should open the house after all,' he said at last, completing the demolition of her beautiful composure by carrying her hand to his lips and kissing it as if she truly was important to him. 'I selfishly wanted to keep you to myself, Thea, but that will not answer the gossip I fear.'

'Thank you,' she murmured, trying not to give credence to the absurd idea that he really wanted her exclusive company.

'I have given you little enough reason to be grateful to me today. Indeed, I still have to humbly beg your pardon, so pray don't interrupt me.'

'Are you never intending to be serious again, Marcus?'

'Laughter helps me choke down all the humble pie.'

'Perhaps some tea would wash it down better,' she said solemnly, then smiled at his revolted expression. 'I thought not, so let's forget this afternoon. You can tell me what you want done with your house instead.'

'That I leave to you, so long as my bookroom remains untouched. I have an affection for libraries. I never know what wonders I may find in them.'

'Then yours will be exempt from my brooms and dusters.'

'As my cousin's was most of the time I suspect. You're not thinking of playing housemaid again, I hope?'

'No, a maid I once knew told me it was a very hard existence.'

'No doubt she wanted you to appreciate her efforts all the more.'

'Her life would have been much easier had a certain gentleman not thought as you do, husband, that she was of little ornament and less use.'

'Never once did I say or even think that, my Thea.'

'Good, then I promise not to scrub the floors or wax the furniture.'

'Of course not, my dear, such tasks would be considered most improper for a lady,' he told her with a perfectly straight face.

Thinking about the events of the day as she prepared for bed, Thea decided that her new life was unlikely to prove dull. If only she could be content with a marriage of convenience, she might even be happy, but how could she resign herself to so little when she was fascinated by her handsome husband and knew they could have so much more, if he let them?

She cravenly pretended to be asleep when Marcus finally came in. Lying perfectly still, she fought to keep her breathing even, until he murmured a soft goodnight and blew out his candle. While her heartbeat was racing at the closeness of his strong body, her husband of a day had turned over and gone straight to sleep, despite knowing perfectly well that she was awake! Thea thumped her pillow and muttered something rather rude at the insensitive brute sleeping next to her as if he hadn't a care in the world.

Over the next few weeks Thea's small army of helpers moved through Chimmerton like a spring tide. She and Marcus joked about the chaos, but she sometimes wondered if she had imagined the raw feeling that had raged between them in his bookroom that first day. In the end she concluded she had behaved like a wanton and given him a disgust of her. Now he had forsaken her bed as well and it was her own fault, her stubborn mind insisted. At any rate, she now looked back on the first days of their marriage with ridiculous nostalgia. She also got little sleep, despite her exertions, and looked so tired and pale one morning that Marcus suggested they took a stroll outside after breakfast instead of launching into their usual tasks.

'And why not accompany me to the Home Farm this afternoon and try out your new mare, Thea?'

Goodness, she must be looking wan to warrant that much attention.

'I have so much to do.'

'Let Mrs Barker take charge, she'll think you don't trust her at this rate and you could do with a day off from all this self-imposed duty—you're making me feel like an idler.'

Anyone less like a lazy society beau she found it

hard to imagine; every day except Sunday he rode out early and came back late, looking weary and often muddy, as if he insisted on doing some of the hard work himself. If she needed an easy morning, he would benefit no less, so she might as well agree to something she wanted anyway.

'Maybe you're right, and it is a beautiful morning.'

'Meet me on the terrace in half an hour then and we will explore the wilderness.'

Thea joined him in much less, and fought hard not to blush as he tucked her hand in the crook of his arm and heat shot through her as usual.

'Perhaps we should leave all this to Nature,' she said with a jerky wave at the riotous shrubbery to divert his gaze from her hot cheeks.

'We would have to rope any guests together so we didn't lose them.'

'Maybe, but a young lady addicted to the gothic would love it.'

'I am no romantic villain, so they would be disappointed anyway.'

Thea would rather cast him as her hero, but put that conclusion aside.

'Could we restore it? I dare say the original plans still exist.'

'You don't want to tear everything up and start afresh?'

'No, I rather like it.'

'The woodsmen could clear the paths and avenues

of willow and ash seedlings, then we could see what
we have left to work with I suppose. Lydia is passionate about her gardens, she could help.'

'Yes, your relations must be faced sometime.'

'True, so why not invite all the tolerable ones for
Christmas? I should like to show you and my house
off at the same time.'

Thea cast him a sharp look, but there was nothing
of mockery in his steady gaze and she began to
realise that he truly thought her pretty.

'The thought of it makes me shake in my shoes,
but they have to be faced sooner or later.'

'With any luck my stepmama will stay in town
with her new husband, for she will take you in
strong dislike.'

'Why?'

'You're too healthy for one thing, and far too lovely.'

'Flatterer, but does your brother share her preju-
dices?'

'Not he—Colin values his freedom far too highly
to covet my title.'

And you, Lord Strensham? an insidious voice
whispered in Thea's head. Do you mourn yours?
Luckily he could not read her thoughts and was
warming to his subject.

'With the support of my family, your presentation
at court won't seem so bad,' he said blithely as Thea
felt a fine bead of perspiration form on her forehead
at the very thought.

'I will be terrified, whomever I meet in the meantime.'

'I have faith in you, Thea. Perhaps it's time you had some in yourself.'

'If this avenue was restored and the brambles removed, would it lead up to that building in the distance, Marcus?' she asked, determined to steer their conversation into safer avenues.

'Yes, and make a fine place for a summer picnic.'

Thea wondered if they would still be polite strangers by then. 'It would be a nice change not to attend one as what Miss Rashton termed a "common servant".'

He gave a crack of laughter that warmed her heart and made her long to just reach up and kiss him, as she had seen Lady Lydia do with her husband, but such spontaneous intimacy was not for them.

'I thought you a most uncommon servant girl, then and now, my Thea.'

'Because I saved you from Miss Rashton.'

'Oh I couldn't marry a woman who wanted me to run her wretched mills before the ink was dry on our marriage lines. That would have been far too wearisome.'

'You're not afraid of hard work, Major, so don't pretend to me. You hated the thought of profiting from a business too close to slavery.'

He was silent for a few moments, his eyes distant

as he contemplated the congested surface of an or-
namental pond.

'You do me too much honour, my lady. I am no
perfect gentle knight.'

'No, but I think I told you before that I find you
a vast improvement on Sir Granby Winforde.'

'And you're a wife without equal,' he told her
lightly, then turned her attention to a tumbledown
summerhouse. 'See those carved stone animals
piled up like children's toys in a box? My grandmother banished them from the terrace when they
gave her guests a shock one dark night.'

Squirrels and badgers sat cheek by jowl with lions
and tigers, monkeys and bears, as well as more
mythical beasts and Thea was enchanted.

'I should love a quiet garden that wasn't solemn
or improving, and we could fill it with beasts instead
of classical statuary.'

'The children will love it.'

Thea drew in a sharp breath and turned to gaze
out over the once-ornamental pool in her turn,
trying to hide her blushes as well as the fierce
longing that ripped through her at the very thought
of bearing his children.

As his wife tried to forge a path to a fanciful
bridge marooned among the rushes, Marcus decided
glumly that they would be celebrating their first
wedding anniversary before they had truly shared a

bed at this rate. Then he re-examined his agreement to her inspired suggestion and grinned wolfishly. She obviously thought he meant their children, not the tribe his various friends and relations were blessed with. The idea of their own children playing in such a magical garden did something strange to his heart, and he found the prospect of a pack of tur-quoise-eyed brats running wild about Chimmerton acutely appealing.

He might need to stalk his elusive lady skilfully, but the rewards would undoubtedly be worthy of the chase. His body responded to the idea with such eagerness that he had to hastily think of the farm accounts, before she turned round and gauged his sorry state for herself. Even at Rosecombe, the idea of trusting any other man to wed her had revolted him. Now, he intended to bind her to him with every tie known to man and, if any other male dared to look at her with a tithe of the desire that tortured him so mercilessly in his eyes, he might just have to kill him!

Unaware of the piratical nature of her husband's thoughts, Thea felt distance yawn between them as they wandered idly back to the house for a quick luncheon. She changed into her very stylish new riding habit and studied herself in the mirror, cursing her unfashionable looks. If only she was blonde and beautiful like Lady Lydia, Marcus might look at her as Sir Edward did at his lady.

* * *

It was only when they were riding away from the Home Farm a couple of hours later that Thea discovered what had put the frown between Marcus's dark brows. He had been riding at her side, breaking the silence only to point out the odd landmark to her.

'I suppose I must learn my way if I'm to visit your tenants.'

'You must never do so alone,' he said abruptly. 'It's too dangerous.'

Recognising her mulish expression, he gave her a hard look, just as if she was a raw recruit under his command, she thought rebelliously.

'Winforde won't turn his back on a fortune that easily. He has been threatening all sorts of mischief toward you, according to Clatmore's spies,' he warned, his gaze urgent on her mulish expression.

'Then I'll take a groom with me,' she finally conceded.

'Take two and stop me behaving like an anxious old dotard.'

'I'll take half a dozen if it will prevent that,' she told him with an urchin grin, before digging her heel into her willing new mare's side and tearing off into the distance.

The thunder of hooves behind made her urge the eager mare on and they flew along the grassy ride, neck and neck for long seconds. Thea crouched low in the saddle and held off the challenge for a few moments, but inevitably Hercules drew ahead, first by a nose, then a head and, by the time they had to draw up, by a full length. Marcus watched her neatly rein in her sweating mount with lavish praise, and let their horses set the pace on the way back to their stables.

'Now I have caught you, whatever shall I do with you, my lady?' he asked softly and hot shivers ran down Thea's spine.

'You could help me rub down my horse, then order me some hot water and perhaps it would be as well if you fed me, before I expire of inanition.'

'And there I was, intending to neglect you and starve you and in all likelihood beat you into the bargain.'

Suddenly his eyes were watchful, his shoulders tense, as memories of her past misadventures rose in both their minds. Thea knew he would for ever walk round her on eggshells if she gave in to the urge to drop her eyes and hunch her shoulders. Instead she urged Dark Lady over to the mounting block and dismounted smartly without his help.

'I always knew I was jumping out of the frying pan into the fire—now I shall go and consider my strategy,' she told him brashly. 'You wed a shrew and not a mouse, I'm afraid, Marcus.'

'Not so, Thea, I married a lioness,' he replied huskily, and if she ever thought his grey eyes cold, the blaze in them now informed her of her error.

Telling herself to grab hold of the courage he

seemed determined to award her, she met his intense
look with one of her own, and they gazed at one
another in charged silence for a long moment.

'Speaking of which, wife…' he began, suddenly
holding her so close that she was overcome with the
most ridiculous shyness and lowered her eyes, only
to find herself fascinated by the way his powerful
chest rose and fell with his accelerated breathing.

Surely he was so fit that their race could not still
be troubling him? She raised her eyes in question,
then her own breathing quickened as she read the
answer in his heated silver gaze.

'Where be you, Master Marcus? Yon beasts are
half-blown and me with more than enough to do
already,' the old head groom bellowed from all of
two yards off, and they sprang apart like a pair of
guilty lovers.

'Here I am, man, as you can very well see.'

'More than them new stable-lads you promised
is,' the tyrant told him—what else could they do but
attend to their sweating mounts forthwith?

'Strangers bin askin' questions at the Feathers,'
Merry observed, once they were all busy.

'What kind of strangers?' Marcus asked tersely.

'Usual kind, Master Marcus, ones as I don't
know.'

'You know very well what I mean,' his employer
snapped, and fixed the old man with a look Merry
rarely encountered, despite his cross-grained ways.

'One's London bred, right enough, t'other a flash fool.'

Thea's heart began to beat faster as she fitted these descriptions to Granby and Carter, and found they meshed perfectly.

Marcus tossed the old man half a crown. 'Find out more and I might let you have that cottage you keep nagging me about,' he said, and followed Thea out of the stable-yard as if he had heard nothing untoward.

'Forewarned is forearmed, Thea,' he reassured her. 'I'll send for Clatmore and Mad Nick and when Winforde realises he's outnumbered, he'll soon turn tail.'

'But what can he want with us? We are married now and he can't do anything about it or we would have heard of some suit by now. Will I never be free of them, Marcus?'

'Of course you will, my dear. We'll soon send him packing between us,' he said with a grim smile that promised Granby an uncomfortable meeting.

'He's dangerous and his mama even more so. You must take care.'

He gave her an odd look, then smiled so dazzlingly she quite forgot to worry as they departed for their separate dressing rooms to prepare for the evening ahead.

That night her husband slept elsewhere once more, and, warm and cosseted in Lady Strensham's

splendid bed, Thea felt as if bleak continents sep-
arated them, making the promise of the day seem
cruel against her current loneliness. She tried to be
glad Merry had interrupted them this afternoon and
was still trying when she slid into sleep at long last.

Chapter Sixteen

Thea's turmoil followed into her dreams and she was running frantically through Chimmerton's vast corridors, searching for safety as Granby and his mother hunted her down with a pack of savage hounds. The fact that he was dressed as a chimney sweep and his mother as the Queen of Hearts only added to the terror of it all. At last gripping fingers reached for her, just as she heard a lively party going on in the Great Hall and opened her mouth to scream. She tried again and again to attract attention to her plight, but the music was so loud nobody heard her frantic pleas for help, and her pursuers taunted her as her mouth opened and shut uselessly. At last she shouted to such effect it all faded away, and she was awake and sitting bolt upright in Lady Strensham's vast bed.

'It was just a dream, Thea, you're quite safe,' Marcus told her, in a voice so calm and certain that her fears were already dying away when she came fully awake and sank back on her snowy pillows.

'I'm sorry I woke you,' she said, mortified. 'I wish I could stop these dratted nightmares.'

'There's no point castigating yourself over what you can't help.'

'It's stupid and childish.'

'Fear is no respecter of age.'

Relighting her candle, he returned to his dressing room by the faint glow of the fire and came back with a small glass of cognac.

'I'll soon be a toper at this rate.'

'I doubt it, but this will calm you enough to tell me all about it.'

She grimaced, disliking the taste of the spirit even as its fiery strength lit a trail down her throat, then bloomed into warmth.

'I don't want to talk about it.'

'I had the most appalling night horrors as a child. They went once my grandfather coaxed me into talking about them.'

'You were a child, Marcus, it was natural to have unpleasant dreams.'

'There's nothing shameful in being human. I wanted to turn tail and run from my duties more times than I care to recall in the Peninsula.'

'You never did, though. I ran as fast as I could from my enemies, which makes me a miserable coward.'

'It makes you a sensible female up against two unscrupulous villains.'

'But I was a spoilt, silly creature until Grandfather

died,' she mumbled reluctantly, hating to admit it to the man whose good opinion she craved.

'And now you're independent to a fault and stubborn as a train of mules. Your strength was only lying dormant until you needed it.'

'Really?'

'Yes, and you're very high in the instep when crossed. I first noticed it when you were pretending to be Hetty the housemaid. You'd do well to study humility if you ever feel the need to assume such a guise again.'

Thea thought hazily that when he looked at her with that warm, teasing smile in his eyes, she would tell him almost anything. 'What do you want to know?' she heard herself ask and almost groaned at her own stupidity.

'I'm incurably inquisitive.' He quirked a quizzical eyebrow at her, then was completely serious. 'Just tell your tale, Thea, it might do you good.'

'It's a long story and not particularly edifying,' she murmured.

The idea of him knowing everything made her shiver uncontrollably until she forced herself to be still.

'We have all night, my Scheherazade,' he told her soothingly, then spoilt the effect by climbing into bed as he had those first few nights of their marriage, making her shiver for a very different reason.

'I intend to get some more sleep,' she told him, hoping for a reprieve.

'Tell me, then we can both prepare for another busy day,' he said calmly, lying back against his pillows as if he was prepared to lounge there until daybreak, like the sultan in the tale he referred to.

'Oh, very well, then.'

Thea took the warm hand he held out to her, and for once found only simple comfort in his proximity as she wondered where to begin.

'My grandfather wanted a grand title and a life of privilege for his only daughter, but she defied him and married a mere lieutenant. She died when I was three, and Papa was killed at Seringapatam. Grandfather took me in and, apart from insisting I take his name, indulged me quite shamefully. I grew up thinking myself a very important personage. When I was old enough I wanted a London Season, although I see now that I would never have received vouchers for Almack's, or invitations to exclusive parties.'

'Débutante balls are full of bread-and-butter misses and empty-headed young fools, so I dare say you wouldn't have enjoyed them anyway.'

'I think that may be a *little* harsh. Anyway, Grandpapa's grand plans for my mother might have come to naught, but he was determined to choose my husband for me. He invited a succession of titled men home to look me over, as if I was a prize filly he was thinking of offering for auction.'

'I warrant one or two very rum customers consented to that scheme.'

'I wonder he did not put a placard round my neck offering me to the noblest bidder.'

He hid a smile at her affronted expression, thanking heaven that one of the fools sent to look her over had not seen her unique quality and snapped her up.

'He had no right to sell you to a fool with a title.'

'No, my lord,' she said demurely.

'Minx, you won't divert me that easily. Carry on, your ladyship.'

'Oh, very well,' she agreed with a sigh. 'He wanted a titled husband and acceptance into society for me, and couldn't imagine I would disagree. Well,' she added fair-mindedly, 'at least I did once I saw the sort of man I would have to marry. Until then I was as enamoured of the idea as he was himself.'

'You refused?'

'Yes, although most could not bring themselves to sticking point after I had made my opinion of them all too clear.'

'I dare say,' he said with a smile that told her he did not believe her.

Comforting, but mistaken. Thea acknowledged her past sins to herself, but could not quite face convincing Marcus of them. She must force the idea that if he approved of her the rest of the world could go hang firmly to the back of her mind as well.

'Then Sir Granby Winforde and his mother came to stay and I'm certain Grandfather had no intention of me marrying him. His manor and estate are long gone, and if he ever had entrée to good society he's certainly lost it now.'

When he heard the note of terror in Thea's voice, Marcus wanted to hit Winforde hard, then force him and his harridan of a mother to beg her forgiveness on their knees. Instead he swallowed his fury and forced himself to gently prompt her for the rest of her tale, as if it was nothing out of the way.

'Why did your grandfather let them stay?'

'For his brother's sake. They were twins and sent to the foundling hospital together as children. He could not turn Uncle Miles's wife away.'

'A shame he didn't consider your well-being, rather than letting Winforde batten on him,' Marcus said grimly.

'Yes, I am a *far* more worthy cause.'

Indeed she was, if only she could be brought to realise it, Marcus decided. His intrepid Thea would never tremble at the very mention of the worthless baronet's name again if he had any say in the matter. He was so lost in his own indignation that he forgot the distance he had sworn to keep from his wife. She needed him, and never had he felt less detached. He ignored the voice of reason and raised her slender hand to his lips.

'Then what happened?' he prompted gently, gallantly turning his back on the incendiary ideas her soft flesh under his eager mouth gave rise to, and nestled their joined hands back among the bedcovers as he congratulated himself on his self-control.

'Grandpapa finally told them to go, but he was taken ill before he could see to it that they actually went.'

'What were his symptoms?'

Marcus hoped her answer would help the case he and his lawyer were building against the Winfordes, but Thea shuddered and her grip on his hand tightened. He only just managed to resist the urge to take her in his arms and make her forget all he was encouraging her to remember so painfully.

'They were truly terrible. He was in the most dreadful pain, as well as raging thirst and palpitations. Mercifully his illness was very short. I could not wish him to suffer so acutely any longer.'

Thea stared into the night for a moment as she remembered those terrible days, then forced herself to carry on.

'Believe it or not, I was actually glad of the Winfordes' presence, until I found out about Grandfather's will.'

'Ah, yes, the famous will.'

'Say infamous, rather! I wasn't surprised to be ordered to marry a man with a title. It was Grandpapa's way of reaching out of the grave. But to appoint Granby my guardian, when he had run through every penny he could lay his hands on and was deeply in debt to the moneylenders? I could hardly believe it, for Grandpapa was nobody's fool. Anyway, Granby proposed to me and I refused him.'

'What sensible female would not?'

If he had been talking of anyone else, Thea would have laughed at his revolted expression; instead she pictured the weak-mouthed baronet, with his growing paunch and greedy eyes, and shuddered.

'He wasn't in the least cast down, but the next day he forbade me to leave the house for fear of a gang of kidnappers who were apparently after my money. At first I was grieving and clung to my privacy, but gradually I found I was a prisoner in my own home. I still wouldn't marry Granby, so they locked me in one of the empty attics until I consented.'

'Damnable!'

'That's what I thought, and next they obtained a special licence and intimidated or bribed a priest to marry me to Granby, as the local vicar would not do so unless I consented. I refused to say the vows and, corrupt as he was, the man would not let them coerce me. That night Granby locked me in Grandfather's room with him, to compromise me so completely I would have to wed him.'

Marcus let out a string of colourful epithets. 'I apologise,' he said tersely, as if more was beyond his self-control.

'I called him every name I could think of at the time, but even Granby can overpower a woman, so

I knew that would not keep him at bay for long.'
Thea swallowed and searched for words to describe
her worst nightmares. 'Then he ripped my gown and
forced his revolting kisses on me, and his horrible
pudgy hands were everywhere they should not be.
I could not endure it, so I bit him on the mouth and
kicked him somewhere quite unmentionable, before
smashing one of his claret bottles over his head for
good measure.'

'Very laudable,' Marcus said with quiet satisfaction, forcing his voice to sound calm for her sake,
even as fury boiled through him like molten lava at
the thought of the bastard mauling his gallant Thea,
even if her solution had paid him back more thoroughly than she probably knew.

'Yes, I did rather enjoy it,' Thea said with some
satisfaction, and he gave a bark of surprised
laughter, before sobering and murmuring that she
might as well carry on now she had begun.

'He could not summon up the least desire for me
after that, and I'm not at all the type of woman he lusts
after anyway, if the mistress he moved into the house
was anything to go by. Anyway, he left off claret and
drank more and more brandy until he passed out. His
mother unlocked the door in the morning, in the
presence of the local vicar and half the neighbour-
hood. She pretended to be deeply shocked and
demanded our wedding take place the next day. If
Granby had not been insensible, I dare say we would

have been hailed off to church then and there, and of course the vicar was prepared to go along with them this time when I was so compromised.'

'I was too merciful. They should be whipped through the streets!'

Marcus was afraid he would frighten her if he gave full reign to his fury, but Thea just smiled serenely. He should have known better, he told himself ruefully. His wife was a woman in a million, and all chivalrous thoughts of somehow contriving her freedom if he didn't suit her went out of the window at that moment. He must win her, or stay lonely the rest of his days, for he would never find another female to equal his lovely and redoubtable Thea.

Resolutions about love that he had thought set in stone were under attack as he rode the fury that her story unleashed and then tempered it to her needs. She was all that mattered here, after all, his own see-sawing emotions could be dealt with when he was alone, he hoped.

'Go on,' he murmured.

'I was hauled back to my attic and locked in, but I waited until it was black dark and forced myself through the narrow light that gave on to the leads and crept down a drainpipe and some scaffolding. After that it was almost too easy.'

'I don't think many gently bred ladies would describe such an odyssey quite so blithely.'

'Maybe not, but I'm not at all genteel.'

'You don't intend to acknowledge your father's family, then?'

'They sent me away, and they're not exactly clamouring to meet me.'

'Do they know about you, Lady Strensham? I should have put an announcement of our marriage in the papers.'

'I have no wish to meet people who only acknowledge me because I wed a viscount.'

'Yes, my lady,' he said solemnly and Thea cast him a look that should have crushed him, but he just looked blandly back and said, 'What happened next?'

'I reached the ground without killing myself, as you see. Then I ran when I could see well enough, and walked when I could not. Once dawn came, I took some clothes from a washing line. Often I slept by day and walked by night, and rested under hedges and in the woods well away from the road. I took bread and an old blanket from a cottage once and felt lower than Granby, even though I left them a few shillings.'

'I dare say they thought the fairies had been. The price for a loaf and that ancient rag you had with you when we met would be far less than that.'

'If you say so. Anyway, that is my story until one night when I mistakenly thought I would not be disturbed in a hovel in Rosecombe woods, and you know the rest, my lord.'

'And how very unwelcome you did make me, you spitting virago,' he told her with a nostalgic grin.

Thea basked in the idea that their meeting had been special to him, but sternly reminded herself of the terms of their marriage.

'You suffered a surfeit of curiosity and disbelieved every word I said.'

'How you did hate me.'

Recalling many times when she had not hated him at all, Thea was silent for a moment. 'Miss Hardy would not have lasted a day as a servant, so I left some of her follies behind with her frills and furbelows.'

'You would have grown out of them, if only you were allowed to.'

His voice was warm in her defence, and Thea badly wanted to cling to his strong hand, or lay her weary head on his broad shoulder and take comfort from his proximity. Gratitude faded and the fiery excitement she was becoming all too familiar with threatened again. Now his touch made her hand tingle pleasantly and her nerves sing, and she was in danger of forgetting she was just another of his responsibilities.

'I wonder if you would have thought so if you had turned up at Rosecombe to find me a part of your cousins' house party,' she mused, doubting he would have liked the spoilt Miss Hardy of old. 'If I learnt to see myself as others did, I might have changed I suppose.'

'Of course you would. You're too intelligent not to, my dear one.'

How she wished she really was dear to him, but she made herself remember their pact. In some ways it had been worth it; in others it was exquisite torture to lie so close and know his thoughts were purer than hers.

'I hope you're right,' she said, as if all her attention was centred on their murmured conversation.

'Husbands always are.'

'And I'm the man in the moon,' she replied sleepily.

He chuckled softly and leaned over to place a swift and rather passionate kiss on her soft lips. 'And I'm not above silencing you by any means at my command, wife.'

He briefly stayed propped above her, and pressed another quick kiss on her startled mouth, before returning hastily to his own half of the bed—much to Thea's silent disappointment.

'Go to sleep, Thea. No doubt there will be more mountains to scale in the morning.'

How she longed for those heart-stirring kisses to be repeated with serious intent. She surreptitiously watched him drop into sleep as lightly as if they had been discussing the weather, and closed her own eyes, to puzzle briefly about the nature of passion and wonder what it would be like to truly make love with her handsome husband.

She was too weary to linger on that tantalising subject, and too shy to turn to him and meet the banked-down desire that rendered Marcus's night hideous. With no notion that his growing passion for his wife would be met enthusiastically, he stayed on his side of the covers and suffered in silence. He wanted his wife almost beyond reason, but swore to himself that duty would have no place between them when he finally introduced her to the delights of the marriage bed.

Bath in October was, the Dowager Lady Prestbury declared over the breakfast table one morning, tedious beyond bearing.

'Really, Grandmama? Then I'm surprised you bullied my father into buying you a house here,' Captain Prestbury replied, not taking his eyes from his letters.

'Since the alternative was living with Lewis and your stepmama and their repellent brats, the North Pole would have looked attractive.'

'If rather chilly. You could have gone for London, or Brighton.'

'One is noisy and smelly, the other rackety in summer and dead in winter. Seemed more sensible to come here and die of boredom, and anyone would think you were trying to hurry me on.'

'Now why on earth should I do that?'

Her ladyship snorted. 'So you could whistle my fortune down the wind along with your god-mother's, I suppose. All those ladybirds you have in your keeping must be devilish expensive.'

'I never take more than one mistress at a time, and not one has had a tongue like an asp, so think how I would miss you. Are you thinking of having yourself put to bed with a shovel by the way?'

'Not before you get yourself wed. Aurelia ain't getting my jewellery.'

'One more reason to avoid matrimony.'

'As if you need one now.'

Nick Prestbury laid aside his correspondence and gave his formidable relative his full attention.

'Why now more than any other time?'

'You don't fool me, my boy. Finding that girl of Marcus's immune to your dubious charms has hit you so hard you're still reeling, and don't try denying it.'

'Ever since I made the mistake of telling you how much I admire her dauntless spirit, you have me pegged down as Lady Strensham's frustrated suitor, which I certainly am not.'

'Prove it, then!'

'How?' he asked cautiously, having too much experience of his volatile grandparent to eagerly volunteer.

'Go to Chimmerton and flirt with her.'

'What?'

'You heard me.'

'Marcus is my best friend, as well as my cousin.'

'Then you won't mind doing him a favour.'

'You have a very odd notion of friendship, if you

think paying too much attention to a man's wife is doing him a favour.'

'And you have an even odder one to stand by and watch him make a mull of his marriage. Imagine promising that chit a white marriage, when anyone can see she's head over ears in love with him! The boy needs a sharp lesson to bring him to his senses and you're just the man to provide it.'

'No!'

'I'll order your half brother to accompany me there for a visit then.'

Nick shuddered. His brother Esmond used a spurious reputation for virtue to pursue vulnerable young wives, who could not demand marriage from him, or publish his villainy after he had suborned them. The thought of him scheming against gallant Thea Hardy was doubly repulsive.

'His attentions would end their marriage rather than bring about the romantic fairytale you expect.'

'Marcus Ashfield only needs a push in the right direction and he'll be as happy a husband as you will find anywhere. I'm shocked that you could turn your back on your cousin in such a heartless fashion, when it would take so little effort to help him.'

'And I that you wish me to interfere between a man and his wife.'

'Because he's too stiff-necked to bind that girl to him when he has nothing but his title to offer her in return—or so he thinks. If you ask me, she would have him as a barefoot fugitive with a whole tribe of dependants.'

'I dare say you're right.'

'There, you see? You do admire her!'

'Aye, far too much to subject her to brother Esmond.'

'Excellent, then I'll leave the rest to you. You have enough experience of women to need no more help from me.'

'Oh, are you intent on helping me, ma'am? Luckily I need no assistance from such an unlikely source. Marcus has invited me to visit them.'

'Why didn't you tell me straight off?'

'And spoil your fun? I trust I'm not that undutiful.'

Lady Prestbury gave a snort that informed him how much she appreciated his duty, and rang the bell for someone who would at least pretend to run about at her bidding.

Chapter Seventeen

The morning after her nightmare, Thea sat at the breakfast table staring into her coffee cup and wondering why she felt as if something very special had slipped out of reach once more, while Marcus read his letters as if he hadn't a care in the world.

'Nick will be arriving in the next few days,' he finally informed her. 'He seems much better, despite the blue devils and his grandmama's tender loving care.'

No doubt the gentlemen would spend their time in sporting pursuits and she would be left to play house.

'There is no better man to have on our side if Winforde is still intent on profiting from your connection to him in some way,' Marcus observed as if he could read her mind.

'Thank heaven for silver linings, then,' she said with careful self-control.

'Aye, I think we have need of one,' Marcus replied, his smile cynical and Thea felt distance yawn between.

If only she did not have such shoddy connections,

and he had less scruples, they might make a good marriage out of this bargain. After last night, the prospect of a lifetime of polite encounters drove her to new efforts to make Chimmerton a welcoming home once more, just to have something to occupy any idle moments that would otherwise have been spent on regrets.

A few days later they greeted Captain Prestbury together and Thea wondered what he really made of their situation. She was grateful for Marcus's warm presence at her side of course, even if their alliance seemed horribly flimsy under the acute blue gaze of his cousin. She and Nick said all that was polite to each other, then he went with Marcus to see to the housing of his sporting curricle and four perfectly matched Welsh greys and she felt more of an outsider than ever.

Luckily Cook refrained from having hysterics and Mrs Barker kept an eagle eye on her new staff as Thea played hostess at her first proper dinner party since becoming Viscountess Strensham the next night. She knew that she should relax and enjoy herself, but found it impossible when Captain Prestbury insisted on flirting with her with wearisome frequency. By the end of the evening she wished she had put the wretch in the Crimson Suite, with the dust and a pair of very regal and uncomfortable ghosts for company.

Nick Prestbury was far too used to charming every female he encountered, be she eighteen or eighty, she decided. If not for her neighbour's cheerful conversation and the excellent meal, dinner would have been rendered hideous by Marcus's brooding abstraction.

Thea felt like the bone being snarled over by two dogs more intent on asserting their dominance than carrying off the prize. She was profoundly grateful when her guests departed so she could seek her bed and get away from them both at last. Hearing the door to his bedchamber slam, she realised Marcus had also chosen an early night and felt unutterably weary herself when he stayed firmly on the other side of the highly polished mahogany door.

At least the afternoon was fine, Thea mused the next day, although her husband's frown had barely lifted since breakfast. The light mist of the morning had melted away from the high ground and now lay in the hollows, so the lake seemed to steam like a hot bath. As she and Marcus rode across the park to meet Nick at Squire Hereward's for dinner and impromptu dancing, Thea felt a pang of anxiety about their return journey in the dark with the added hazard of fog.

She knew perfectly well that Marcus resisted setting up a carriage because he would have to use her money to do so. Then there was Dark Lady, a beautifully trained thoroughbred exclusively for her use, while the spare horses he had purchased were mere hacks. When would he realise her money was more of a curse than a blessing to her? Probably never, she decided crossly, and dismissed the heat behind her eyes as mawkish. If he could not sink his silly pride, she had better learn to swallow her own.

'You are very thoughtful, my lady.'

'Just wool gathering,' she replied, as they took the bridle path over the hills that should crop a mile or more off the journey.

Initially she had been surprised he had not insisted the new grooms come along to protect her, before she spied the rifle he carried behind his saddle. Granby was too much of a coward to risk being shot by a true marksman, even if wild horses dragged him up these windswept hills.

'You mean you're worrying about our visitor's comfort.'

'No, I was just musing about something.'

'When there's no solution, it's better not to.'

'There's always a solution, even if it's not pa-latable. But there's a kestrel hovering over there and it's a beautiful day, so never mind my problems.'

'Your puzzles are my puzzles, Thea,' he assured her enigmatically and she hoped he wasn't still brooding on the Captain's unwelcome attentions. 'I remember dreaming of a day like this when we were being alternately fried and boiled on the Spanish Sierras,' he said with a reminiscent smile, 'so let's not waste it now I have my wish at last. I'll race you to that pine if you're game. Hercules is bored with polite rambles.'

He was a superb rider and completely in sympathy with the noble animal, and Dark Lady reached the lone tree several seconds after he brought Hercules to a halt.

'Is that pretty slug capable of more than a trot? I can't think why Merry landed you with such a slowtop.'

'She follows Hercules about like a lamb.'

His laughter as he watched the mare arch her neck at the object of her adoration was as carefree as a boy's. Thea smiled wryly, knowing she was just as infatuated with Hercules's master, even if she had too much sense to show it. With his clear-cut features, abundant energy and powerful figure, her husband looked the perfect model of an English nobleman, but it was his intelligence and humour that rendered him irresistible to her. Her heart jarred when she finally registered the fact that he was staring back at her with heat and shadows in his smoky gaze.

Marcus was remembering how his wife felt in his arms. Recollection of her ardent response to his kisses was doing terrible things to his self-restraint, and he suddenly wished them back at Rosecombe in the most improper circumstances. Perhaps it would be a good idea to set up a carriage after all, for he could hardly make love to his wife on the open hills where any passing shepherd could see them. Yet the flush of colour on her high cheek-bones, and those wonderful eyes of hers, so full of mystery as they turned from blue to green, nearly drove him beyond the limits of self-control.

'Damn it, Thea, I can't fight both of us,' he groaned and, urging the two horses closer together, he stole a passionate kiss.

She was as eager as he, despite the fidgeting horses and Marcus's treasured Baker rifle. Their lips lingered hungrily, as if neither could abide to part, despite fidgeting horses and the open hillside. She murmured her delight in a husky tone that shot desire through Marcus until he was racked by need. Wooing his Thea never palled, but he was almost at the limits of his control. His body clenched with desire and he fought it, even as he recklessly fed the flames with kisses.

His Thea, knowing nothing of that significant possessive, was upbraiding herself for behaving so badly when Marcus held his horse still solely by the power of his legs and his personality, and lifted her into his lap to deepen his embrace. Lost in the delight of a kiss so full of tenderness and promise that she was hard pressed to remember her own name, she gave up berating herself and snug-gled deeper into his embrace, raising hesitant fingers to caress his tanned cheek.

He groaned and drew in a juddering breath. Moved by the idea that she had brought about such turmoil in this strong man, she brushed a hand round the back of his neck to pull his head down again. Revelling in the outdoor freshness of his bronzed skin, she drew her fingers over his firm chin, then rested her hand contentedly on his broad shoulder, shamelessly trying to wriggle even closer. His kiss was so passionate that she lost all semblance of rational thought and it took the sound of persistent barking to shock them back to here and now.

'Oh, Thea, whatever will the neighbours say?' he murmured huskily.

She struggled weakly and he let her go, boosting her over the gap between the horses as effortlessly as he had pulled her to him a few moments before. Shivering with shock and denied emotions, Thea came down to earth with a thud.

'That I am scandalous baggage, as they have since you married me.'

'Never let me hear you spout such rubbish again,' he ordered abruptly, his dark brows nearly coming together in a heavy frown

Thinking of the stories that must be buzzing round society, she firmed her chin. 'The truth is still out there, Marcus.'

'No, a bundle of ill-founded rumours masquerading as truth.'

'I bring no credit to you, and we both know it.'

'And I refuse to listen to such arrant nonsense!'

'You will have little say in the matter if you insist on taking me to London in the spring.'

'The gossips can go to the devil, I—'

'What a pair of slowtops,' Nick called out as he approached on the Squire's favourite hunter, surrounded by several of his prized hounds.

'Aye, and he can go with them,' Marcus muttered darkly, before hailing his cousin with such carefree bonhomie that Thea marvelled at his capacity for concealment. 'How did you sweet-talk Trojan and those misbegotten mongrels out of our host, Nick?'

'Oh, my fabled charm, you know, and a vague but hopeless belief that he might sell one or the other to me.'

'He would soon realise his error if he had seen you in Spain. I never saw such an ill-favoured pack of breakdowns as you kept in those days.'

'Got us out of trouble more times than I care to remember, though, didn't they? And I might have known you would get lost, coz, for you never could find your way out of a pudding bag. Call this a short cut? I reached the Manor an hour since and am sent like the dove from the ark to discover you,' Nick informed them, apparently oblivious to their tumultuous emotions.

'More like the raven,' Marcus murmured darkly, torn between relief that his cousin had missed that kiss and a primitive desire to wring his neck.

'Much more,' Nick agreed with a sidelong look at Thea that made her itch to slap the grin off his handsome face. 'But I'm devilish sharp set and Thea never did finish telling me what you two got up to at Rosecombe, before I arrived too late to rescue the little darling and carry her off to *my* lair.'

'Tell me, coz, would even Boney's escape from that benighted island relieve us of your presence?'

'He's caught fast enough.'

'If you truly believe he will play toy soldiers on a tiny island in the middle of the Mediterranean for long, you're more sanguine than I am.'

'Plenty of chance of my majority if we're going back on campaign, then,' Nick replied with an admiring glance towards Thea, which made Marcus wonder why he put up with him.

'At this rate you'll miss your precious dinner,' he remarked, and urged Hercules into a trot.

When they reached journey's end, Thea strode out of the stable-yard to find the maid her hostess had promised to help her dress. Marcus hungrily watched her go, bitter frustration racking him body and mind. He abruptly informed Nick he would stroll up to the paddocks before joining in the 'damned flimflam' and the speed of his going discouraged Nick from viewing the Squire's beloved mares and foals as well.

Nick shook his head, ruefully remembering the women who had chased his cousin as they marched through Europe. He hated what he was doing to a man he considered more his brother than any real one. Needs must when the devil drove he decided, and for the rest of the evening he treated Thea with an elaborate courtesy she was far too miserable to notice.

All this time she had been congratulating herself that Marcus was no longer a soldier, Thea berated herself as she greeted her hosts serenely. He had sold his commission, she had reasoned. *She* would never suffer the agony of not knowing if her husband was alive or dead in battle. Then she heard his opinion of Bonaparte's present captivity and that false security dropped away. Marcus would fight again, because he thought it his duty.

If only he had something more than a convenient wife to weigh in the balance, such as a child. She would rather wed Granby than watch Marcus ride away from Chimmerton in the famous green uniform she had once so stupidly longed to see him wear again, knowing as she did so that he might never come back. If he was wed to a woman he could love, he might not take such a terrible risk. If an annulment would keep him safe, she would do it and be glad, she concluded with a militant nod that silenced the curate, who had finally plucked up the courage to address the new Lady Strensham.

When Marcus eventually arrived fresh from the attentions of their host's valet, his cool look convinced her something drastic had to be done. Watching him partake of the toasts more enthusiastically than ever before, she wondered if she had imagined that passionate kiss up on the hillside. All that lovely warmth and urgency seemed so remote now that he had distanced himself from her again. The thought that he only kissed her in temper made her smile empty and her slender shoulders droop, until she realised it and gamely pretended to enjoy herself.

When the gentlemen finally rejoined the ladies after dinner, she watched her husband's steady progress across the drawing room, torn between awe and exasperation. She didn't need Nick's confidential whisper to inform her that Marcus was the devil of a fellow for holding his brandy.

'I see that for myself. Thank you, Captain,' she murmured crossly. 'Since you'll both have terrible heads come morning, nothing will show you the error of your ways as well as time itself.'

'A man needs to kick over the traces now and again.'

'Go and play, then. I'm too busy being shrewish to flirt right now.'

He gave her an unrepentant grin and went off to charm the daughter of the house. Watching him go, she failed to see Marcus frown ferociously, then take an angry pull at the brandy glass he had brought in with him. All in all, Thea was heartily glad when the horses were ordered round at last, until everyone insisted it was far too dangerous for her to ride in the dark.

'What about Dark Lady?' she protested, the idea of two gentlemen in their cups finding their way home safely making her heart hammer in time to the galloping hooves of their mounts as they rode off into the darkness.

'We'll look after her royally and send her over in the morning, Lady Strensham. Never you fear,' Squire Hereward boomed out helpfully.

'You're very kind, sir. Please convey my thanks to your wife once again,' she said and gave the nod to the Herewards' coachman.

There was no point arguing with gentlemen in the condition Marcus and Nick were in by now, but she hoped they would not fall. Marcus was far too good a horseman to come unstuck easily of course and, even if he fell off, something told her gentlemen in his condition fell softly. Anyway, by the time her cautious driver reached Chimmerton, the gentlemen had returned safely and were already closeted in Marcus's bookroom with the decanters.

'I wish they had fallen in a ditch and stopped until morning!' Thea announced, not sure why their carelessness bit so gallingly.

'Never mind, my lady,' Mrs Barker replied soothingly. 'His lordship has never been a drunkard.'

Her assurance made Thea feel worse. Refusing possets and company, she retired to her bedchamber, unable to endure the sympathy of her household. She was still awake and resolutely dry-eyed when she heard Marcus's wavering footsteps in the hallway and her silly heart thumped in anticipation.

'Stupid!' she told herself. 'You're irredeemably stupid!' She thumped her pillow hard.

She heard him speak to Barker with perfect clarity through her not-quite-latched door and decided that if Marcus's step was uncertain, his thoughts seemed remarkably clear.

'Mustn't wake her ladyship, my lord,' she heard Barker murmur.

'Heaven forbid,' her husband replied with such apparent revulsion that Thea nearly rushed in and screamed at him never to trouble her with his empty kisses and false endearments again.

Despair finally overcame fury as the silence from her husband's room stretched out, punctuated by the clink of glass on glass. Why should she care if he preferred the brandy bottle to his wife's bed? She was so indifferent to him that she turned her face into her abused pillow and sobbed silently after all, until exhaustion finally overcame her and she drifted into a troubled sleep.

Having finally dismissed Barker, Marcus reached for the brandy decanter again, then stopped himself as the memory of Thea haunted him. Even the remnants of his common sense could not stop him seeking the delights of his lady's bed, when she responded to him so generously. She had welcomed his kisses with nearly as much enthusiasm as she had Nick's subtle attentions throughout the hellish evening just gone. Damned if he would martyr himself any longer; he would take what he could get and be thankful!

He pushed open the door to Thea's room and the fading glow from the fire showed him his wife, lying fast asleep across the vast bed. She must have been too distracted by an evening spent with the man she ought to have married to wind her long mass of hair into its usual thick plait, and it was spread about her so luxuriantly he longed to reach out and caress her through its dusky softness. Disarmed by the vulnerable curve of her back and the suspicion of tears on her pale cheek, he was almost brought to his knees by a great surge of protective tenderness, even if all she currently needed to be saved from was himself.

His wife stirred briefly in her restless sleep, as if she could feel his hungry gaze on her unguarded profile, and he knew then that he could not wake her and demand his rights, before his damned rake of a cousin usurped them. He turned away with a sigh, moving with the exaggerated care of the half-cut as she murmured something in her sleep. He desperately hoped she would not have one of her nightmares tonight, because offering her platonic comfort was totally beyond him.

Seeking something in her dreams, she tossed and turned until he ached to go to her, but dared not. Then she captured another lace-edged pillow and seemed content at last. He finally dared move and was nearly at the door when she murmured, 'Marcus!' with considerable satisfaction.

He spun round rather unsteadily to stare down at her. Was she awake after all and intent on torturing him? No, the moon suddenly appeared through the clouds and showed him his Thea, fast asleep and clutching that pillow as if it offered her more comfort than any inanimate object rightly should.

He fought off a desperate compulsion to wake her and make love to her until the moon and stars faded from the sky, cast away or no. Disarmed by her vulnerability, he took one last, longing look at his lady by moonlight, all glorious temptation with her hair now wound about her curvaceous body as she restlessly thrust aside her coverings. He gently pulled them back over her, so she would not grow cold in the silvered moonlight, and left before he threw himself at her.

Back in his own chamber, Marcus plunged his head into the cooling water in the wash basin and made himself drink deep from the carafe by his bed. Tomorrow night, after pleasuring them both so mightily Thea wouldn't be able to find breath to argue, he would finally make sure she knew she was his in every way that mattered.

Not that he felt the sort of insane passion for her that his mother had suffered from, he reassured himself. Most of the time he was even capable of rational thought, but Thea deserved a sober husband to initiate her into the joys of the marriage bed, and he wasn't sure what he deserved. He already felt as if he had one of Watt's steam hammers in his head, but anticipation made the pain bearable as he slid into dreams far less innocent than his wife's would ever be at long last.

Next morning Thea woke to the awful certainty that Marcus didn't love her and took childish pleasure in making as much noise as possible, to the descant of Barker tiptoeing about Marcus's dressing room as if treading on eggshells. Once ready to go downstairs, she took a long look in the mirror, then marched out, slamming the door with all her strength. That would give him something to think about besides Bonaparte and the brandy bottle!

Marcus raised his head from a pillow suddenly stuffed with house bricks and doubted he would be in a fit state to seduce his lady this week, let alone tonight. From the sound of it she was in a fine temper and he wondered if his head might explode as she stormed out of her bedchamber.

'Barker,' he murmured softly enough to set off only a minor volley of pains in his head, 'more water and one of Mrs Barker's potions, if you please.'

'She's mixing it now, my lord.'

'Good man,' he whispered, and wondered silently why he had ever been such a damned fool as to think getting drunk solved anything.

Chapter Eighteen

Thea brooded over the late Lord Strensham's secrets, and her chances of uncovering them, while she ate her breakfast in solitary splendour. Could the late Viscount really have left the grandsons he loved so much virtually penniless? Knowing his son's extravagance as he did, he must have hidden something for the benefit of his grandchildren, and he would not expect his heir to predecease him so he would have to hide it very well.

Even if Marcus was too stubborn to believe his grandfather loved him enough to outfox his own son, she thought otherwise. Anyway, he would poker up like a tin soldier if she mentioned her suspicions, so somehow she must find out if part of the Ashfield fortune had been secreted away without his help. Tears pricked her eyes as she thought about her stiff-necked, arrogant, wonderful husband. There was no point in pretending to herself that she didn't love him after last night. She had feared for him so acutely that she had known it with absolute certainty, and she loved him enough to let him go.

She sat frozen in her seat as she explored the full breadth and depth of that love, and, oh, why did it have to hurt so much? If she found his fortune, he would not need her any more. He could marry for love. She could not send him back to the fortune-hunting game she knew revolted him and made him a stranger to himself. In the mundane act of breaking her fast, Thea came to a new understanding of the world. Love, she discovered, was not the shimmering fairytale she had once thought, and she must let her husband go.

He had had ample opportunity to woo her if he had wanted to since they were married. Then there was his declaration to her at Rosecombe that he didn't believe in love. Maybe affection would be enough, a craven voice argued, but she silenced it. What a blind idiot he was, she thought with a tender smile. He would never be truly happy without passionately loving his chosen lady, and he would be a wonderful lover if he did, but unfortunately not hers.

She couldn't stand knowing only money held them together. If all he had to offer was obligation and tolerance, then she must end this marriage, before it destroyed her. As she reeled under her conclusion, something the housekeeper told her the first day teased at her memory. Words slotted into her mind as if someone had whispered them in her ear. The old lord 'used to say he'd see Mr Marcus and Master Colin right, even if Mr Julius and the French finally managed to do their worst.' The more she thought about it, the more sense it made: something was hidden here, something the late Julius Ashfield would never find and only Marcus, or his brother, could discover.

Marcus had said his grandfather had delighted in games and treasure hunts, so why not set him one in earnest? And if her husband was too stubborn to look for the clues, she would have to do it for him. The painful jar as her heartbeat missed, then thundered, told her what recovering her husband's fortune would mean and she was tempted to let it rest. No, it must be done, and there was no time like the present.

So that was why, after a frustrating couple of hours searching the late Lord Strensham's possessions, Thea came downstairs to find her lord recovered in all but temper.

'Where have you been?' he greeted abruptly.

'In the attics.'

'Whatever for?' he exploded.

She might be ridiculously in love with him, but being addressed so abruptly set her hackles on end.

'I was looking for something,' she replied mildly, eyeing the dusty hem of her cambric gown. 'If there's nothing else, I would like to go and change.'

'As it happens, there is,' he snapped, obviously controlling his temper with difficulty. 'Come to my bookroom, and we can discuss it in private.'

Bowing her head with exquisite irony, she marched ahead of him and heard the door snap shut behind them. They seemed to have all their most interesting arguments in this room, she thought with grim humour and turned to face her wedded lord.

'Why were you questioning Nick about Grandfather's will?' he barked.

'I wanted to know what it contained and you were unlikely to tell me.'

'I won't have it, Thea,' he stormed and her own temper flashed out.

'Fortunately I no longer obey orders, my lord.'

'And take your marriage vows selectively,' he replied furiously, then looked disconcerted when she blushed at the thought that some of them were all too appropriate. 'So are you going to tell me what you are up to, of must I find out from the servants?'

'Your business, since you refuse to see to it yourself.'

He stepped forward as if he was about to shake her and she waited with shameful eagerness. He usually found it expedient to kiss her when he was in a temper, and her silly heart raced at the prospect. Unfortunately he stopped short and imposed an iron curb on his emotions. It was most disappointing, despite her noble resolutions.

'Your grandfather loved you, Marcus. He wouldn't leave you penniless.'

'You don't know what you're talking about.'

Loving him herself, she would move heaven and earth to protect him, even if that meant giving him his freedom.

'There's no need to be rude.'

'There is every need,' he told her in a driven voice.

'I would free you.'

'Free yourself, more like.'

'Think what you like,' she gritted, hurt by his assumption that she actually wanted to leave him— it would be the hardest thing she had ever done.

'First we will prove this whole business is a mare's nest you came up with because I dipped too deep last night.'

'No, for I would have told you directly if that was all it was.'

'You did, my lady, very directly.'

'Did I disturb you, my lord?'

'Always,' he ground out, and it was more of an accusation than an admission. 'Come,' he snapped, and going over to the desk unlocked a drawer and drew out a document heavy with legal seals and red tape. 'My grandfather's will. Read it if you wish. It contains no clues to some mythical fortune, hidden as if it was a game played on a summer picnic.'

'Is that what he used to do?'

His hard mouth softened momentarily into a reminiscent smile. 'Only if we were very good, but this is just legal waffle.'

'Nothing odd at all?'

'Only his blessing and something about clean shirts.'

'Where?' she asked eagerly, for that seemed a very strange thing to put into a will to her.

'Here,' he said pointing to the parchment in his hands. '"I exhort my grandsons to keep a clean conscience."'

'We could all benefit from one of those, what else?'

'"They should also remember there is nothing half so essential to a gentleman as a well-laundered shirt and a fresh cravat."'

'I wonder…'

'What?'

'Where does a gentleman keep his shirts, Marcus?'

'In a clothes' press in his dressing room.'

'The same one your grandfather used?'

'Of course.'

Their eyes met in a brief moment and she knew the hunt was on, whatever the consequences.

Ten minutes later she had carefully laid all the shirts he passed her on the truckle bed, only to give a sigh of frustration as they contemplated empty drawers. Seeing doubts stay him, she felt down the back of one of them herself, and it moved so abruptly she thought it broken. Then a false panel slid aside, just large enough for the paper nestled inside it.

'Oh, it was true, then,' she gasped, but his stern expression softened not a bit. 'Should I leave you to read it?'

He gave her a hard look and held the letter out to her. 'You must be desperate indeed to get away from me to clutch at such straws.'

She stared blankly at the much-folded parchment, then her gaze sharpened. 'Marcus, there's more to this than there looks at first glance.'

'It's nonsense.'

'Yes, but it's meant to be. Only imagine if your father had found it first.'

'I dare say he would have burnt it.'

'Your grandfather took a terrible risk. He must have trusted you to understand his message.'

'I was sick with grief and worry and didn't think twice about it.'

'You had too much to worry about at the time.'

Thea took the paper and read it aloud:

The lady of the vines loved to sport
With the old instrument of Dan Cupid's court.
Discover the best and vilest truth,
That naught could save our dearest Ruth.
Even Mammon could not forestall
The foulest murder of them all.

Yet if you learn harmony she may
Help you find a prosperous day.

'Even I can see it's about music,' she concluded.
'My aunt Lavinia was musical and music is the
food of love, according to Orsino in *Twelfth Night*.
My aunt he cast as Ruth amongst the alien corn, and
his vile truth must be a pun on the word viol.'

It was so simple once he explained that Thea felt
remarkably stupid.

'Then it must be in the Music Room,' she said and
sprang into action without waiting for him. It seemed
better not to when he was frowning so darkly.

'I wonder which of those antiques is a viol?' she
mused when they got there, still in tense silence.

'One of these, unless he meant a bass viol, I
suppose,' Marcus muttered almost as if he was
alone, reaching for the first of two instruments
hanging on a wall of antiquities, kept as much for
curiosity as use.

She took it from him and was engulfed in a cloud
of dust. When he took down the next one and
examined it she waited impatiently.

'You're very eager for release, are you not?' he asked
as he used his long fingers to delve into one of the instruments and produced another folded paper. The
silky danger running through his deep voice took her
straight back to their improper encounter in the library
at Rosecombe, but his coldness made her shiver.

'No,' she replied, and set her mouth in a stubborn line in case it started to wobble. She refused to squirm under his icy scrutiny, and imperiously waved his attention to his grandfather's message.

'Very well, but we will have a reckoning for this.'

'Just read it, my lord,' she said wearily. Later the only reckoning he would make would be of what he had spent, and never would a small fortune be received so ungratefully.

He sent her a dark look and moved a little further away, ostensibly to catch the light, but she felt he was isolating himself from her as he read out the next clue.

From the royal tree, survey your wide domain
Where dreamed a maiden now sublime.
Then stand in her allotted space again
And know that life is full of folly,
Seek not joy in reason's cold confine
When life is food for melancholy.
Music is the key to delight and salvation
So seek your blessings in contemplation.

'My aunt Lavinia again, but what is he trying to tell us?' Marcus mused. 'The royal tree must be the Queen's Oak, but as it was cut down twenty years ago, he can't have hidden anything there.'

'Checkmate,' Thea said disgustedly.

'Just check, and the Gainsborough will enlighten

us,' Marcus told her, the thrill of the chase catching him at last.

Thea sped along at his side, wondering how he would feel if this turned out to be a wild-goose chase. Maybe she should have left well alone, but she couldn't help hurrying after him all the same. In the saloon, long shafts of autumn sunlight slanted onto the magnificent portrait and the unlucky Lavinia looked as if she might step down and greet them.

'The setting is key, I suspect,' Marcus told her distantly. 'So we might as well ride to the site of the oak.'

'I'm sure you don't need my help now.'

'I'm not letting you out of my sight that easily, madam wife. God knows what you'll get up to if I do, run off with the coal man perhaps.'

'Why didn't I think of that?' she muttered sulkily as he marched her to the stables and set about saddling their horses himself.

She couldn't just stand and watch, so she ran for the tack, saying nothing as she bridled her mare and handed him Hercules's light bit. Two could play the silence game, she decided, but when he threw her into Dark Lady's saddle as if she weighed no more than a child, she could not quite suppress a moan at the effect his strong hands closing about her waist had on her, totally against her will.

'What was that, my lady?'

'What was what?'

'I thought you spoke.'

'Well, I didn't, nor do I want to.'

'Just as well.'

Thea tried to force all expression from her face as a dark pit of misery seemed to yawn at her feet, and managed to show him a blank face when they finally reached the tree stump. Marcus dismounted and sent her a cool look as she took Hercules's reins, and turned Dark Lady so she could look at the remains of a once-magnificent tree.

'The church tower is behind her left elbow in the picture, so if I move to the right and look north…' He paused as he surveyed his domain. 'I can see the house, chimneys, and a good many trees.'

'Perhaps we recently employed the richest chimney sweep in England.'

'Of course it's difficult to judge exactly where Lavinia is looking in the painting,' he went on as if she hadn't spoken. 'Of course! That's it!'

'That's what?'

'The Temple of the Muses, of course.'

'Of course, so what else does it say?'

Marcus took the dusty paper from his pocket and handed it to her.

'"Music is the key"—now what's all that about?' she asked, forgetting they were at outs in her eagerness.

'One of the Muses. We will have to go and look, if you are coming?'

Since he had demanded she came with him, he really was the most contrary, bad-tempered man she had ever come across. 'What's the point of having the dismals alone?' she sniped crossly.

'Don't blame me if it's a fool's errand, then.'

Contemplating the loss of his trust and the precious intimacy that had once seemed so close, Thea considered her bleak future on the ride to the folly. Marcus had never pretended to love her, but their passionate friendship seemed the height of luxury, now he had cut himself off from her as if they inhabited different continents.

At least he had possessed the foresight to ride back and take the key from the muniment room, she conceded numbly as he took it from his pocket. It took him some effort before the rusted lock moved and Thea was awed by the length of time the old Viscount must have kept his secrets. Finally Marcus gave the doors a mighty kick to force them open. That should earn him a scold from Barker for marring the pristine glory of his glossy top boots. Although, if they solved this enigma, he could probably buy himself a pair a week and kick as many obstacles as he chose.

Marcus entered the shuttered building and Thea reluctantly followed. Soon she would know exactly where she stood, and blindly tagged along because falling into strong hysterics would be ridiculous. Marcus opened enough shutters to light their way and she saw that the marble interior was dull with neglect. She shrugged off the ghostly presence of lost summers and stared at the nine statues arranged around the walls, looking for the 'key' in Antony Ashfield's deplorable poem.

'I think Terpsichore dances and sings, and Polyhymnia,' she said with a frown at the assembled goddesses. 'Euterpe's poetry and music seems most likely, given your grandfather's versifying.'

'The lyre is a bardic instrument,' Marcus mused, 'although the sculptor looks to have used the same model for all nine.'

'They are not masterpieces, are they?' agreed Thea abstractedly, as she searched for a clue. '"Music is the key to delight and salvation/ So seek your blessings in contemplation." What did he mean?' she muttered, staring at the heavy-limbed goddesses.

'That one is pointing at something,' he observed, and Thea was climbing onto the statue's podium before she remembered it wasn't ladylike.

'The staircase? Nothing could be concealed there,' she said, trying to pretend ladies climbed the statuary all the time.

'The angle is not right. She's pointing at something on that wall.' Marcus ran up the steps to examine the delicate frieze a more inspired artist had carved into the marble. 'I only hope it's not another piece of paper,' he observed, just as he slipped on something unsavoury and put out a hand to save himself. He fell against one of the figures on the wall and fought even harder to regain his balance as he felt it shift under his touch.

'It's loose, Thea! We've done it after all!'

He twisted the mechanism that levered the stone out of place and gazed into the gap it revealed. Heart thumping with excitement, Thea scrambled up the steps and saw into a small chamber, piled high with boxes and bags. For long moments they gaped at the horde, before fear of discovery spurred them into action.

'The rest can stop here till morning,' Marcus announced as he pulled out a soft suede bag and examined the fabulous diamond necklace inside. 'My grandfather must have been buying gold for decades if that stash of boxes is anything to go by.'

Thea remembered her conversation with the housekeeper on her very first day at Chimmerton.

'He was determined to save you from your father's depredations and invasion by the French,' she said and, for the first time today, her eyes met Marcus's in perfect understanding.

'He never could be persuaded that our army and navy between them would see Boney off.'

Thinking back to the invasion scares of ten years ago and Bonaparte's many victories, Thea could not altogether blame him.

'He must have seen the way things were going since the year twelve?'

'My father was well on the road to ruin by then,

and Bonaparte rallied after the Russian débâcle don't forget. By the time he was routed Grandfather was probably too ill to care and I expect he waited for me to get home and untangle it all.'

Thea reached out to offer him comfort, then let her hand drop as he shrugged and turned to purely practical matters without appearing to notice.

'Nick can help me move it into the strong room this afternoon. It'll keep him out of mischief,' he said with a stony look she found hard to meet.

Sighing, she followed him outside and untied a restless Dark Lady's reins and moved over to a convenient stone bench ready to mount. Marcus confounded her by seizing her about the waist and tossing her up into the saddle. Breathless and trembling after so brief a contact, she drew in a stuttering breath and told herself not to be an idiot.

'Your brother will be glad,' she remarked lamely.

'At least he won't be able to come up with any more hare-brained schemes to restore us Ashfields to our former glory,' Marcus remarked with the first sincere smile she'd seen all day.

'From the look of it you have glory enough for half-a-dozen brothers to share,' she answered unwarily.

'And to think that you married a fortune hunter, Lady Strensham,' he said bitterly.

Wondering why her remark had stung him to urge Hercules into a gallop that left her behind, Thea wistfully watched her husband's powerful figure until he was hidden from sight then made Dark Lady follow more sedately. She had thought he would be delighted to be once again the proud owner of a wealthy estate and honourable heritage. Wrong again, Thea, she thought rather mournfully and contemplated the future with a sinking heart.

Trotting into the stable-yard long after her husband had left it, Thea persuaded Dark Lady into her box, whispering sweet nothings about long gallops on the morrow as she groomed her and then fed her a carrot. Eventually Thea had to go back to the house, and maybe after a change of clothes she would feel better, but somehow she doubted it. Her money had done as a stop-gap, but, now what of the goose-girl?

Thea came downstairs and found her husband impatiently pacing her sitting room; her heart sank at his grim face and searing gaze.

'I suppose you want your fortune back so you can offer it elsewhere?' he said harshly. Thea raised one haughty eyebrow and a flush of angry colour flared high across his cheekbones as he glared at her. 'Be careful how you provoke me now you are so close to your goal.'

'What goal?'

'Oh, don't act the innocent with me, it doesn't suit you.' He looked away from her as if she was too low to look upon. 'If you intend leaving Chimmerton, then I beg you to do so without delay,' he told her stonily.

'If I'm to be thrown out like a discarded servant, I would know why.'

His laugh was bitter and he turned to stare bleakly out of the window as if he couldn't bear to look at her.

'They say the husband is the last one to know, do they not? I was completely taken in. I was…well, never mind that. I think, after all, that it would look a little out of the ordinary if my bride departed the house before our first guests. You will stay until after Christmas.'

Thea flinched at his harsh expression, and the prospect of two more months of wedded strife. Surely he hadn't been hiding such revulsion for her all along? She swayed under a wave of pain that was too acute to examine as she contemplated such a terrible idea.

Chapter Nineteen

'I see I was mistaken in judging you a gentleman,' she said at last, 'but why dispense with me so summarily? Will it not cause a scandal?'

'Spare me the act, Thea.' Marcus gave a humourless laugh. 'I should have enjoyed your favours after all. Your lover will do so soon enough, so I should have forgotten my scruples and taken you.'

His anger seemed to build with his harsh words, but they gave her hope. He didn't look indifferent as he seized and held her so forcefully that all her breath left her lungs in a rush. She should have been furious, of course, but she glimpsed such anguish in his beloved face. He was no more capable of hurting her physically than he was of flying to the moon, but he gave a fine imitation of a possessive man in a berserker rage as he took her mouth in a hard kiss that deprived her lungs of air.

A few heated moments went by as she responded helplessly and his hands wandered ruthlessly over her slender curves. She almost gave in and welcomed his rough caress, excitement threatening reason as she felt the hunger behind his fury.

'No! I will not let you treat me like some back-street whore whenever you are out of temper, however much I love you,' she insisted once she could get her mouth free, but luckily he was beyond hearing that admission.

He crushed her mouth under his furious one again and this time she did not force her head aside, but met him fury for fury as their mouths clashed with a heat that seared and burned almost beyond control. Then his mouth softened and his sensuous kiss let in the passion under all that anger. He broke it far too soon and looked down at her with molten silver eyes as she battled love and hurt.

'Why not tell me you planned to leave me, Thea? I would have let you go, however much it hurt.'

'I have no lover!' she countered, struggling with a sunburst of hope that he must care for her to sound so driven.

'Damn it, tell me the truth, Thea,' he demanded, giving her a brief shake as if he must get an answer somehow.

'You wouldn't recognise it if it stood in front of you with a flaming sword, but I won't go because of some ridiculous fantasy wrought out of nothing.'

Despite her elation at that passionate kiss and his veiled assertion that he had strong feelings for her after all, she was smarting from his bitter words and lack of faith.

'Nothing to say, my lord? Then I will see you at dinner tonight,' she informed him haughtily and left with a regal swish of skirts.

Evidently he put his fortune first, as she was left to brood over her accounts until it was time to change for dinner at last. Not that she felt particularly hungry, but she would not retire to her bedchamber like an invalid!

For Marcus the evening was rendered hideous by Nick's determined flirtation with his wife. He should consider himself lucky to have escaped such a nauseating spectacle while they retrieved his fortune, but as he had been tortured by jealousy the whole time he was away, it had not helped. Nick didn't deserve her. He had chased every beautiful woman he came across, and caught most of them. Marcus would never trust his spirited, lovely Thea to such a rogue.

He would make her his after all, and, given the way she responded to him, he knew he could make her seduction sweet. If she had chosen a worthier lover he might have held back, but Nick would break her heart. The uneasy suspicion that he was using that as an excuse, made him more taciturn as the evening wore on, and Thea was looking enchanting in a gown that matched her unique gaze, and he wanted her outrageously. He was in nearly as irrational a state as he had been the night before by the time he entered her bedchamber, with no help from the brandy bottle.

'Nick is completely besotted with you,' he accused abruptly, after ordering Maggie to bed and banishing Barker to perdition, before following Thea into her room and slamming the door.

'No, he's playing some devious game,' she stormed back.

Nick might not be a perfect gentle knight but he loved his cousin, and how could Marcus think she would encourage him if he were serious?

'He's in love with you,' Marcus insisted starkly. 'And you wanted your money back so you could bestow it on him.'

His tanned face was stern, his eyes as wintry as when they first met and Thea could have sunk to the floor and wept. He had completely misread her quest for his lost fortune.

'Nick Prestbury is no more in love with me than I am with him.'

Marcus's eyes were iron dark now and she sighed wearily, wondering how everything could have gone so wrong.

'I'm a married woman and Nick always flirts with ladies who see through him.' She considered this statement for a moment. 'Other than those females I'm told inhabit the fringes of the *ton*. They probably take him very seriously indeed.'

Her own temper ignited as she met his smoky gaze, and saw he hadn't listened to a word. No matter, she decided militantly, it was better to meet his stupidity with pride than tears.

'Never consider setting yourself up as one of that ragtag company,' he barked, looking as if the words might poison him.

'And stop pretending you care a jot for anything but your precious name,' she raged. 'I dare say I could go to the devil with any careless rogue who wanted me for myself alone, if I did not share it.'

'Try it and I'll show you how mistaken you are. Look at another man as you did at Nick tonight and I'll lock you in your room.'

'I look at him as a friend, and why does it matter? You don't want me yourself. It's just pride talking, my lord Strensham, nothing but stiff-necked, possessive, dog-in-a-manger pride. I hope it keeps you warm at night.'

His expression was implacable—bitterly cold and yet hotly furious—and Thea stared back with such misery in her heart that she was beyond tears. He moved inexorably closer and she had to force herself not to back up against the bed.

'I intend to swallow it and take a real bedfellow tonight, instead of one who cowers behind my honour and a sheet. I might as well sample the wares, if they're shortly to be put on show.'

'How can you even think such slander, let alone

speak it?' she whispered, knowing that saying the words aloud would hurt too much. 'Why do you suddenly believe me so base, Marcus?' she added, her own fury dying as pain knifed into her.

'Guess!' he said, and it came out more as a groan than an accusation as the last shreds of control snapped.

Abruptly he pulled her into his arms and ground his hungry mouth against hers. For moments that seemed to stretch beyond their usual measure, she felt herself go rigid with shock against his iron-hard body.

Of course it wasn't really happening, she assured herself in a daze of hurt, curiosity and seemingly indestructible desire. He had roused that in her the first moment she set eyes on him, so tall, proud and handsome that she bitterly wanted her blown reputation back so she might meet him as an equal.

In the morning she would wake up and her urbane husband would face her across the breakfast table, his gaze ironic as she greeted him with this odd fantasy rendering her tongue-tied and uncomfortable. Except it didn't feel in the least imaginary, her bemused brain informed her, as the explicit arousal of her husband's hard body informed her he was fact. Her inexperienced imagination could never conjure up such awesome need!

The desperation in his stormy gaze suddenly disarmed her. Even if he wanted her against his will, he unmistakably wanted her. Fury died as she felt the

fine tremor in hands intent on drawing her inexorably toward his mighty body. Outraged stiffness
drained out of her like wax from a heated mould. Fire
raged through her in its stead, as she revelled in the
feel of his rigidly muscled torso hard against her.

Some nameless new need opened every pore and
sinew to the merciless wanting she sensed in him
now, and fervently bid it welcome. Tomorrow she
would regret this, feel the pain of his ridiculous accusations cutting to the quick, but tonight her traitor
senses were in control. There had never been much
doubt what they wanted, once she had laid eyes on
Marcus Ashfield, Lord Strensham and shamelessly
wanted him; despite everything she had learnt of
fortune hunters.

He had kissed her before she assured herself, and
she had survived it. Yet never before had she felt so
undefended, so ready to open herself to him. The
hurt of his ridiculous accusations still lingered of
course, and a stern voice tried to insist he didn't
deserve her complete surrender after that tirade, but
she reached up to smooth away the fierce frown
drawing his dark brows together.

The feel of his firm skin under her sensitised fingers
and her temper fell away. She moved against him as
sensuously as a luxuriating cat, her fluid curves
stretching and settling against masculine hardness.
He pulled a great gasp of air into much-tried lungs and
she could only suppose he liked her boldness, nearly

as much as she did the fire-and-ice novelty of being so close to him she could feel him breathe.

With his eyes pure silver with heat and passion, Marcus lowered his head and kissed her eager mouth. His firm lips wooed hers, as demand gentled to supplication and he seemed to forget his fury. Now he sipped at her mouth, gently coaxing her to open for him and truly let him in. She knew it would be the ultimate surrender if she did, no more pretending to be friends who had wed each other. No chance of leaving him to wed another, no more ridiculously noble sacrifice.

It was a decision that took no time at all. She was flesh and blood, not an impossibly worthy heroine, so she boldly met him need for need. Her body sang under his knowing hands as she opened her lips and surrendered without a shot, let alone a battle. He rasped air into his lungs, and she felt her knees give up their struggle to hold her. His tongue danced with hers, so knowing, so gentle that it echoed his questing touch, and she returned his caress with a demand she barely understood.

His strong, long-fingered hands braced the curves of her bottom and took the weight from her failing legs, and she was only relieved. Lifting her even closer to his eager body, Marcus left her without breath to protest, even if she wanted to, and walked her inexorably in the direction of her vast bed, just as one of those gasps for air filled her pent lungs for a change. Then all power of rational thought flew away, as he impatiently ripped through her knotted laces and her gown fell open to reveal her waiting breasts, shamelessly aroused by the awed adoration in silver eyes, heavy lidded with desire.

'Beautiful, you're so unbelievably beautiful,' he murmured as he cupped one of them gently, his hot gaze urgent and awed on her expectant nipple.

She gasped again and his eyes met hers, wonder at what they could do to each other in their gazes, as they held that look for endless seconds and his long fingers caressed her so intimately that fire shot through her and pooled between her unsteady legs.

All the blue suddenly burned out of her extraordinary eyes and Marcus watched his sea-witch go green-eyed with desire. Tenderness and such an indescribable need it nigh on brought him to his knees surged through him as he watched her untried passions ignite. Only for her could he fight off the driving need to take her without further ado, and relieve the agony of desire he had fought so long. For his wife all must be as perfect as he could make it.

'Wife?' he murmured, savouring the word as if it was unique to them and defying the stars to do their worst.

He should leave before they changed the world, but could no more go to his lonely bed tonight than he could stop time and hold back the dawn. His hand stilled on her breast, and his eyes looked into hers

with a question in their silver depths. If she asked him
to stop he could, just because she was owed better
than raging jealousy and boorish demands.

'Please?' she whispered huskily, and with a heart-
felt sigh, he lowered his head to that eager nipple
and took it in his mouth to suckle on her.

His wicked tongue played there, even as his long
fingers teased her other breast, and the hot pool of fire
at the very core of Thea's body began to scorch and
demand more than this wonderful intimacy, before
she melted into a passion-racked heap at his feet.

'Ah, stop! No, don't ever. I couldn't bear it. Oh,
Marcus, I want you so much,' she groaned, as he
transferred his mouth to her other breast and freed
his hand to wander.

'And you shall have me, lovely Thea,' he
murmured huskily, leaving his task long enough to
meet her wide eyes, and promise more with his own.

Feeling her skirts being pulled aside only when his
warm hand brushed her smooth thigh, Thea was too
far flown to find the cool air on her bare skin in any
way shocking. Instead, emboldened by passion and
feelings she dare not question just now, she gave her
own hands licence to roam and revelled in his touch.

Oh, but he was a wonder to her unsteady touch she
decided dazedly, as she discovered iron-hard
muscles covered in satin-smooth skin, where he had
ripped his starched cravat off with an eagerness that
would have horrified the dandies. She had longed

to explore his broad shoulders more intimately from the moment she first laid eyes on him, she finally admitted to herself, and now she had the chance to do so she wanted it even more.

She eyed his dishevelled hair, as he butted against her breast with ever more demanding desire and dropped a butterfly kiss on his wildly disordered curls, then rested her head on his bowed one, in a moment of such intimacy that her breath almost failed her. Raising his head at last to meet her passion-hazed gaze, Marcus's eyes blazed and demanded and begged all at once.

'Now?' he asked simply and, unable to find a single barrier to raise against the storm, she met his eyes and nodded.

Kissing her again, he half-walked, half-carried her the few remaining steps to her bed, and heat shot through her so sharply that her legs sagged weakly against his heavily muscled limbs. Then she was swung triumphantly into his arms and laid on the bed before she had time to even think. Lying down was an absolute necessity at any rate she decided gratefully, but, as her remaining garments yielded to the inevitable force that was her husband, she began to wonder at their inequality of undress and grew restless.

Beyond speech now, she pushed at his superfine coat and wondered he had not had the sense to remove it long ago. Distracted from his task of summarily dealing with her garters, he looked up with the wickedest smile she had ever seen quirk his dear mouth and obediently shrugged it off. She eyed his waistcoat with reproach and, with a hasty unbuttoning that would horrify Barker, that was gone too. As cool air peaked her nipples to almost painful hardness, she tugged at his shirt and was only happy for him to renew his incendiary attentions when he peeled it off impatiently.

Now her hands were free to roam his magnificent body unimpeded at long last, so she happily settled to the task while he returned to her garters and, kissing each creamy thigh, peeled her stockings down and finally spared time to look at the beauty he had uncovered.

'Oh, Thea, what a wonder you are,' he breathed as if he hadn't seen her doubts for revelling in the sight of her, and instinct made her arch the body he seemed to like so much towards the one she quite shamelessly adored.

'Please?' she murmured again, need now growing nigh unbearable within her, even as she wondered what it was she wanted so desperately it was almost consuming her.

With one mighty movement he ripped off the last of his own clothing, quite beyond patience with so many layers of gentlemanliness, and it was her turn to gaze in awe. The pool of heat between her thighs began to throb with undeniable need, even as a question jumped starkly into her slumberous mind. Six months of misadventures had given her an un-ladylike insight into what men and women did together in a bed, but there was a vast gulf between theory and practice.

'How shall we fit?' she asked, her voice so husky with passion she hardly recognised it herself.

'Ever since Adam and Eve, our kind seem to have contrived to do so, and I dare say we will do the same. Would you like to try?'

'Ooh, yes,' she gasped, then caught herself being immodest in the most extraordinarily com-promising position known to woman. 'If you don't mind, Marcus?'

'Mind? Oh, Thea, I think I shall expire of sheer need if I don't take you very soon,' he husked and sucked in a great breath, as if the need he spoke of ground as fiercely in him as it did in her.

Her eyes lingered on the awesome evidence of his manhood, as her mind went to work on the gnawing need for completion within her.

'Well, then,' she demanded, quite reasonably in her eyes, 'why don't you get on with it, my lord?'

'Your wish is my command, termagant,' he replied and moved over her, waiting for her to accept the closeness of them, skin to skin, before he attempted more.

As she ran her hands desperately over the heated satin of his muscular back, he began to caress her to the verge of desperation, even as his mouth on hers urged her to match him need for need. She took little urging and the most exquisite excitement ripped through her as he took her with one long, desperate thrust and nearly overrode the pain as he breached her virginity.

'I hurt you,' he gasped in remorse, halting above her even as they were finally joined in the most intimate way possible.

Riding that momentary smart, she wondered at the extraordinary novelty of this sense of fullness, of completion, and feeling him inside her was so exhilarating that she shook her head, momentarily beyond words. He began to move and yet another wave of acceptance, of opening to this, and to him and her like this overtook her, and pleasure sighed from her passion-swollen mouth as pain became a memory.

'Wonderful,' she moaned, when she could spare the breath, and his rhythm increased gently, driving them both to ever-increasing heights of desire and urgent necessity.

Part of her wanted this glorious, fiery intimacy to go on and on, for the stroke and hungry drive of his heavily muscled body, to keep him sheathed in her wet silk softness for ever and a day. Another was warming to the idea that something even more wonderful, and ever more desirable, lay at the end of the journey they were striving to travel in such perfect harmony that her muscles instinctively adjusted to his thrusts and deepened them with the motion of her slender body, despite her inexperience. Then he quickened his pace at last, and her breath panted in time to his increasingly desperate demand, as pleasure she had never dared dream of danced and beckoned just out of reach.

For endless moments it seemed that she would journey, but not achieve her destination, then he drove one final, mighty thrust so urgently into her welcoming softness that mere passion exploded into a fiery starburst, way beyond human imagination. Her body rocked with great convulsions of pleasure, even as spasm after spasm of ecstasy drove him desperately into her and sent her spiralling, at last, into a place where they were alone on the peak of an experience that felt unique.

As he finally spent himself in her warmth, her body still quivering with lovely aftershocks of pleasure, they curled together in a haven new to both of them and found out, at last, why lovers risked the world for this, why that very world faded and grew unimportant next to their fiery conjunction.

'Now I see why Helen started the war of Troy.'

'And I why Paris let her,' he teased, even as the lingering spasms of the most earth-shattering completion he had ever experienced shook him. 'Even now you cannot let up on your precious Greeks and Romans, my bookish Thea,' he husked as he dipped his forehead to hers in a caress that felt even closer than a kiss.

'Even now I cannot let up on *you*, my lord. When can we do it again?'

He eased himself off her gently, and rolled over with her nestled in his arms so she lay on his heaving chest.

'Far sooner than we should if you don't stop doing that,' he protested as she ran an inexperienced, admiring hand over his manhood and he felt it spring to attention, despite everything they had just done. 'You will be sore, my lady, and it's best if I just pet you for the rest of the night.'

'Stuff, I had rather be a little sore tomorrow than very unfulfilled tonight.'

'Unfulfilled? After I just pleasured you so mightily you miraculously lost the power of speech for all of two minutes together?'

'Then why not try for five this time, husband?'

'Oh, Thea, you're a very demanding wife, but I'll do my poor best,' he promised, and succeeded to such effect that it took three cups of tea the next morning before she lost the husky tone her voice had acquired from gasping out her extreme satisfaction at his efforts.

Chapter Twenty

Over breakfast Thea watched Marcus surreptitiously. He seemed happy, she concluded with a dreamy smile. She was so far gone that banked-down excitement was shamefully ready to glow into life at the slightest provocation. And what a scandalous fire having Marcus embrace his husbandly duties so enthusiastically seemed to have lit in her!

They had to avoid one another's gaze just to get through breakfast with any semblance of decorum, and even then Thea shifted under the knowing eyes of Captain Prestbury. Despite it, she would have joined Marcus in a furtive tryst just about anywhere he suggested, but Nick carried her husband off somewhere, so she tried to concentrate on her duties, and failed.

Of course Nick had deliberately driven Marcus into such a savage state of jealousy that he had, thankfully, forgotten his silly scruples and truly made her his wife at long last. Thea didn't know if she should kiss the overly gallant captain, or be offended that he had interfered between man and wife.

A dreamy smile overcame her frown as she dwelt on that intimacy, and felt her knees wobble and her head spin. She plumped down on the window-seat in the bay window that lit the stairs of the Tudor wing and allowed herself to gloat. After all, she would only be a new wife once, so she might as well enjoy it when her husband had made her initiation to the marriage bed so spectacular. She yawned like a well-fed cat and felt her eyelids grow heavy as she remembered, but if only Nick had not intervened, she might be revelling in her husband's amorous attentions at this very moment.

'Amorous,' she repeated to herself, liking the feel of the word on her tongue, murmuring it again through lips that were still plumped and rosy from her lover's kisses. '*Amour,*' she experimented and then sat up straighter with a frown drawing her slender brows into a line.

Amour was French for love, and Marcus had not mentioned that word once last night. He had even woken her again with the dawn so they could climb beyond the world once more. Could he have given her such joyous satisfaction, if he felt nothing more than mere desire? All trace of the satisfied, sleepy-eyed woman he had made of her vanished as she realised that yes, a man could probably find such wondrous gratification with any available woman he desired, even if he did not love her.

Was she receiving the benefit of his former lovers' experience, or maybe her husband was a genius at the art of making a woman feel so special that they were briefly certain there was no other?

'Thea, where are you?' Marcus's voice was urgent.

'Here,' she called rather hollowly as he ran up the stairs toward her.

'Nobody knew if you were inside or out.'

'And why should they?'

For some reason that comment made him more agitated and he began to pace the gallery. 'Nick's wrong,' he finally concluded and turned to face her again. 'Winforde never returned the jewellery your grandfather had in his safe to me, despite Clatmore's demands.'

Thea shrugged, 'Most of it was hideous.'

'But valuable, and now he's sold it, probably to buy the help he needs to get you, Thea.'

'Why should he bother?' she asked, exasperated that he was worrying about Granby, when she was struggling to fit her whole life together.

'Because he thinks we cheated him.'

'He was lucky to keep his freedom after what he did.'

'A mistake I'm rapidly repenting.'

'Why? He can't force me to wed him now, my lord.'

He stepped forward and placed his hands on her

shoulders as if he was tempted to shake some sense into her, but as always his hold gentled and he stood looking down at her with all sorts of mysteries in his eyes.

'Don't you see that there is more than one way of profiting from you, Thea? If he and his mother imprisoned you for gain once, they will not balk at doing it again.'

'You mean they might kidnap me and demand a ransom?'

'Of course, it's an obvious solution to their difficulties.'

'And would you pay it?'

'What a ridiculous question.'

'There's no need to be rude.'

'There is every need.'

He ran his hands through his already dishevelled dark hair and Thea watched steadily as his stormy gaze cooled and his set mouth gentled into a rueful smile. To think she had once thought him so self-contained she could not read him, and she felt an answering smile kick at her own mouth, despite her worries.

'He must never hurt so much as a hair on your head again, Thea,' Marcus told her rawly, and she saw that he felt more for her than she had ever dared dream. The question remained—was it enough, when she loved him so much?

'You will stop him doing so,' she reassured him huskily as she moved closer and raised a hand to smooth his dishevelled locks, then ran it down his lean cheek. 'He's really not very clever, you know.'

'Who isn't?' he asked absently as he took every advantage of such a promising opening to pull her into his arms.

'Granby, but I wasted enough time worrying about him these last six months,' she informed him with a very encouraging smile.

'True,' he murmured, flying in the face of all he had just tried to convince her of, and bent his head to take her lips in a kiss of such desperate need it was as if they had been parted for days instead of hours.

Surrendering eagerly to such a storm of passion, she made no protest at all when he lifted her up in his powerful arms and carried her back to the newer part of the house.

'I hear that many fashionable ladies take a rest in the afternoon,' she remarked distractedly, as he opened the door to her bedchamber and informed Maggie that her mistress was very tired and would ring once she wished to dress.

'I'm not that feeble, Marcus,' she told him when they were alone.

'Then my husbandly attentions cannot be urgent enough,' he replied, and set about refining them.

'I don't think there's anything wrong with your technique at all,' she gasped after a considerable interlude.

'Practice makes perfect,' he informed her virtuously and went back to seducing his wife with a will. 'I'm well aware that you're distracting me,' he told her, as she struggled to hold back a purr of satisfaction when he divested her of her morning gown with ruthless efficiency.

'Is it working?'

'All too well.'

'What a bad woman I am.'

'Oh, I don't know,' he murmured as he reared over her and gazed full into her open eyes as he surged into her, and she received him with eager awe. 'I like you just as you are, my sweet,' he assured her huskily as he drove into her silken depths with a passion that went a very long way to reassure her he really did want his wife very badly indeed, when she was capable of thought. 'I like you very much indeed,' he murmured and proved it.

A long time afterwards Thea stirred restlessly in his arms. 'Like, Marcus Ashfield?' she murmured at her sleeping husband and leaned over him to examine his beloved features one by one. 'Like? I'll give you "like", you idiot,' she promised vengefully and settled down for that rest after all.

'Promise me that you will at least be careful?' Marcus asked urgently when they awoke at last and found it was high time they were dressed for dinner. 'News of my recovered fortune will only make them more resentful.'

Her heart did a somersault at the sight of him so rumpled and ruffled by passion and anxiety.

'Of course, anyway you already send me about with an armed guard, so I cannot see what else I can do but bear it.'

He turned back and gave her a long, breath-stealing kiss. 'One day we will be free of them, Thea,' he promised.

'I hope so, I might be tempted to shoot them myself if I am to be guarded like the crown jewels for the rest of my life.'

'Once I lay hands on him, I'll make sure he never troubles you again,' Marcus declared grimly.

Several hours later, Marcus yawned widely as they finally climbed the steps after waving off the last of their dinner guests and remarked how thankful he was for country hours. 'I thought our guests were in danger of staying to breakfast.'

'Lucky the Squire was as eager to seek his bed as you are, Marco, if for very different reasons,' Nick teased with an amused glance at where his cousin's arm curled possessively round Thea's waist.

'Mind your own business for once, Niccolo,' Marcus told him lazily and whisked Thea away with a lofty injunction that everyone was to go to bed and leave the clearing up until morning.

'You, madam wife, have been driving me half-mad all evening,' Marcus told her once they were

alone and could set about the happy task of reliev-
ing that frustration.

'One does one's poor best,' she gasped when she
could find breath.

'Reward me for my ingenuity like that, my torment,
and your best will undoubtedly be good enough.'

'Please, Marcus,' she pleaded brazenly and, as
she drifted on a fuzzy cloud of satisfaction very
much later, not one single inch of her felt neglected
and unloved any more.

She smiled besottedly, safe in the knowledge that
he was asleep and, even if he was not, could not see
her face from where he lay with his dark head
pillowed on her breast and one hand clasped possessively over her hips. His long body was sprawled
across the bed where he had landed after their last
bout of lovemaking and, if only it wouldn't wake
him, she longed to explore his body as he had just
mapped hers, for love alone and not because she
desired him beyond reason. Not *just* because of
that, anyway.

She eyed his sleeping form in the last remaining
glow of the fire, and recalled with a wince she fought
to control that he bore the marks of his former profession on his athletic body. There was the scar of a
bullet wound high on his left shoulder; among his
crisply curling hair she had traced the healed furrow
of another; and down his right arm there was the fine
silver scar he said came from a sabre wound. She

realised with a shudder how close she had come to never knowing her remarkable husband.

'Cold, love?' he murmured sleepily, not lifting his head from the luxury of her silky smooth skin.

'Far from it, husband,' she murmured, but he lazily shrugged the covers over their temporarily spent bodies and snuggled even closer to her before falling back into contented sleep.

'Love?' She lay there questioning, long after his breath had grown deep and even again.

Had he meant it? Or was that precious word a convenience, in case a gentleman forgot the name of his bedmate in the heat of passion, or the sweet lethargy of its aftermath? He had probably told more women than she cared to think of that he 'loved' them, before moving on to a new battle, another siege and a different country, full of more potentially beloved women. He had been a soldier, after all, and constantly in danger of his life, so who could blame him for taking comfort when it was offered?

Not even she could, she reluctantly concluded, but hoped against hope that her presence in his bed meant as much to him as it did to her. She had a lover who considered her extravagant satisfaction before he took his own, so should that not be enough? It was more than she had dreamt of when they made their agreement, so she should be grateful.

The sinking feeling that she might never recover if he sought out a mistress when he grew tired of the marriage bed nearly made her wince again, but she held still with an effort. The feel of him so close, and so determined to hold on to her, was a comfort she could not bring herself to think an illusion as she drifted into sleep.

Towards dawn he woke up, desire once more smelting his grey gaze to fiery silver and she opened sleepy eyes to meet them and bid him welcome.

'Do you mind that our agreement seems to have gone by the by?' he asked her, as one long finger found the secret place at the core of her femininity and set about driving her to the very edge of sanity.

'Does it feel as if I mind, husband?' she managed and evidently the sight of her desperate for his amorous attentions was answer enough, for he gave up driving her to distraction to bury himself in her to the very hilt again and again.

Rocked by the relentless waves of fulfilment, they reached a climax of such fierce power she all but lost her senses and lacked the breath for further conversation.

When she awoke alone to full morning, she wondered what would have happened if she had the courage to admit her feelings to him and watch him draw away. It was a risk she dare not take, and she condemned herself as a weak fool as she scampered round his chamber, picking up her discarded clothing, washing in the cold water on the night stand and assuming her pristine nightgown. By the time Maggie came with her morning tea, she was neatly demure in her own bed, as if refreshed after an innocent night's sleep.

Maybe if Marcus had not gone before she awoke, she would have had the courage to meet her maid's knowing glances. Well, he had gone, and didn't that prove her deliberations in the still of the night had been right?

Of course it did, sensible Thea told her wilder, more rebellious side and went downstairs to supervise breakfast. When it was over she would treat herself to a walk in the gardens to clear her head of wistful fantasies. The mistress of Chimmerton needed all her wits about her, after all, and she was sure Granby would not venture so close to Marcus's home.

A couple of hours later, Marcus knocked impatiently on his wife's door, but the room was as empty as the adjoining boudoir. As he ordered the house to be searched fear twisted his mouth into a grimace at the thought of his Thea in the hands of two ruthless people with nothing left to lose. Somehow the Winfordes had evaded his watchdogs and he cursed himself for not keeping an eye on them himself. He had been too busy seducing his wife to take proper care of her, and desperation tore, at him at the thought of her in their hands again. He had to find her before they did her more harm, and it felt like a sword to his gut to think of her hurt and needing him.

A nightmarish vision of her being carried off to the Continent, drugged and abused out of some warped desire for revenge, made him shudder with fear. He received the news that she could not be found in grim silence and strode toward the stables as fast as his legs would carry him. Maybe she was at the horseshoe lake again. He could not see Winforde miring his boots or breeches in that mud and fervently hoped Thea was just wandering the grounds, convinced she was safe in her own gardens.

She would appear any moment now, he assured himself. Furious with her for wandering off when he had warned her so emphatically and increasingly uneasy, he hoped her horse would be gone and the new groom along with her, but Dark Lady looked back at him from her stall, more than ready for a good gallop. He could not search alone, and forced himself to take time to organise a wider search.

'Can't you keep a better eye on yon pretty wench that you keeps losin' of 'er?' Merry had the effrontery to say.

'Never mind that, saddle up and help me find her before they do!'

Marcus leapt up onto Hercules and set himself to search the woods.

* * *

Half an hour later he returned, heart sinking at the gloomy faces of the other searchers, then Merry returned—carrying Thea's precious Kashmir shawl.

'Where was it?'

'By the south lodge.'

'Someone must have seen her,' he shouted and the men obediently filed out of the yard once again without complaint to question their neighbours.

Thea had won many more hearts than his own since her arrival here, he realised, and turned Hercules towards the main gate, intent on finding the local magistrate.

'Marcus, stop!'

Blessing Nick's parade-ground bellow, he turned Hercules back towards the house.

'Barker found me trussed up in the bushes the other side of the lane, Marcus. I heard the scheming evil bastard!'

'Hurry up and tell me, Thea's life could be at stake.'

'Sorry, they hit me,' Captain Prestbury explained disgustedly. He raised his hand to the back of his head and it came away covered in blood.

'Try to remember, Nick. I'm like to run mad without her,' Marcus admitted quietly.

'I saw a carriage and pair and knew no sane person would use a rutted cartway to get to the main road, but I was a fool not to take evasive action and they caught me watching.'

Marcus clenched his fists until his knuckles whitened.

'No sign of Carter,' Nick managed. 'Cut his losses, I dare say.'

'That's something.'

'They said something about Bristol, Marcus,' Captain Prestbury insisted as he swayed ominously on unsteady legs. 'That's all I know,' he managed before he finally sagged into Barker's waiting arms.

'Deal with him for me?' Marcus asked, and his henchman looked back at him with something uncomfortably close to pity.

'Aye, Master Marcus, but you'd best hurry.'

'That I had. God knows what they will do to her this time.'

Thea hazily remembered wandering into the Yew Walk once she had gone through all the business of the day with Mrs Barker and finally managed to escape. Hearing a twig snap behind her and suspecting Marcus had put someone on her tail, she turned round with an order to leave her be on her tongue and got an unwelcome shock.

'Ah, Alethea, it's been such a long time.'

'You!' she cried out in disgust, wishing she had not been so complacent. Obviously desperation had lent Granby some courage after all.

'You have made me wait far too long, cousin,' he

replied, seizing her hand and kissing it, despite her wild struggles.

'I'm no cousin of yours, and let me go, you fat toad!'

'I've better things to do than argue with a whore, and we'll miss the tide.'

'I won't stir a step with you, let alone sail anywhere.'

Granby gave an impatient sigh and looked beyond her. 'That's it, Fielding, make sure you get the gag on her before she screams.'

Turning sharply to confront Granby's repellent valet, she had only an instant to realise how she had been tricked, before a sharp blow from Granby's weighted cane fell on her head and deprived her of her senses.

When she finally woke from a serene pit of unconsciousness, her immediate impulse was to slip back into it. She had no idea if she had been out for minutes or hours, and the closeness of some heavy cloth was making her feel horribly sick. She moaned softly, as the floor of a carriage lurched under her poor head, sure she would cast up her accounts very soon.

'Take that blanket off her, Granby, we don't want her smothered before the fool pays her ransom.'

Thea's relief as the heavy rug was pulled off was mitigated by the knowledge that she was in Lady Winforde's unscrupulous hands again.

'I feel sick and will shortly be so over your breeches, Granby.'

At this generous warning, he kicked out and added a sharp bruise on her side to the score she had against him.

'I told you to fetch her, not assault her, my son. This is all of a piece with everything you have done lately.' For once the lady sounded less than fond of her unattractive son. 'We need her healthy if this is to work.'

'I won't hit her again, but I ain't travelling another step with her looking so green. The stupid wench will be ill all over me.'

'Not so stupid as she makes out, as we have good cause to know.'

Her warning fell on deaf ears, for Granby was squeamish as a Bath Miss in his own cause. Banging sharply on the roof of the coach, he ordered the coachman to stop. Ignoring his mother's protests that they couldn't afford to waste any time, he climbed down and ordered the men to wait while his guest recovered from the effects of a rocking carriage.

He tried to act the gentleman toward a female he loathed as he handed her down. Thea might well have found such a tableau irresistibly amusing, had she not been preoccupied with being wretchedly sick. If only her fuddled wits were not buzzing, this could be her chance to escape, she thought, when her poor stomach was finally empty. She risked looking up, winced at the brilliance of the autumn sun low across the valley and gasped a demand for water.

'Come, child,' Lady Winforde intervened. 'A walk

in the fresh air will do you good. Is there a stream nearby, coachman?'

The coachman shrugged unhelpfully, an extraordinary idea dawning that he knew the younger lady, and would be better out of this murky affair.

Eager to get her victim out of sight, Lady Winforde bundled Thea off the road and down to the wooded valley bottom. It was a blessed relief to breathe in cool air and Thea's head began to clear at last, although she clung to her captor as she was marched toward the noise of running water as if her legs could not hold her. At last they came to a stream, yards wide and less than a foot deep. Thea subsided on a rock with a weak sigh, and Lady Winforde moved away to soak her handkerchief in the icy stream, her stays creaking with protest all the while.

Thea held her head in her hands as if she felt worse. 'I'm going to be sick again!'

She staggered to her feet and was savagely amused to see Lady Winforde back away in alarm. When she was close enough to the stream, Thea ran at her foe and nearly whooped with joy as she toppled.

It seemed to take for ever for Lady Winforde to hit the water, and Thea wasted precious moments watching the astonished dread on her enemy's face. With a loud splash and a hoarse grunt, Lady Winforde sat in the middle of the shallow river, her skirts floating about her like a grotesque purple island.

Thea plunged across the river. She knew she

couldn't evade capture for long and, given their vindictive natures, did not relish being at the Winfordes' mercy again, but she had to slow them down until Marcus caught up and dealt with them once and for all. The thought of leaving England without him was simply not to be borne, so hearing a commotion in the distance, she blindly forced her way through a thick stand of trees and looked round frantically for a place to hide.

She was safer on this side of the river, but night would soon overtake her and, goodness, she was cold. Stumbling over a tree root, she muttered an unladylike curse. Liberally covered in mud and wet from the knees down, it took all her courage to climb the side of the valley. She was beginning to wonder if it might be better to let herself be recaptured, rather than spend the night in a ditch, when she heard the noise of a horse's hooves behind her.

Granby must have made the post boy come after her. She couldn't outrun him and looked desperately for a hiding place, despite her reservations. Choosing a fine oak tree, she sprang for the first foothold she could see and was up among the sheltering branches faster than she could think. Lying still on a broad branch, she wrapped her skirts as tight to her body as she could, and prayed her pursuer would not look up.

Chapter Twenty-One

Listening for the noises of her pursuers with her heart beating like a drum, Thea concluded the horse was picking its way over the uncertain ground below her. Fighting to keep her breath from rasping a warning, she dared not look down. She squeezed her eyes tightly shut and clung to the rough bark as the rider paused beneath her tree. Holding her breath, she tried to melt into the tree.

'If you're planning to become a *guerillo,* never take a soaking first, my love. I feel as if I'm caught in a shower of rain,' Marcus's deep voice observed laconically.

She gasped and nearly fell off her branch. 'You might have called out, you frightened me half to death!'

'Nice to think we both know what it feels like, then. Are you planning to stay up there and argue, or have you the common sense to get down before you take an ague?'

Thea found the courage to look down at his beloved face, and saw that he was in the grip of some powerful emotion, and she was not sure if it was fury or relief. 'You don't seem very pleased to see me, Marcus.'

'How could you wander about alone with Winforde on the loose, Thea, after Nick and I warned you not to?' he raged and Thea could think of nothing to say in her own defence.

It had been both arrogant and stupid of her not to listen, but how could she explain that something in her would not stay inside the house like a prisoner, after being locked up in her grandfather's home by her enemies? Anyway, Marcus didn't look to be in the mood to listen to reasons she barely understood herself, or to concede that her recklessness had at least drawn the Winfordes out of cover.

'Dammit, woman, will you get out of that tree before we both succumb to an inflammation of the lungs?' he snapped, obviously still furious with her.

Ignoring his language with a dignified sniff, Thea accepted his help, but, once she was back on the ground, faced him with her chin raised as she silently dared him to comment on her parlous state.

'You think me amusing?' she demanded belligerently.

'No, but your dressmaker would never believe how little regard you have for her creations. Give me your hand.' Thea folded her arms. 'Don't be ridiculous,' he snapped. 'You'll take a fever if I don't get you home soon. Show a little consideration for your household, if not for me.'

'I dare say *you* would survive,' she told him, then reluctantly took his hand and was swung upward with little concern for her dignity, or the fact that she was showing a good deal of muddy leg. 'I'm not decent,' she cried, as Hercules began to pick his way over the uneven ground.

'Madam, I'm not in the least concerned, and it amazes me you should be after this latest escapade.'

'Would you rather I tamely allowed myself to be carried off next time?'

'Rather than run about the countryside in such a lunatic fashion risking life and limb, yes, I would.'

Thea felt that her cup was full to overflowing. 'I have the headache,' she informed him and tried to hold herself proudly aloof.

'You'll have a lot more than that if you don't stop acting like a bodkin. We'll both land on the floor before we can go five yards.'

She gave an expressive sniff and told herself pride alone prevented her from turning into the sobbing creature he deserved to be burdened with.

When they reached the road after an interminable journey through the darkening woods, they found the coachman engaged in a heated argument with Granby, while Marcus's keepers kept their guns trained on both. Lady Winforde was sitting by the roadside, haranguing anyone who would listen.

'Sound the yard of tin, man. I have her ladyship safe,' Marcus ordered the guard in a voice that implied it was no fault of her own she was not drowned in the river, or lying with a broken head at the foot of the tree in which he had discovered her. 'If she will only keep still, that is,' he added. 'Do you wish to unnerve poor Hercules into bolting with us both, madam?'

An ear-splitting blast was repeated three times and Marcus nodded his satisfaction. 'Good. Now, coachman, turn your rig about and follow my men.'

'I hired you, my man, you will drive on to Bristol as we agreed.'

'Madam,' said Marcus in a very bored voice, 'do as you are bid and I might let you both live.' He turned to his head-keeper. 'See to it, Grantley,' he ordered and galloped off with a still-protesting Thea.

'Hercules can't carry a double burden so far, Marcus.'

'We're only five miles from the south lodge, so will you just hold tight and stop arguing? Or would you rather travel with your aunt?'

'She's not my aunt,' Thea muttered in a dark undertone.

They arrived at the lodge gates sooner than she would have believed possible. Slowing down out of what seemed to her to be respect for his horse rather than his wife, Marcus trotted the great stallion up the drive and round to the south portico.

'Home,' Thea murmured, with a great sigh of relief. 'Thank you, Marcus,' she said abruptly, forgetting her righteous wrath in profound relief at the sight of Chimmerton's mellow golden stones, still seeming to carry the warmth of the sun in the autumn light.

'You can thank me? After all I have put you through?' he asked, halting Hercules and jumping down to lift her from the great horse as if she was made of eggshells.

Thea suddenly felt as if he was growing ever further away, and slid towards his muscular arms and into unconsciousness. She came round quickly this time, to see a rather startled Mrs Barker leading Hercules to a well-earned rest, as Marcus carried his wife through the front door. He continued up the stairs, despite her telling him she could walk.

'You'd tumble from one end of the staircase to the other, so just be quiet and keep still for once. If you continue to wriggle, I'll drop you.'

Maggie awaited her with a hot bath, possets and warm towels. Thea was reminded of the progress of an important invalid to the hot baths in Bath and almost had the giggles. She was deposited on the day bed without any other farewell from her husband than a gruff order to do as she was told, and watched Marcus disappear with an expression that revealed too much of her feelings for him. Maggie tutted, silently forming a resolution that, master or no, she would give his lordship a piece of her mind if he didn't mend his ways.

'Look at the state of this gown, your ladyship!' she exclaimed as she gently stripped her mistress of her muddy skirts. 'It'll have to go for rags and I doubt these petticoats will wash clean either.'

'And after the trouble everyone took to bring me into fashion as well.'

'Never mind fashion!' her maid amazed them both by exclaiming. 'You're safe, milady, and that's all that matters to any of us here, and you'll feel much better after a bath.'

Awed by such loyalty, Thea docilely agreed, and was even persuaded to lie on her bed, where she fell fast asleep before her head had hardly touched the pillows.

Meanwhile Marcus was taking out his feelings on their enemies. 'If you so much as set foot in the British Isles again,' he informed the unsavoury pair, 'the warrants my lawyer has secured against you will be executed. I mean executed in every sense of the word of course. Stay away and the sum of one hundred pounds a year will be paid you by the governor of his Majesty's colony at Botany Bay. If you leave that place, all payments will cease and I will hunt you down to the very ends of the earth.'

'The place is full of felons!' blustered Granby.

'Then you should feel very much at home. As your own kind will undoubtedly see straight through you, you might even be obliged to do a decent day's work for once in your worthless life.'

'Sir, you insult us,' cried Lady Winforde, the angry flush on her plump cheeks all but matching her puce pelisse.

'Is that possible?' he asked disdainfully. 'No doubt you have more brains than your son, so understand me once and for all, madam, if you make any attempt to hurt my wife, even by proxy, you will regret not dying at the executioner's hand.'

'It is no simple matter to execute a lady of quality.'

'But you will find it's easy enough to hang a thief, a fraud and a murderess, even if her rank were far more elevated than your own.'

The colour left Lady Winforde's cheeks and she looked grey.

'You have no proof.'

'Oh, but I have. Sworn statements from apothecaries and lawyers, servants and so-called friends and confederates. Giles Hardy did not die of any natural illness, and nor did his brother. In the last few weeks I have gathered enough evidence to hang you both, even if you were of the blood royal. You should have been a little kinder to your tools, my lady, and they might have repaid you with loyalty. But make the mistake of believing me too much the gentleman to use this information, and it will certainly be your last.'

Meeting his implacable gaze, Lady Winforde evidently decided it was time to relinquish any idea of brazening out a trial they would surely lose.

'I accept,' she said regally and, when Granby tried to protest, held up a queenly hand. 'Be silent, you have proved a fool from first to last,' she informed him coldly, and Granby subsided into a corner to console himself with the brandy decanter.

He contented himself with making muttered comments that did no harm to anybody as the unsavoury pair awaited their fate. At last the hired carriage set off again with an armed escort, and did not stop until the vehicle reached Bristol. Neither Merry nor Barker took their eyes off the Winfordes until their ship was so far offshore that no detail remained distinct through Captain Prestbury's spy-glass.

'Your relatives are fond indeed, my lady,' remarked the ageing captain, noting their costly raiment and deciding they would bear cultivation.

'Relatives? Oh, no, sir, devoted serving men, quite lost without us. I'm a lone widow with only my dear Granby to support me in this cold, hard world.'

Her dear Granby was about to say the men on the quay were no servants of theirs and as for relatives, he wanted none of them, when the tip of his mother's elbow was thrust very hard into his bulging midriff. He tried to protest, but the tip of her parasol was applied sharply to his foot, so he retired to his cabin to contemplate the future. It appeared shorn of all hope, but he didn't despair of his mama bringing them about, somehow or another.

Thea awoke to find her headache gone, and her scratches and bruises subsiding to a dull ache. It was dark, but at this time of year that told her very little, and the clock on the mantelpiece had been stopped. She climbed stiffly out of bed and put on her wrapper before heading for the door. It was much too long since she had eaten and her stomach rumbled loudly. Her hand was on the door handle when Marcus's dressing-room door opened and he surveyed her coldly.

She bravely faced his chilly gaze, despite bare feet, hair wildly tumbling down her back and decidedly flimsy attire. He looked so intolerably handsome that her knees trembled, but if he wanted a meek little echo he should never have married her. A disconcerting glitter lit his eyes as he took in every detail of her appearance. She told herself not to be ridiculous as a long, slow shiver of awareness trickled down her spine. It was no use; her heart leapt in sinful anticipation as she recognised the hot glow in his silver-grey eyes.

'Taking a midnight stroll, Lady Strensham?'

'How was I to know it was midnight? And I'm hungry.'

He raised his eyes to the ceiling and muttered something Thea was glad she could not hear.

'When I came upstairs Cook was arguing the privilege of feeding you with Maggie and Mrs Barker. Even Merry scolded me today for not taking better care of you.' It was her turn to mumble something indistinct, and he sighed and moved over to the fire to rake it viciously. 'Come and sit down, Thea. I'll ring for whoever won to bring something to eat.'

'I'm not an invalid.'

'Through no fault of your own,' he said wrathfully and gave the bell-pull a savage yank.

'Would you have me meekly allow them to carry me off?'

'I would pay over your entire fortune and mine with it, rather than put you through what you suffered today. What if I had not found you until tomorrow, after a night out in the cold? You could have contracted an inflammation of the lungs, or fallen out of that wretched tree after that blow to your head.'

'An addled wife being the last thing you need?'

'What I need is you, Thea, and only you.'

At that crucial moment Maggie entered the room with the merest tap at the door and Marcus swung away from his wife, as if caught out in some guilty act, and bent to inspect the fire again.

'My lady, you should be in bed!'

'I'm quite happy where I am, thank you, Maggie.'

'Her ladyship is hungry. Maybe a glass of milk and some stewed fish?'

'And maybe not. Some chicken if Cook has any left, Maggie, and some of her apple tarts, if you please. Even then I am not sure I shall not perish of inanition before morning.'

Thea glared at her husband, who laughed, just as if he had not been plaguing her with his abrupt questions and confusing statements moments before.

'I rather doubt it,' he said more cheerfully. 'Very well, Maggie, could you find something short of a twenty-four-course banquet for my wife?'

'Yes, my lord, something light and a cup of tea, perhaps?'

Thea regarded them both with disfavour, but Maggie finally left, after wrapping Thea in a shawl and covering her feet with a rug, which she discarded as soon as the door closed. Marcus frowned and she told him she was more like to succumb to heat exhaustion than the ague at this rate.

'Very well, then, but you will keep the shawl.'

'I'm really not as weak and helpless as I must look.'

'None of us doubt that you possess a will of iron, my lady.'

'But I was so afraid, Marcus,' she whispered.

She met a steady gaze that made her heart turn somersaults. He grasped her hands in his strong ones and crouched in front of her to look closely at her face.

'And I was terrified they would take you beyond my reach, Thea. Although you must be more exhausted than I thought, my darling, to admit even that much.'

On the verge of making the declaration she had longed for so deeply, he jumped up and turned away, disgust apparent in every movement as another knock sounded.

'Curse it, is our entire household intent on spiking my guns?' he asked and Thea struggled with her own frustration and a nervous desire to laugh. 'I might as well try and be alone with you in the middle of Almack's. Better, for I might snatch the odd moment of private conversation there,' he exclaimed disgustedly.

'You must be a very accomplished philanderer.'

'I can't even make a chance to declare myself to my own wife!' he muttered darkly.

Confused by a warm rush of triumph and love, and a distinct feeling that, after this afternoon, she should not make life too easy for him, Thea sent a warning glance towards the door.

'As the rest of the world seems to know my business, I don't see why whoever it might be should remain in ignorance,' he declared, and when the knock was repeated, called out impatiently for the visitor to come in.

'He would come,' Mrs Barker told them with a nod at Nick, who sported a pristine bandage around his dark head and had obviously received a far more severe blow than Thea.

'Oh, poor Captain Prestbury,' Thea cooed, 'you will be the object of pity to all the young ladies in the area,' she told him mischievously.

'I can see you are better, my lady.'

'My wife is thriving under the care of her *many* well-wishers.'

Nick ignored Marcus's broad hint that he was *de trop*. 'Now you have your fortune and your wife back, little cousin, I hope you'll hold on to both a little better in future.'

'I'm quite capable of managing my own affairs, thank you,' Marcus assured him silkily.

'D'you remember that time you fell out of a tree in Green Park and your stepmother wanted to send for the undertaker?'

'Wishful thinking, but you should be in bed. Kindly go away before you fall over and I have to carry you there.'

Mrs Barker obviously agreed for she took another look at the Captain's pale face and shooed the tall and powerful man in front of her as if he was twenty years younger, and decades less dangerous. Thea and Marcus were left in peace for all of thirty seconds, until Maggie knocked perfunctorily on the door and urged her party inside, with the anxious look of a mother sheepdog supervising her unruly puppies.

Marcus sat down on a spindly-legged gilt chair with the look of a man resigned to waiting, and Thea, who was very hungry indeed, wished he would go away for a while and let her concentrate on her dinner.

'You'll do well to get through the half of that,' he observed laconically.

'I told you I was famished.'

'If you eat it, you have a better appetite than my half brother, and Colin could eat for England.'

Thea pulled a face. 'It's not at all gallant of you to say so.'

'I don't feel gallant. Thank you, wine for me, but none for my lady.'

'Cook sent up some lemonade especially, my lord,' Maggie said reproachfully, as if he had accused her of giving her mistress poison.

It seemed she had yet another protector, and Thea had a vision of being pursued by the whole household whenever she so much as set foot outside the front door and chuckled. At Marcus's enquiring look, she shook her head and turned her attention to Cook's delicious chicken in aspic. When she finished her dinner, she helped herself to a generous piece of apple tart. Finally, with a regretful look at the fruit bowl, she declared that she couldn't eat another thing.

'I thought I would be obliged to sit here for as long as it takes to wade through a dinner at Carlton House. I really must introduce you to Prinny, my dear, I feel sure you will have a great deal in common.'

'Thank you, but I don't need to be hoisted onto my horse!'

'Keep eating like that and I'll trade Dark Lady for a cart.'

'Will that be all, my lord?' Maggie asked repressively.

'Do you require a baron of beef to stave off night hungers, my lady?'

'If I do, I shall seek it out for myself. Pray thank Cook, and tell her I feel quite restored after that delicious meal.'

'And you may safely leave her ladyship in my care, she is obviously well enough to outface a hostile army once more.'

As the door closed behind her maid, Marcus got up and turned the key in the lock.

'Before the scullery maid or the stable lad decide they need personal proof that you're not lying at death's door,' he explained in a driven tone. He knelt down by her chair and said in a raw voice, 'I'm not good at describing my deepest feelings, Thea. Lately I have held back, because I couldn't put them into words, but I think I must have loved you from the first moment I set eyes on you. I refused to admit the truth even to myself, fool that I was, and today

I was so afraid I would lose you and never be able to say it.'

A wonderful smile lifted her mouth and her eyes glowed as the completeness of his declaration dawned and warmth and joy flooded through her. Suddenly she was the one who could hardly put her feelings into words.

'I thought you the most arrogant and ridiculously handsome man I had ever laid eyes on, and I tried so hard to hate you,' she told him, but her eyes also deepened to a dreamy blue he had never seen before and Marcus was encouraged to continue.

'I knew you were trouble the instant I saw you across that hovel. One look made me doubt everything I knew. Marry for mutual advantage and to the devil with love was my creed, until you made a liar of me. Now I love you, I know that my mother felt no more than a twisted sort of infatuation for a man she couldn't have. I probably wouldn't die without you, Thea, but my life would be barren.'

Thea reached out a gentle hand and smoothed it over his beloved face, looking deep into his eyes and trying not to cry with sheer happiness. 'I would not have you kneel to me, love,' she said gently, 'and I think you are so very good at describing your deepest feelings that I shall try and borrow your eloquence. If I were ever parted from you, Marcus, the snow and ice of January would be all one with midsummer, for I would not feel the difference. I was so afraid you had decided to make the best of a bad job by making me your true wife that I hardly dared hope you would ever come to love me.'

'Looking back, I know your plight was an ideal excuse to tie you to me irrevocably. I wanted you so badly that it nearly drove me demented, and when you offered me that infamous bargain, I had a hard time arguing. I wanted to tie you to me by every bond known to God and man.'

'I thought you married me out of charity.'

'I'm not that wonderful a being, as you should know by now, my Thea. I already knew no other woman in the kingdom would suit me half as well, and when Nick began making up to you, I had a job not to rip him limb from limb. He's damned lucky I didn't try and put a bullet in him.'

'What a fearsome lord I have married.'

'Say rather what a crass fool and you might be closer to the mark. I really wanted to break Winforde's worthless neck today, so no wonder I could only rave at you when I found you. It was either that or crawl into the nearest cave with you and kill anyone who came near, and I thought you would prefer not to be soaking wet, sick and starving when I finally put my fate to the test. Now, is there anything else we need to discuss before I kiss you?'

Making a show of thinking about that offer and finally coming to a conclusion, Thea looked at him with loving provocation. 'Probably not,' she said at last.

Rising fluidly to his feet, Marcus seized her in blissfully compelling arms and carried her to the bed, where he kissed her until she felt boneless and witless. His warm mouth moving on hers set up such a whirlpool of longings and such elation Thea hardly knew how to bear it. She murmured an inarticulate protest as his mouth lifted and he looked down at her.

'You're in no fit state for this, my love,' he said, in a voice that was not altogether steady.

'I'm in no fit state for you to stop!'

He laughed and turned her to face him as he lay down on the bed again, looking deep into turquoise eyes shining with unguarded love for him.

'I prefer my lady's senses to be spinning from the effects of my kisses rather than a blow to the head,' he said in a huskier voice than usual.

'It would take more than a bruise to keep me out of your arms. Please don't leave me longing for you tonight, Marcus.'

'My darling, you're unique.'

'Because I don't mind telling you how much I want you? And what have I said to make you laugh at me now?' Thea asked softly, preoccupied with the pleasure of being close to him again as much as the reason for his bark of warm laughter.

It was such a delight not have to guard her tongue

and it felt so good to be close to his strong body.
Pleasurable shivers were running up and down her
spine at the prospect of getting even closer, and she
wriggled deeper into his arms, despite his gallant
attempts to keep a cool head.

'You're so honest about your feelings, Lady
Strensham.'

'You mean I'm a fast baggage?'

She ran her hand over his heavily muscled chest
and sighed her appreciation. She couldn't quite
remember when they disposed of his cravat, but it
was a delight to be free to touch him again. She felt
a tremor run through his powerful frame and her
own body began to shiver with delighted anticipation. Then he took her hand and put it firmly back
by her side.

'No, you're my beautiful, and nigh on irresistible,
wife. So don't put words into your long-suffering
husband's mouth. I refuse to make love to a woman
suffering from the after-effects of being knocked
out, my siren.'

'I hope you never think of making love to any
other woman, for I'm going to be a very possessive
wife, Marcus. Indeed, I dare say you'll soon become
sadly impatient with me,' she said, all the time
letting her hands rove boldly over his intriguing
torso in defiance of his edicts.

'Never be jealous, love, I have no intention of
seeking out more trouble.'

He gave a muffled gasp as her exploring hands wandered lower.

'Good, now when are you going to believe that I'm more like to faint of frustration than concussion?' she said, then looked at him with a blaze of emotions in her now brilliantly green eyes, following up her questing hands with a series of teasing kisses.

He groaned and pulled her back into his arms to kiss her passionately, his own hands working such magic on her body that she was lost in a whirl of desire and love.

'You believe it to be medically expedient, then?' he asked at last.

His eyes were shining like polished silver and a burn of colour ran across his hard cheekbones. She ran an exploring finger over them, then drew in her breath sharply as he seized her finger to nuzzle it with his mouth.

On fire with love and desire, she still managed to say, 'Essential, and you would not want Lady Strensham to be driven out of her senses, would you, Marcus, not when you possess the means to avert such a disaster?'

'Oh, I don't know,' he said, and stopped her indignant cry with a kiss of such disturbing power that she had to fight to remember to breathe.

He broke it and let his lips trail down her slender throat, to honour the hollows at the base and then brush lower, until she was gasping and on fire with need for him to linger, but also to do something urgent to assuage the heat building within her. Then he recalled a far more mundane matter and stopped to rub his chin ruefully.

'I need a shave.'

'I would rather have you kiss me than a hundred smooth-chinned gentlemen.'

'No, love, you can't have thought about it. There isn't room for even one more cavalier in this bed, only your very possessive husband.'

Thea giggled and gazed up at him. 'I do love you, Marcus, despite your ruffianly looks and managing ways,' she told him.

'And I love you, despite your black eye.'

'I haven't got a black eye, have I?' He nodded and she put a hand up to touch the tender spot. 'I must look like a prize-fighter.'

'You look lovely,' he said with admirable composure.

'Then why won't you make love to me?'

'Because I don't know if I can be gentle tonight,' he said in a voice rough with passion and frustration.

'Good, as I'm close to melting, husband, I don't want gentle,' she replied and pulled him down to meet her eager mouth again.

As another of those drugging kisses rendered her helplessly yearning, a need to be so close to him that no more barriers could ever exist between them nearly overwhelmed her.

'Tonight you will have gentle, if it costs me my sanity. Tomorrow will be soon enough for anything wilder you have in mind, wife.'

'Oh, you mean it gets wilder than this?' she gasped as he raised his head so they could breathe, his wickedly roving hands busy about her eager body, delight in his every touch.

'With you anything is possible, but whatever we do, we will do it together—and you will always have my love, my one and only lady,' he replied, looking happier than she had ever dared dream he might to be her beloved husband.

'Ooh, well, what are we waiting for then?' she said eagerly and tried to pull him even closer.

'Woman, will you never let me have the last word?'

'Yes, if you say that you love me, for I adore you beyond reason and it does seem only fair,' she said hopefully.

'For ever and beyond, my torment,' Marcus said firmly and pulled her to him so urgently it was a very long time before Thea said anything at all. 'I love you,' he murmured into her very receptive ear and then proved it to her complete satisfaction.

HISTORICAL

LARGE PRINT

THE VANISHING VISCOUNTESS
Diane Gaston

The prisoner stood with an expression of defiance, leather shackles on her wrists. Adam Vickery, Marquess of Tannerton, was drawn to this woman, so dignified in her plight. He didn't recognise her as the once innocent débutante he had danced with long ago. Marlena Parronley, the notorious Vanishing Viscountess, was a fugitive, and seeing the dashing man of her dreams just reminded her she couldn't risk letting anyone get caught up in her escape…

A WICKED LIAISON
Christine Merrill

Anthony de Portnay Smythe is a mysterious figure. Gentleman by day, he steals secrets for the government by night. When Constance Townley, Duchess of Wellford, finds a man in her bedroom late one night, her first instinct is to call for help. But the thief apologises and gracefully takes his leave…with a kiss for good measure. And Constance knows it won't be the last she sees of this intriguing rogue…

VIRGIN SLAVE, BARBARIAN KING
Louise Allen

Julia Livia Rufa is horrified when barbarians invade Rome and steal everything in sight. But she doesn't expect to be among the taken! As Wulfric's woman, she's ordered to keep house for the uncivilised marauders. It would be all too easy to succumb to Wulfric's quiet strength, and Julia wants him more than she's ever wanted anything. But what future can there be for two people from such different worlds?

MILLS & BOON
Pure reading pleasure

HIST0508 LP

HISTORICAL

LARGE PRINT

A COMPROMISED LADY
Elizabeth Rolls

As a girl she was full of mischief. As a woman she seemed
lost in the shadow. But Richard Blakehurst couldn't miss the
flash of connection between them when his hand touched
hers. Seeing Richard again brought back the taunting memory
of a dance they had once shared. But Thea *must* tame her
wayward thoughts; because she doubted even her
considerable fortune could buy Richard's good opinion
of her if he ever learnt the truth…

RUNAWAY MISS
Mary Nichols

Alexander, Viscount Malvers, is sure the beautiful girl on the
public coach is not who she says she is. Her shabby clothing
and claim of being a companion cannot hide the fact that she is
Quality. He's intrigued. This captivating miss is definitely
running away, but from what – or whom? Lady Emma Lindsay
knows she must keep up the pretence no matter how strong
her feelings grow…so Miss Fanny Draper she must remain!

MY LADY INNOCENT
Annie Burrows

As the nobility jostles for the new King's favour, Maddy is
all alone. Landless and friendless, she accepts a bridegroom
she has never met, intending to find peace at home. But
peace is in short supply when Maddy marries Sir Geraint,
a powerful protector and passionate man. Fiercely loyal to
the King, Geraint cannot trust his Yorkist bride – but
neither can he resist her!

HISTORICAL

LARGE PRINT

THE DANGEROUS MR RYDER
Louise Allen

Jack Ryder, spy and adventurer, knows that escorting the haughty Grand Duchess of Maubourg to England will not be an easy task, but he believes he is more than capable of managing Her Serene Highness. However, he's not prepared for her beauty, her youth, or the way her sensual warmth shines through her cold façade…

AN IMPROPER ARISTOCRAT
Deb Marlowe

The Earl of Treyford, scandalous son of a disgraced mother, has no time for the pretty niceties of the *Ton*. He has come back to England to aid an ageing spinster facing an undefined danger – but Miss Latimer's thick eyelashes and long ebony hair, her mix of knowledge and innocence, arouse far more than his protective instincts…

THE NOVICE BRIDE
Carol Townend

As she is a novice, Lady Cecily of Fulford's knowledge of men is non-existent. But when tragic news bids her home immediately, her only means of escape from the convent is to offer herself to the enemy as a bride! With her fate now in the hands of her husband, Sir Adam Wymark, she battles to protect her family…

⊚™ MILLS & BOON®
Pure reading pleasure

HIST0708 LP